Sweet Girl

Also by Rachel Hollis

Party Girl

Sweet Girl

A NOVEL

RACHEL HOLLIS

LAKE UNION
PUBLISHING

Text copyright © 2015 Rachel Hollis

Published by Lake Union Publishing, Seattle

www.apub.com

Amazon, the Amazon logo, and Lake Union Publishing are trademarks of Amazon.com, Inc., or its affiliates.

ISBN-13: 9781477829516
ISBN-10: 1477829512

Cover design by Elsie Lyons
Cover photo by Cortnee Brown

Library of Congress Control Number: 2014920770

Printed in the United States of America

For my big sister Melody Daily, the greatest baker I know.

Sweet Girl

Chapter One

"Landon, I swear on all that is holy—" I growl without looking up from my laptop.

"Max, don't break a commandment! It's not even dark outside yet!" she calls from across the living room.

I assume she means to sound fierce, but the twang in her accent kills whatever force the reprimand might have taken on, and in typical Landon style, her reasoning makes little sense to anyone but her. I glance quickly at the sliding doors that lead to the miniscule balcony off our apartment to confirm her statement. It's past six, but because summer is just around the corner, she's right—it's still not dark out.

"So it's OK to use the Lord's name in vain after hours?" Even as I ask, I still avoid looking up. If I have to review another one of her outfits today, I might start bleeding from the eyes.

"Of course not; it just seems a little less offensive. Like drinking a wine cooler, or going braless in front of company. It's never really the right thing to do, but at least after dark it's less pronounced. Besides that, you promised you'd try to work on your language, remember?"

"That promise was made under duress," I grumble.

"That promise," Landon challenges, "was made under vodka. That's not the same thing and you know it."

I snort inelegantly and continue to scroll down the page on my Mac until I'm momentarily distracted by the picture on the screen.

. . . topped with caramelized bananas and a buttered-rum sauce.

I drag the photo from Pinterest into a file on my desktop and try to ignore my roommate's mewling on the other side of the room.

"Please, Max, *please*? Scout's honor—I really think this is the one!"

"You dress yourself every day, and you seem to have made it this far in life without my help." I whip one hand off my keyboard. The bracelets on my left wrist jangle in protest as I run my fingers through my messy pixie cut. "I'm not exactly the reigning fashion plate."

I point out my faded *Charles in Charge* T-shirt. It's the one where Scott Baio is wearing a suit and casually looking over his neon Ray-Bans like an eighties creeper. The shirt is classic, but my pairing it with faded gray thermal pajama bottoms and the disposable flip-flops I wore home from my last pedicure should deter anyone from asking me for fashion advice.

"And yet when you need to, you can somehow bust out a designer ensemble and makeup inspired by *WWD*," she says, working her way across the living room. "And yeah, you only wear black nail polish, but you and I both know it's Chanel. You know, at first I thought your bipolar style was accidental, but then when you did that smoky purple eye for Miko's party and it was *exactly* like the last Burberry ad, I—"

"Oh, for freak's sake!" I slam my laptop closed and look up at her with a scowl. This little interlude has gone on long enough. "Look, you've been my roommate for six months—"

"Seven and a half." Landon cuts me off with a smile.

I ignore the correction.

"And in that time you've managed to start *and lose* a job working at one of the biggest event-planning firms in the nation. I get that your boss was a soul-sucking nightmare, and that likely made your first months in LA feel like a profound life experience. Then, in sheer defiance of the laws of reality, you and Miko start your own company—"

"All because of your support and encouragement," she interrupts again.

Again, I ignore her.

"—and you've actually managed to grow your client base, which is, frankly, way more than anyone expected so soon. Top it off with the fact that you're officially dating Brody now."

Her happy sigh travels all the way across the room.

"That's a lot of big things in a short period of time, and I can understand how you'd think that somehow bonds us or whatever, but—"

"Oh, come off it, Max." She giggles. "I just want you to help me figure out what to wear. Like it or not, that's what friends do, and despite your gruff exterior, your constant scowling, and your pretended indifference, that's what we are. Now"—she wiggles her eyebrows—"what do you think of this one?"

She poses expectantly in between our dinosaur of a TV and the breakfast bar that separates the kitchen from the small living room. She's waiting for my opinion on the eighth—wait, no. This is the *ninth* outfit she's tried on. I recognize that at this point it's easier to acquiesce than to keep rebelling against the idea of playing fashion police.

This time she's chosen something a bit more sophisticated than you'd normally find her in. A tight white T-shirt tucked into a tea-length pleated silk skirt, with black booties and a little black leather jacket. Her hair is in a chic chignon. It's the smallest I've ever seen her typically gigantic blonde mane.

I get what she's going for here; it's all very Parisian cool, and she's actually totally pulling it off despite the fact that she's neither Parisian nor cool. Even though she's annoying the hell out of me, this look is actually really pretty, and I start to tell her so. But before the words fall from my mouth, something about that little leather jacket sparks a memory. That memory flares to life, and I remember another girl, years ago, who wore her black leather jacket every day. If this look reminds me of her, then surely it'll remind him of her too. That can't bode well for their first date.

"Not that one," I say, before quickly looking away.

"Really?" Landon does a little twirl and the skirt flares out dramatically just as she intended. "It's so cute, though."

She looks down at herself as if trying to guess what I dislike about it. But that's impossible; it'd take a shared family history to understand what's wrong with this look.

"Really. Put the red one back on." I open my computer back up and hope that she gets that I'm over this conversation.

"You don't think that's too loud? Too, I don't know, colorful for Hatfield's?"

No such luck.

I don't need to look up at her to know she's biting her lower lip nervously. I hate seeing her second-guess herself all because she's putting so much effort into impressing a man. It pisses me off.

"Clearly he likes loud and colorful, or he wouldn't be dating you, right?" I demand. "Honestly, I hope you're embarrassed by the way you're acting. I know drag queens who don't spend this much time debating what to wear!" I scowl down at my keyboard.

I hear her giggle as she turns to go back to her room, presumably to try on thirteen more outfits before he gets here.

Her ability to laugh off my bad moods is one of the things that makes our friendship work. That and the fact that she's not easily offended, which is vital to hanging out with someone like me since I basically hate everyone.

"You're right, girl. I know you are. It's just our first *real* date." I can hear the smile in her voice, though I don't understand what it's for. "I wanna look nice. I needed a second opinion on what he might like."

"Yeah, because I'm the reigning intellect on what a man wants!" I call after her.

I can't even remember the last time I cared enough to try to impress a man—or actually, I can, but I do my very best not to.

"—do too." The sound of her voice breaks into my thoughts, and I blink hard to pull myself back into the conversation.

"What?" I ask, still distracted.

"You do too know what a man likes. Particularly when the man in question is your brother!" she calls back with a laugh.

She's right, obviously, but I refuse to validate her comment with a response. Imagining your best friend dating your big brother is eight kinds of wrong, and so, like all the other uncomfortable thoughts, I just try not to think about it.

———

I'm fully immersed in the images on my screen. Some of them I save for later, but most of them I mock. I know it's rude, because a lot of these food bloggers are trying really hard, but picking apart a recipe is my favorite hobby. Actually, it's my only hobby—and we should all be allowed one, right? I can't help checking my Pinterest feed every day to see what's new. In some cases the visual is gorgeous, but if you read through the recipe, you can tell that there's no way those ingredients would actually taste good together. In others, it looks like they took the photo in a dark closet with an iPhone 3. No matter how delicious a recipe might be, nobody is going to give those mutant cookies a chance.

Though it would shock anyone who knows me, I get way too excited about people like Ina Garten or Joy the Baker. Both are chefs who use quality ingredients to reinvent the classics and present them beautifully. I'm never going to be a food blogger (I can barely style myself, let alone a photograph), but I love following people who are, and Pinterest is baker mecca. My favorite is when everyone online fanatically jumps on a recipe bandwagon. For instance, why is everyone so obsessed with covering everything with sprinkles right now? Is this 1987?

I can fall down this rabbit hole for hours, so when I hear the knock at the front door, I have no idea how much time has passed. I look at the empty hallway with a sigh. There's no way she's going to answer the door herself, because my roommate lives to make a grand entrance. I close down my computer and head to the entryway.

Our peephole dates back to the seventies, along with the rest of the building, so the view is slightly yellow and distorted, but it's easy enough to make out Brody standing there. I open the door to let him in.

He's dressed to the nines, but the slightly disheveled hair and the tan from spending the morning on a surfboard always make his style seem effortless rather than overly polished. Landon will probably have a seizure when she sees him.

I acknowledge him with a nod. "Captain."

"Tennille." He smiles back indulgently.

It's the same smile he's been giving me since I first met him sixteen years ago. I was a shy nine-year-old and was utterly terrified to meet the Ashton brothers in the lobby of their father's hotel. They were teenage boys, after all, and I wasn't sure how they'd treat my little sister and me, especially after the recent announcement of our parents' whirlwind engagement. I made myself sick imagining every possible scenario and prepared for the worst. I expected that they'd be angry or, best-case scenario, that they'd just ignore us. It's not like I had any other men in my life for comparison. I walked into that lobby prepared to meet bullies; instead I met my two big brothers.

Brody and Liam accepted Malin and me from the very first moment, and I always thought our relationships were stronger than those of regular siblings because we didn't have a blood obligation to love each other; we chose to, which is way more powerful.

I turn and head into the kitchen, and I hear the front door close as Brody follows me. He walks around to the other side of the bar, and he's smart enough to sit on the one barstool that isn't warped and janky. Guests only make that mistake once.

I start to pull ingredients out of the cabinets to make drinks like I have on a million other nights. Only this time we aren't headed to a family dinner. This time he's not here for me, which is awkward.

"What are you in the mood for?" I ask over the sound of ice cubes hitting the bottom of the shaker I'm filling up.

"Scotch, I think."

I turn around in surprise. I always mix him a cocktail. Straight scotch is reserved for nights when he's stressed out from work or when we're headed out to meet whatever asshole Malin has convinced herself she's going to marry this time. I look closer at him, trying to figure out why he needs a strong drink. He's fidgeting with his phone on the countertop, pulling the protective case off and snapping it back on again. He does it over and over like a nervous tic, which wouldn't be weird for a twelve-year-old but looks ridiculous for a man in his thirties.

"You seem—wait, are you *nervous*?" I half hiss, half laugh at him.

His fingers pause on the phone, and he checks over his shoulder to make sure we're still alone. He looks at me sheepishly.

"It's just, I've screwed up once already and—"

"And so has she," I remind him pointedly, and turn to grab a lowball glass from the cabinet. I own exactly two nice glasses for this purpose alone; I don't want to get crap from Brody and Liam when they slum it down to my cruddy Hollywood apartment for a drink. Everything else in our cabinets is a hodgepodge. It's a plastic menagerie of juice glasses, old Tupperware, dollar-store coffee mugs, and a handful of reusable plastic cups Landon received as part of a kids' meal. God forbid she order a normal-sized dinner like an actual adult.

"Yeah, but she was being naive," he says. "I was just being a prick."

I hand over two fingers of the Glenlivet 18 I keep at the back of the shelf for him.

"Well, she'll have to get used to that if she's going to date you," I say.

"True." He laughs once before taking a sip. "How is everything with you?"

I force a grin, mildly annoyed at his fishing.

"Probably the same since you asked me that yesterday."

I start to muddle together mango and mint for my own drink, and I stare down at my hands while they work. He doesn't respond, so I know he's waiting for me to elaborate. Honestly, you'd think he'd be used to limited conversation with me by now. When I finally glance up to grab the bottle of Ketel, his eyebrows rise an inch in invitation.

"It's fine, I told you. I'm fine," I say, a little more strongly.

"Any thought on what you're going to do with that master's you just worked so hard to get?"

"Is my mom harassing *you* about it now?" I sound petulant.

I am petulant.

I pour an extra bit of vodka into the shaker and start mixing it with more aggression than fresh fruit deserves.

"I imagine Viv would harass you herself if you'd answer your phone when she calls."

I knew it would come to this.

I knew when I didn't call her back this week she'd eventually sic one of them on me. But even knowing it would happen doesn't temper my anger. It might be irrational to get so upset so quickly, but this is a sore subject, and Brody has the disadvantage of being the one who broke this pissed-off camel's back. I am just so sick of everyone hovering!

I slam the shaker down on the countertop so hard that the coffeepot rattles on its stand.

"You know, one of the perks of living in this hovel and supporting myself is not having to answer to anyone!"

"She just wants to make sure you're OK," he says calmly.

He's purposefully refusing to rise to my level of annoyance, which only irritates me more. I take a swig of my drink, barely tasting it, as I reach for my bag. I only have to dig around for a second before my hand finds the small plastic device. I pull it out and toss it on the counter. The glucose tester skids to a stop right in front of his glass. The last readout is still on the screen from when I used it an hour ago. He tries to appear uninterested, but I watch his eyes take in the numbers before he looks away.

"That's not what I meant by OK." He sounds almost bored, but it's a practiced tone.

I look him right in the eye. "That's exactly what you meant."

For a second I think he won't answer. Brody has had years of experience deflecting my attitude, so he's an expert at it. But in this rare instance, his aggravation starts to peek through the veneer.

"You scared us," he says, exasperated.

It's not what I expected him to say, so I gape like a fish. I didn't think he'd bring it up, but now that he has I have to fight the urge to reach up and touch the scar that's hidden under my short hair.

Because nobody has asked me to talk about it in the months since it happened, and I can't remember much anyway, I thought we had an unspoken agreement to let it lie. My refusal to discuss it drives my mother insane, since she treats meddling in her children's lives like a part-time job. Lucky for all of us, Daddy was raised by the WASPiest people alive. My parents have politely argued the point for as long as they've been together, but since he typically puts his foot down with her about everyone deserving privacy, we stay silent. In fact, "don't ask, don't tell" could be the family motto. We don't ask about where my biological father is now, nor do we discuss how many guys my little sister has worked her way through to try to make up for his absence. We don't talk about the time Brody went off the deep end, or why I don't date, or how no matter how much money he has, Liam still works more hours than he sleeps. We don't discuss any of it at all.

And as far as that night is concerned, I only remember bits and pieces of it anyway. The night I was so busy studying that I forgot to check my levels. The night I felt disoriented and knew I needed to eat something, but on the way to the kitchen the confusion only got worse, and I couldn't remember what I'd gone in there to do. I started to fall, but my memory ends before my head hit the edge of the counter and I bled all over the floor I'm standing on now. It took the landlord three weeks to replace the tile, but we didn't talk about it then either. Even with a reminder staining the grout.

When I woke up I was in a hospital room, and Landon was clutching my hand like a limpet. It wasn't until later that I discovered how she'd found me and realized how scary that must have been for her. She'd had to call Brody, who called my parents, who spent God-knows-what chartering a private jet in Whistler to bring them back to LA immediately. Four sets of eyes stared down at me that morning, and the air in the hospital room was so heavy with their concern and my disappointment in myself that I felt helpless. For a brief moment in time, it was another hospital room and I was nineteen again. I was immobilized by the memory, and I couldn't find the words to argue with my mom or to explain what had happened. I just sat there hovering between the lost teenager I'd been and the grown woman who couldn't seem to find the courage to speak. Landon was the one who stood up to my mother's overwhelming concern and my brother's anger. She couldn't have recognized the lifetime of family drama she was inserting herself into, but she must have seen the desperation in my eyes. She must have seen that I was incapable of explaining any of it to them, just like I was six years ago. Because Landon, who's all soft edges and sweetness, had to speak up for me like I was a child, the shame of that memory still makes me sick to my stomach. I lash back at it with anger.

"It was months ago!" I yell.

"It was yesterday." Brody shakes his head and stares down into his glass, where a single swallow is left. "It feels like it was yesterday."

The sadness in his tone takes all the fight out of me. I know how terrified he was for me that night and during the weeks that followed. I know how terrified they all were. I wish I had it in me to be sweet and biddable and to let them fuss over me like they want to. But I don't. True to form, I'm being prickly and rude. I don't even know why they keep trying with me.

"Hey." The word comes out as a croak, but he looks up anyway. "I'm fine, I swear. I don't know what I want to be when I grow up, but I'm taking care of myself. I promise."

He opens his mouth to respond, but that's the moment that Landon decides to come breezing into the kitchen. She'd changed back into the red-and-pink Kate Spade dress her parents bought her for Christmas. It's loud and pretty, with a skirt that's almost as voluminous as her hair. It's totally her. She reaches for my glass without asking permission and takes a sip. She's purposefully avoiding the moment where she has to acknowledge the man in the room who's looking at her like she's the best idea he ever had.

"That's a good one." She sets the drink back on the counter. "Is that pepper in there?"

I didn't really pay attention while I made it, but I likely added some pepper to balance the sweetness of the mango.

"Just a little."

"I like it—gives it a little kick." She smiles down at the glass and then finally looks across the bar at Brody.

"Hi," she says, suddenly acting shy.

"Hi," he responds.

"I'm a little nervous," she says conspiratorially.

She's the only person I know who would tell her date that he makes her nervous.

His whole face breaks into a grin. "Me too," he tells her.

She lets go of a breath I didn't realize she was holding. The smile she gives him then is so big it would be embarrassing, except that he's looking at her the exact same way.

For a moment they just grin at each other like idiots. Their expressions are so sweet and full of promise and hope that it actually hurts me to see them. That kind of look is dangerous, something you're not supposed to let someone see when you've only known each other a minute and a half. I'm not sure if they realize how easy it is for someone to hurt you when you look at them that way.

"Well, this is weird," I say loudly enough to snap them out of it. "I've got to get ready for work."

I grab my glass off the countertop and turn to head into my room. I'm sure if they're left alone long enough they'll figure out the steps necessary to make it down to the car instead of staring at each other across the Formica all night.

"Don't forget," Landon calls out after me, "tomorrow you're supposed to help Miko and me design those drinks for the Riverton Espresso party."

"Much to my chagrin, I haven't forgotten. Espresso-flavored tequila is wrong on multiple levels."

I don't turn around and she doesn't answer, so I'm not sure if she even heard me or if she's currently so wrapped up in staring at Brody that she's lost her ability to respond.

Chapter Two

The bar at Gander is already packed when I arrive, and it's fairly raucous for eight o'clock, which means at least I'll stay busy and the night won't drag.

I stash my Tumi under the bar and immediately jump on the line. As usual, I'm working next to Singer-Songwriter, who I've never seen sing or song-write in the two months he's been here. On the other side of him, I'm Not Really a Waitress is making a customer a really strong old-fashioned or a particularly weak manhattan—you never can tell with her since she's forever getting the glassware wrong. Typically our GM is pretty strict with the mixologists he hires, but I'm Not Really a Waitress has boobs the size of regulation soccer balls, and they're forever on the verge of toppling right out of the white button-down we wear as part of our uniform.

LA fact: cleavage trumps skill-set or reading at grade level when you work for a skeezebag.

Jorge, my favorite busser, hustles behind me on the way to deliver food to a group of Eurotrash at the end of the long wooden bar. I give him a slight nod as I start to grab beers for the first order screamed my way.

Honestly, beer is such a pedestrian order. I don't have an issue with beer in general, especially when we have so many great craft beers on our menu. I have an issue with tourists who order beer because they're fearful of picking a cocktail they've never heard of or overwhelmed by the thought of paying eighteen dollars for a single drink. If the drinks seem overpriced to you, you probably shouldn't be in that particular bar in the first place. This same motto can be applied to most areas of life.

"*Necesitas algo?*" Jorge asks on his way back through.

I look around at my supplies while I pour vodka into the shaker in front of me.

"We're low on the purple basil, lemongrass, and chipotle. Will you have Hector replenish when he has a moment?"

Jorge scans the smorgasbord of ingredients on the counter in front of me with a nod, then grabs a bin of dirty dishes to haul back to the kitchen. The food runners, bussers, and expo guys on the line are the hardest-working people here, and most of them have been doing this twice as long as I have. The others—bartenders, hosts, and cocktail servers—don't stick around long. I don't even bother to learn their names. Because it's never just a name: *Hi, I'm Sara*, or *Hey, my name is Mike*. It's always a name plus a qualifier: *I'm Sky. I just auditioned for an NBC pilot*. Or *Hey, I'm Avery. I do slam poetry on the weekends*. They're forever pushing their taglines on others, as if who they *might* be somehow makes them more interesting than who they actually are. Doing their jobs well or staying with the same employer for more than three months at a time is what might impress me. But they rarely manage to do either, so in my head they'll always be known by my private set of nicknames, and if I acknowledge their existence at all, it's with as little communication as possible.

An hour or so later, two overplucked, over-forty divorcées squeeze their way up to the bar and flail their arms in my direction. They're already speaking to me before I even get close enough to hear what they're saying.

"—drinks from you? We've been trying to order from that hottie over there forever, but that group keeps crowding in."

She points down the bar with a spray-brushed acrylic nail. I glance in that direction to see Singer-Songwriter shamelessly flirting with a group of junior agents in casual wear. Unfortunately for my new customers, they aren't about to garner much of his attention unless they've got an Adam's apple to go along with their cocktail order.

"What can I get you both?" I ask.

The taller one checks out the liquor on the shelf behind me like it's a particularly difficult sudoku puzzle. Her friend seems equally confused by the cocktail menu on the bar. I can't really blame her either; the names of our cocktails are so overly precious and self-aggrandizing, you'd think Jay Gatsby owned this bar. Her lips move silently as she reads each option, and her consternation only grows as she examines the ingredient list. Hibiscus fizz, homemade bitters, egg-white foam, infused liqueur—there's no way she knows what any of them are. She's going off menu.

"Could I have a lava flow?" she finally asks.

Of course she opts for the alcoholic slushie.

I valiantly fight the urge to point out that this is not a Ruby Tuesday, and I am *mostly* sure the annoyance I feel can't be seen on my face.

I lean towards the wrong side of a bad mood most days, but I really do try not to take it out on the undeserving. These two are clueless, which isn't necessarily a crime, unlike the twinkle in her eyes as she asks again for a lava flow. As if I'd be caught dead serving a drink that requires a prepackaged mix!

"No blender." I stare at her, willing her to get with the program.

Some people—Landon, let's say—would hold her hand and explain to her how a bar like this works. Landon would be kind and funny, and make her feel at ease. But I'm not my roommate, and I don't really do the whole bonding with strangers thing. I just want them to hurry up because I have a hundred other people to serve.

"How about a sex on the beach?" she tries again sheepishly.

"No schnapps," I answer with a raise of one eyebrow.

Her friend glances back and forth between me and the mountain of liquor on the wall as if it might attack her. She's probably worried that she'll be called on next since she appears to be unfamiliar with any of the names on the bottles. I look down at the acrylic nails she's tapping nervously on the menu in front of her. Even upside down, I can read the tattoo on her left wrist: *To Thy Own Self Be True.*

The tattoo is fairly new; it stands out against the worn-out, sun-damaged skin of her forearm. I'd wager my Prius that this is the big vacation to find herself after finalizing her divorce paperwork.

She got herself a new tattoo, a too-tight wardrobe from the Victoria's Secret catalog, and a new hairstyle because she thought they'd make her into a new person. And while her friend should have warned her off a bob, because she really doesn't have the bone structure to pull it off, I still empathize with this person. I'm shocked to find some common ground with a woman who's wearing an unironic asymmetrical hem. But I do. I recognize the desire to chop off your hair or to carry around a reminder on your skin. I know what it feels like to want to change every single thing that made you who you were, as if becoming someone new might give you power over the mistakes you made.

But even as I empathize, I hate recognizing any part of myself in someone so clearly lost, because, well, what does that say about me? I grow more irritated.

She opens her mouth to ask for another drink and then snaps it closed. I see her glance nervously at the exit and then back at her friend, and suddenly I feel . . . not *bad* for her, but at least embarrassed that she's gotten herself into this position.

"Look." I glare at her. "I'll make something for you guys. What kind of liquor do you want as a base?"

They exchange a glance, each willing the other to answer. Finally Asymmetrical Skirt speaks up.

"Gin?"

"OK," I say, grabbing some of my tools. "Do you like savory or sweet?"

"Sweet," they answer in unison.

"Berry or citrus?" I ask, pulling together more ingredients.

"Either. Why don't you choose whatever is best?" she answers. *She's learning.*

I muddle together strawberries and a little jalapeño in the bottom of my shaker. I add in a splash of citrus-infused simple syrup and then the gin. It's uncomplicated, but when you're using in-season farmers' market produce, you don't want to cover it up with too many other flavors. Everything gets a tumble with the ice until the outside of the stainless-steel shaker fogs up with condensation, a sign of the perfect temperature. I'm sure they'd be more comfortable with a martini glass, or even a plastic tumbler for that matter, but I don't give them one. To a mixologist, a real one, glassware is sacrosanct. The shape and size of the vessel are chosen based on what will best display both the look and the taste of the cocktail. I strain the drinks into two lowball glasses filled with our giant spherical ice cubes. Customers think the ice is so elegant, but they don't realize it takes up more than half of the space in the glass. It's management's way of tricking people into buying more of these overpriced drinks, so I compensate by adding extra alcohol into the mix. I garnish each glass with some cilantro just to throw them off and slide the drinks across the bar. They both take a tentative sip, and grins light up their faces. I'm already printing out the bill and sliding it next to their cocktail napkins.

When I pass by again half an hour later, the divorcées are getting up to leave—to find a two-for-one happy hour somewhere that's more their speed, I'm sure.

"Thanks so, so much." One of them waves the bill and a handful of cash at me.

I take them from the woman, and her friend calls over the music, "You keep the change. We really appreciate your help!"

I look down at the two twenties in my hand. I'm not rude enough to say something ungrateful, even if any other bartender here would be offended by the two-dollar tip they each left.

"Thanks," I grumble, and head off to my next customer.

————

By the time I finish closing out that night, it's nearly three in the morning. I'm exhausted from a heavy shift and probably from the argument with Brody earlier too. I mean to drag myself right back to the hotel's employee parking lot and straight home to bed, but my feet start to move in a different direction. I pass the entrance to Gander and wind down a series of employee hallways before coming out into a small side lobby. I skirt the fountain and walk through the elevator bank and past the gift shop that doesn't have a single thing that costs less than a hundred dollars.

I find myself in the exact same spot I end up almost every working night.

The lobby of the Buchanan is cavernous but broken down into unique individual sections, so it manages to feel cozy. When the hotel was remodeled six years ago, the owners shocked everyone (and by everyone, I mean people like my family, who follow the hospitality industry like others follow sports or politics) by luring Marcus Balmain away from a restaurant in New York. In a totally unprecedented move, they handed nearly their entire lobby over to the famous young chef and gave him carte blanche over everything from the budget to the design. Nobody believed any single menu was worth that kind of financial gamble, but with a James Beard award and two Michelin stars under his belt, Balmain had proved them wrong. For the owners of the hotel, it was a visionary move in a town that was rapidly being overrun by wannabe foodies. The men in my family scoffed at the salary the chef had negotiated as part of his deal. But six months into the new opening, there were lines out the door and press by the bucketload, and Brody, Liam, and Dad were trying to figure out how to steal Balmain away for themselves.

On the far side next to reception sits Primi, which features dark whimsical furnishings and austere elegance. Its long tables and leather sofas are typically teeming with people enjoying drinks, appetizers, and a wine list you'd need a special degree to fully understand. Tucked next to Primi is the entrance to Secondi, the hotel's five-star restaurant and crowning glory. Reservations are booked six months out, and even then you'll likely be eating at five thirty on a Tuesday unless you know someone in management. And last, in front of me now, a pink haven sits in the middle of the room, bright and sweet like a dollop of whipped cream. This small collection of marble tables, French Regency prints, and ornate, gilded chairs has no place in the otherwise brooding lobby. Its purpose is to stand out, to tantalize, and it does. Behind those tables is an open kitchen separated from the rest of the room by a long white bar. This bar doesn't serve alcohol, though; it's covered with apothecary vases of every shape and size, and each is filled with one of the perfect handcrafted desserts that Dolci is famous for. Balmain designed the three spaces to function together so that guests might flit from one spot to the next and, by the end of the progression, have a complete dining experience.

Just like every other time I've stood here, I watch through the glass as the early crew starts their work for the day. This is just the prep team; the actual pastry chefs won't come in for a couple hours yet, but I still can't help but watch as they practice the minutiae of spinning sugar into something delectable. Eggs are cracked and separated, brown sugar is measured out into giant mixing bowls, and so much flour is sifted at once that it hovers in the air like fog. I have the urge, like I always do, to walk through to the back and see it all up close. I want to know exactly how much butter they use in their flaky tart crusts or what the hell they put into the *fleur de sel* cake that makes it as addictive as crack.

But that urge comes from the memories of another person entirely, and I ruined her dreams along with everything else. So I don't walk back; I don't acknowledge the crew at all. I watch a moment longer before turning and heading in the other direction. I give myself only as long as it takes to get back to my car to think about those dreams and the little girl who they belonged to.

———

"OK, Miss Mackenzie"—my mother smiled down at me while tying her apron around her waist—"what's the first thing we have to do before we start a new recipe?"

I was overeager to answer, and I nearly tripped over the untied lace of my Keds as I ran across the kitchen to her.

"Oh, I know, Mama!" I crowed as I hurried to climb up onto the chair she had set at the counter for me. "We preheat the oven!"

When her face fell a little, I knew I'd said something wrong. She leaned down to tie my shoe before she responded.

"That's almost right, sweetheart, but that's the second thing we do. Can you remember the first? It's very important."

My six-year-old brain scrambled for the right answer, and then my shoulders slumped when I realized what it was.

"First"—I recited the line she'd told me a kajillion times already—
"we have to check my levels to make sure it's OK if I have some sugar
before we bake."

"Exactly!" She beamed her approval. "Now then . . ." Her voice
trailed off as she held my index finger in her hand and used a tiny
machine to get a sample. I used to hate this part, but I'd been doing
it for so long now that I could mostly ignore it when it pinched me.

While we waited for the readout, I washed my hands (that's
step three for a good baker, Mama says) and came back over to the
counter.

"You're all set, Kenzie!" She smiled and put the monitor back
into the cabinet. "Now, what should we bake today?"

My mind spun with the images of all the yummy things we'd
made last time she'd had a day off like this. Mama and I loved to
bake, and because it was so close to Christmastime, we got to make
even more things than usual. Then we bundled them up in pretty
paper and handed them out to the neighbors in our apartment
building.

"Um . . ." I trailed off, trying to come up with a fun idea for us.
"Maybe—what about peanut butter cookies? The kind Malin likes."

"Mmm, that's a good idea," Mama said, running her fingers back
through my hair. "Then she can have a cookie when she wakes up
from her nap. OK, so peanut butter cookies."

She walked across our small kitchen and began pulling ingredients from the shelves. She got out our big blue mixing bowl and
my favorite spatula. Next came the flour and the sugar and a jar of
peanut butter. We liked chunky, not smooth.

"What can we do to give these cookies a Kenzie-spin?" she asked.
"What should we add to make them more special?"

I wasn't surprised when she asked. Mama usually asked me for
ideas to experiment with a recipe. I didn't always have a good answer,
and she helped me a lot, but sometimes I came up with really fun creations. Like that time I asked her if we could put cookie dough into

our brownie dough, and the dessert we made was so good. We called them brookies because they were brownies plus cookies. I wanted to come up with something just as good for our recipe today.

"Um . . . what about if we add gummy bears?" I asked hopefully. Mama made a grossed-out face, and I laughed.

"Kenzie, remember how we do this? Try to think of something you've had that you already know tastes good with your main ingredient. This time we're using peanut butter, so maybe we could do jelly or—"

"Chocolate!" I yelled, so excited at having come up with the idea.

"Shhh," she whispered. "Malin is still asleep, remember?" She spoke quietly, and I tried to lower my voice too.

"But chocolate works, right? Like a peanut butter cup?" I danced in place.

Mama reached into the pantry, pulled out the chocolate chips, and placed them on the counter with everything else.

"Chocolate is a great idea, smart girl." She smiled at me.

What seemed like a billion years later, the first batch of cookies had cooled down enough that Mama let me have one. It was so yummy that I felt like peanut butter and chocolate were having a party in my mouth. I told Mama that and she laughed.

"Mama," I said as I licked the last of the chocolate off my fingertips, "I can't wait until I'm all growed up."

"Grown up," she told me while trying a bite of her own cookie. "And why is that?"

"Because when I'm grown up," I told her happily, "I can marry David H. from my class. Not David C.; he's the one who pinched me on our science-day field trip. But David H. is my friend, and he said he would marry me if I gave him my red slap band. So then I can be married and have babies, and they'll have a mama and a daddy just like Marissa's family. Then I can bake every single day because that's my job, and me and David H. can eat all the cookies we want

because when you're growed up you get to be in charge of yourself. Right, Mama?"

When I looked up at her, she had a funny expression on her face. I didn't know what I'd said that was wrong, but I could tell something was. She seemed sad. She had to swallow a few times before she could answer me, even though she didn't have anything in her mouth.

"You know what I always loved most about baking?" she asked me.

I wasn't sure what this had to do with David H., but I was happy she didn't have that look on her face anymore. I shrugged my shoulders so she would continue.

"I always love how happy it makes other people to try a special treat. It makes me feel good inside when I know that they're enjoying something I made just for them."

"Me too!" I said happily. "That's why it's gonna be my job some-day." I thought for a second and then asked, "I can do that, right? There are people whose job it is to bake things."

Mama reached out to run her fingers through my hair. "You," she said with a smile, "can do anything you set your mind to." She made a silly face that made me laugh. "Just don't mix gummy bears and peanut butter."

Chapter Three

I make a hurried grab for the caramel while still holding the mixing bowl, and chocolate batter splats across the kitchen floor. I curse, happy I'm home alone because Landon would definitely screech in reaction to my using those two words together in the same sentence.

"Girl, you have the mouth of a sailor!" my roommate calls from the entryway.

So I'm not home alone, after all.

I can hear her shuffling and struggling with the door, her bags, and whatever else. I look around, realizing I need to clean up ASAP. I've thoroughly trashed the kitchen trying out this recipe, and I'm supposed to help her come up with drinks to make that espresso tequila palatable tonight. As if that's possible.

She's mumbling to herself as I pull on my mitts and slide the pan halfway out of the oven.

"Are you wearing clothes?" she calls out accusingly.

I drizzle another layer of caramel over the nearly finished brownies and sprinkle them with a layer of this round's add-on.

"Of course I'm wearing clothes. Since when do I run around here nude?" I call back. I bend over to slide the pan into the oven as I hear her walk down the hallway to the kitchen.

"It's not nudity I'm worried about, but your typical shocking lack of"—I'm still adjusting the brownie pan with my oven mitt when she walks into the kitchen and gasps—"pants."

At that same moment, I hear a decidedly masculine choking sound. I glance behind me and see Landon's whole face turn every shade of red available in the spectrum. Her friend Taylor stands next to her, eyes wide in shock before they dart away from the sight of me bent over the oven door wearing a partially buttoned flannel and a miniscule pair of boxers I got in the preteen boy's section. Yes, I *am* dressed, dressed enough to hang out with Landon and Miko, but the threadbare shorts barely cover up anything.

Good effing grief! Who brings a man over without even a text message of warning?

I stand up to glare properly at them both, and when I put my hands on my hips, I realize that I still have a lobster-claw oven mitt on each hand. The fact that I look ridiculous isn't helping my annoyance level.

"Hey, Princess," I hiss, and she has the sense to look contrite. "I thought we talked about bringing douche bags back to the apartment."

Taylor looks back at me, and I meet his challenging stare with one of my own. He's taller than I am (which is saying something), with dark-brown hair and eyes. Landon and Miko think he looks like a built version of Adam Levine. They offer this up like it's some kind of compliment, but I think Maroon 5 are my mom's favorite band . . . which pretty much sums up their level of cool.

Taylor leans up against the wall with his arms crossed like he's settling in to watch a show. I'm momentarily distracted by the tattoos that cover both of his arms in a kaleidoscope of color. When I follow the line up towards the sleeve of his white T-shirt, his bicep flexes. My gaze snaps up to the humor dancing in his eyes. He thinks I was checking him out. I glare at them both.

"Max, don't be rude. You know Taylor isn't, well, that. He's helping Miko and me with the layout for the party, and since we're sampling cocktails anyway, I thought it'd be easier to do it all at once."

"I wasn't aware I make you so uncomfortable, Jennings," Taylor says with mock sincerity. "I'd be happy to come back another time."

I start to point an angry finger in his direction, but then I realize my hand is still covered by a giant fabric claw and slam it back down to my side.

"In order for you to make me uncomfortable, I'd first have to give a damn, Bennett." I purposefully use his first name since only his friends call him by his last. We're definitely not friends. In fact, I assume the only reason Landon and Miko like him is because they all worked events together. Based on the dark circles under Landon's eyes during the latter part of her time at SSE, I'm guessing working events together is sort of like being in the same platoon. I don't care if they think he's great, or that he's some kind of wunderkind in event production and uses that knowledge to help them out. He might play Boy Scout with them all he wants, but he's gone out of his way to antagonize me since the moment we met.

He responds with an amused grin, which I ignore by turning back around to clean up the rest of my mess. Landon walks through the kitchen with her bags and, in her typical style of avoiding conflict, refuses to acknowledge our bickering.

"I'm going to change out of these work clothes. Y'all try not to kill each other while I'm gone."

I start to pile dirty dishes into the sink and pick my way through the destroyed kitchen. Chocolate- and flour-covered bowls and spatulas are everywhere. Broken potato chips are strewn about as if I threw them into the air like confetti. I am not a tidy cook, and it takes several minutes of scrubbing before I can even see the countertop again. Taylor doesn't speak or move, but I can feel him watching me. I'm positive that if I turned around now I'd see him grinning like a jackass.

When the last dirty spatula sails into the sink with the other dishes, I turn to grab my brownies from the oven. Mindful of my audience, I don't bend down this time as I use my lobster claw to pull them out. As soon as they are visible, Taylor gasps, and I turn my head to face him.

"Dear Lord, are those potato chips?" He pushes himself off the wall and comes to stare into the pan as if I'm holding plutonium. I look along with him, surprised that my desire to push him out of my personal space is warring with the excitement I hear in his voice.

"It's"—I clear my throat—"it's a mixture of potato chips and pretzels. It's a play off of salty and sweet. I'm hoping they still have a crunch, but it's a new recipe idea, so I can't be sure."

I have no idea why I just explained all of that to him, and I utterly loathe that I've now initiated a conversation. I put the pan on the stove, grab the edges of the parchment paper, pull it out along with the brownies, and set them on a wire rack to cool.

"Can I try one of those?" he asks.

I can actually hear the chocolate-lust in his voice.

"No!" I snap.

"Why?"

"Because they're mine."

"What are you, five?" he accuses.

I realize that on some level I am acting like a five-year-old. I made the brownies for other people to eat; it's not as if I can enjoy them myself. But this guy hasn't done anything but antagonize me since the moment we met, and if he tried the recipe and offered any criticism, I'd have to bash his head in with the brownie tray. Then blood would get all over the already-messy kitchen.

I'm saved from further conversation when the doorbell rings and he turns towards it.

"It's my door to answer!" I bark.

Taylor just shrugs as if he's totally unaffected by my attitude and leans back against the countertop. I walk off to the entryway and throw the door back without even checking to see who it is first.

Miko is on the other side of it, looking gorgeous but also sort of as if she just left an outdoor music festival.

Honestly, when did macramé become a thing again?

"Did you just come back from Burning Man?" I ask as she walks past me into the apartment.

She turns towards me with a somber expression.

"It's too much, right? I knew it was, but I couldn't help myself." She lets out a long sigh, as if she's about to admit something truly upsetting. "Dude, I think I'm finally too old for Urban Outfitters. It used to be just a little edgy, but now everything there is like half-shirts and acid washed and I'm just always going to be too—"

"Asian?" I tease as I follow her back to the kitchen.

She throws me an annoyed look over her shoulder.

"No, short. I was going to say I'll always be too short to pull it off."

"Six of one, half a dozen of the other." I can't help but smirk at her.

Miko doesn't break stride as she pulls her giant shoulder bag off of her arm and lets it fall to the floor with a thud.

"Ooh, you're extra grouchy today. Why is that?"

No sooner is the question out of her mouth than she rounds the corner into the kitchen and sees Taylor hovering over the brownies.

"Ahh." She smiles at me as if she's got me all figured out.

"I am not extra anything, I—"

Taylor turns towards us, already chewing. He's holding a brownie the size of his hand and wearing an unrepentant expression.

"I can't be held responsible," he tells me before I can even open my mouth to yell. "It's all my favorite food baked together in one pan," he says almost desperately. "It's like kryptonite."

Miko rushes forward to inspect the cooling rack.

"How are they?" she asks, already cutting herself a square.

It actually takes me a second to find the words, because I'm so shocked by their total lack of manners.

Who eats someone else's baked goods without being invited to do so?

I open my mouth to rip into them just as Taylor actually sighs into his next bite. "They're incredible. Possibly the greatest thing to ever happen to my mouth."

My lips snap closed.

How do you scold someone who just gave you a compliment like that? I want to, based on principle, but I can't do it. Because truthfully, if potato chips and chocolate are his kryptonite, then people liking my recipes is mine. Taylor's smile kicks up to one side as he chews, and a single perfect dimple appears. He looks from Miko to me.

"Well, there was that model last summer—"

"Big-Lips Chloe?" Miko asks between bites.

"The very same." He answers her but looks at me. "So this was, I guess, the second greatest thing to ever happen to my mouth. But that's still a wild endorsement for your skills in the kitchen, Sebastian." He looks pointedly at the lone lobster mitt I still have on my hand.

"Sebastian was a crab, not a lobster," Miko says, hopping up on the counter behind her.

"You're right." He smiles at her indulgently. "My knowledge of crustaceans as immortalized in the annals of cinematic history is surprisingly sparse."

I clench my fist inside the ridiculous oven mitt, but I refuse to give him the satisfaction of my taking it off. Since when did guys with perfectly sculpted arms and massive tattoos start using words like "annals"?

Since when did I start noticing his sculpted anything?

"What's surprisingly sparse?" Landon asks as she walks back into the kitchen, wearing her workout clothes.

She makes a beeline for the brownie pan and cuts herself a sliver.

"The number of quality historical novels involving a Viking love story?" Miko answers helpfully.

Landon throws the little weirdo a bemused expression.

"That only really makes sense to you. You get that, right?" she says, cutting a slightly bigger sliver this time.

"Doesn't make it any less true," Miko answers wistfully from her perch. "Now then, someone promised me booze, and if I don't have a cocktail in my hand soon, I'm going to eat whatever's left of this pan of stoner-delight. Landon, stop cutting one miniscule bite at a time and just take a whole piece." Landon stops midslice to argue, but Miko ignores her and looks at me. "And Max, go put on some flipping pants, because Taylor can practice nonchalance for only so long, and I'm not sure he can help us with our timeline if he's surreptitiously staring at your Iron Man chonies all night."

I open my mouth to answer her, but between the *Little Mermaid* reference, Landon slowly hacking away at my brownies, the Vikings, and Miko's bossiness, I've lost some of the steam behind the tirade I was about to go on.

I turn and head out of the kitchen, going the long way, all the way around the breakfast bar, to avoid walking past Taylor. If that jackass is inclined to check out my shorts, I'm not going to give him a clear line of sight.

———

"And this one is?" Landon takes a sniff of the cocktail in her hand.

The other six options I created are lined up on the coffee table between me, her, and Miko. Taylor took off right after they finished working out the timeline for the party this weekend. I stayed in the kitchen mixing the drinks, but I heard him claim he had other work to finish up that evening. Since it was after eight o'clock, I couldn't help but wonder if his "work" had an IQ that was at least as big as her bra size.

"That one"—I point at the lowball glass in Landon's hand—"is an espresso margarita made with a citrus-infused simple syrup and a cinnamon-sugar rim."

"Well, that sounds like—" Miko starts in cheerfully.

"The best I could come up with given the required ingredient." I roll my eyes. "I told you both already, espresso-flavored tequila is an abomination."

I take a sip from my own cocktail, which remains espresso and tequila free. Landon does a weird little dance as she sips on the cocktail in her hand and then grins as she sets it to the side.

"Well, abomination or not, Riverton Tequila is our biggest client and is currently making it possible for me to pay rent on time," she says while making a note in the giant event binder she carries around for each party.

"And how bad can it be?" Miko asks, pulling the tequila bottle over and pouring some into a shot glass to taste. "Tequila is good. Espresso is good." She gives it an exploratory sniff. "It smells interesting."

I watch with a grin as she shoots the entire glass into her mouth and swallows, but I don't fight my laughter as she battles the urge to spit it all back up again.

"Oh my, *no!*" Miko points an angry finger at the bottle. "*Why? Why* would someone do that to perfectly good liquor?"

I don't need to say "I told you so"; I assume my smirk says it for me.

Landon sips the next drink and smiles over the rim of the glass. "This one isn't bad. What's it called?" she asks.

"Espresso Sunrise," I tell them, folding my legs underneath me on the couch. "Except I used both dark- and white-chocolate liqueur to get the gradient color."

"You're so creative, dude," Miko tells me as she reaches out to grab the glass.

She takes a sip and almost immediately fights a gag reflex.

"Gods, I hate this stuff." She glares at the glass in her hand.

Landon laughs at her. "Why do you keep drinking it, then?"

Miko shrugs. "Most liquor tastes terrible. At least this one has the added bonus of caffeine. Plus, if the client asks I want to be able to speak about the menu intelligently."

Landon sips the third drink and promptly sets it to the side distastefully. I guess my play on a Tom Collins didn't go over well.

"Speaking of the menu," Landon asks, "what are we going to name these things?"

"Ooh, how about we play off famous literary references, like Tequila Mockingbird!" Miko pipes up happily.

She never misses an opportunity to allude to anything book related.

I purse my lips in irritation since she felt the need to yell loud enough for the neighbors to hear. Landon happily picks up the gauntlet.

"The Polar Express-o." Landon giggles helplessly. "And it's—I don't know—chilled or something."

"Good enough!" Miko tells her.

They both look at me like eager puppies.

"Um, Tequila Flat?" I try.

"Boo!" Miko says through laughter. "Nobody under a hundred will get a Steinbeck reference!" She runs her fingers back and forth through her already-wild hair. "Hmm, I wish I could think of some play on *Graceling*. Not necessarily a classic per se, but I *adored* that trilogy. We could have a drink that is two different colors, which would be totally esoteric, I know, but if anyone got it they'd be way stoked."

I rarely know what Miko is talking about, but my little buzz from half a cocktail is making me feel benevolent. I try to speak her bookish language.

"Is that the one with the different factions?" I ask.

Miko gasps in outrage.

Landon scowls at me.

"You know better than to bring up *Divergent* around her," Landon says emphatically.

"But I thought—"

"I'm still not over it, OK?" Miko says seriously.

I'm confused. "But didn't you read those a while ago?"

"The pain doesn't ever really go away." She stabs a straw down into the drink closest to her before taking an angry sip. She only gags once this time, then continues her diatribe. "There were just so many other possible endings and it was—"

"We know, girl. Let's try not to focus on it, OK?" Landon says while glaring at me.

I glare back.

If they expect me to keep track of all the fictional characters and subplots that might send Miko into a tailspin, we are going to be here awhile.

"Let's move on." Landon pats Miko's shoulder reassuringly. "Drink number four has a cinnamon stick as a garnish. Isn't that fun?"

"Four!" Miko cries sadly.

I look at Landon, at a loss.

I don't know what that means, I mouth to her.

"It's OK, sweetie," she tells Miko with a roll of her eyes and a smile.

The best option now is just to play along and try to divert her attention. She's had at least a whole drink now between all of her sampling, and Miko's theatrics are always exacerbated by liquor and the mention of young adult fiction.

———

The next morning my alarm goes off way too early. Of course, anytime I have to set an alarm, it's too early for me. I roll out of bed, and I'm already in the bathroom brushing my teeth before my mind is even fully awake. In the mirror I can see that last night's mascara is smudged in every direction, but I don't wipe it away. I put it on thick, and only a three-step process or an act of God is going to get it off. First things first, though, I need coffee.

I walk out into the hallway and head for the kitchen, with my eyelids open just wide enough to see the way.

I smell the coffee before I see it, and then I turn into the kitchen and find Landon there drinking her own cup. I'm so thrilled at finding the caffeine already waiting for me that I almost smile, or at least sort of grimace in an upward direction. Landon beams at me over her mug with way too much enthusiasm.

"Happy Sunday!" she calls.

I hate morning people.

"I'm gonna go to church, and then I thought I'd hit the farmers' market. You wanna come?" she asks when I don't respond to her greeting.

"Work," I grumble in reply.

She looks around the kitchen; for what, I don't know. Finally she gives up the pretense.

"Your mom called me!" It bursts out of her mouth like a cheer, and she instantly starts biting her lip when I scowl in response.

"She said you won't answer your phone. She said you're being prickly and combative, and you're going to force her to do something drastic."

I swallow my first sip of coffee too quickly, and it burns my tongue. I am instantly awake and annoyed.

"She doesn't need to check up on me," I bark at her. "I am not a child!"

Landon smiles at me, and it's just short of patronizing. At twenty-three she's younger than I am, younger than everyone we hang out with, actually, but that's never stopped her from trying to offer an opinion to anyone who will listen.

"Then maybe you should stop acting like one," she says, before raising her cup and taking a demure sip.

I am way too flipping tired to be having this conversation with her.

"Oh, you can just stop your scowling right now. It hasn't worked to scare me off yet, and it likely causes premature wrinkles."

I stare mutinously at the neon hearts covering her pajama pants. The fact that someone wearing so many shades of pink at one time feels comfortable lecturing me just shows how far off track my life has gotten since she cartwheeled into it last year.

"I don't want to talk about this right now," I growl.

"We have to. You're never ever awake this early, so it's the perfect time. Plus I have an event tonight, so we can't talk then. What's going on? Why won't you return Viv's calls?"

I refuse to answer the questions simply because she thinks she can ask them. I latch onto the first part of her reasoning.

"I'm awake this early because I have to meet with the produce supplier to approve the new selections for work," I yell, and make a beeline back to my room. "You acting like a harpy is going to make me late!"

"Why won't you stay and discuss this?" she demands, stamping her foot.

"Because I don't want to," I say. Then I throw out the most mature statement of the century: "And because I don't like you very much right now!"

"Yeah, well, I don't like you right now either!" she yells back.

I'm actually kind of impressed; that was pretty stern for Landon.

"Max?" she calls sheepishly.

"What?"

"Take an umbrella. It's supposed to be unseasonably drizzly today."

All trace of her aggravation is gone. She sounds more worried about my getting caught in bad weather than my yelling at her.

I sigh so loudly that she's got to be able to hear it even back in the kitchen. That's the problem with Landon; she's always quick to get over an argument, and ridiculously thoughtful and kind. She makes it sort of impossible to hate her. It's one of her most annoying qualities.

———

The meeting with the hotel's produce supplier is in the back of the industrial kitchen. The room itself is roughly the size of a small island nation because it supports all the restaurants and bars on-site. The assembled motley crew in the room are gathered around a long stainless-steel table that's covered with every imaginable bit of produce you'll find in season. Since we're in California and it's early summer, the assortment is extensive.

Fresh fruits, vegetables, and herbs are spread out in every direction and are being sampled, sniffed, and discussed by the sous-chefs from all of the hotel's restaurants. They're all tattooed and grizzled, and every one of them looks as delighted to be awake before ten in the morning as I do. Since almost all restaurant-industry employees work late, we aren't typically known to be joyful early risers. As the supplier hands out different seasonal produce to sample, it doesn't escape my notice that I'm the only woman in this crowd and the only one who isn't actually a chef. Typically the general manager of Gander should make all the decisions, but he doesn't know anything about mixology, which is why I'm here instead. I step forward and sort through the herbs directly in front of me. In turn I pick up basil, rosemary, thyme, and lavender and rub them between my fingers until their scent saturates the air around me. All of them can be muddled in my drinks, infused within a simple syrup, or used to make a flavored spirit. The goal with any of them, at least as far as I'm concerned, is to find flavors that complement each other in unexpected ways. Like the bite of black pepper with the tartness of a fresh mango, or a dirty martini served with a white-chocolate truffle on the side. Or the acidity in heirloom tomatoes muddled against summer strawberries at the height of the season. Actually, we might just be close enough to that part of the season to try a version of that drink.

I reach out to sample a berry, but a tiny hand slaps mine out of the way.

What the—

I turn to snap at my attacker, but the words die on my tongue. She can't be more than five feet tall, and half of that height appears to be made up of salt-and-pepper hair that's pulled up high in a topknot that defies gravity. She's wrapped a scarf around her head too many times to count, and the effect is a brightly colored turban. Even though she just attacked me, she's not even paying me any notice now. Her eyes are entirely on the berries, praising them like a beloved pet.

I never knew it was possible to be jealous of fresh fruit.

I've watched Avis Phillips through the window of Dolci more times than I can count. I've tried every dessert she's ever served on her menu, and I've read all of her cookbooks cover to cover. I've seen celebrities and musicians; hell, I met the president a few years ago when my parents bought a table at his fundraising dinner. But I've never been as starstruck as I am now.

"I am such a massive fan of your work!" It bursts out of my lips and falls in the space between us. I'm so shocked that I said it that I take a step backwards, as if the distance will erase my mortification. I look down, surprised to see my words aren't actually flapping around on the ground like a dying bird.

Avis squints up at me through gigantic purple bifocals.

"What's the best dish on my menu?" She barks it like an order.

I take a step forward.

"My favorite is—"

"I didn't ask your favorite, Stork; I asked what was best."

She looks back down at the table before her and starts inspecting the blueberries. I don't even question the nickname. I'm tall, she's short, whatever. Frankly, she could call me any name at all and most of the curse words I know, and I'd still answer to it. My career-crush on her is that bad.

"The orange-zest *Baumkuchen* with the white-chocolate ganache." I answer her without giving myself time to debate it.

She barely moves her eyes from the berries, but there's a little flicker of notice, and it's enough that I can see I've caught her attention.

I keep talking.

"It's incredibly labor intensive, and almost impossible to pull off. Most people wouldn't attempt more than ten or twelve layers, but yours has thirty-eight—I've counted them. More than once."

She snorts in response and starts to manhandle a loquat like she's checking it for concealed weapons. After another couple of minutes I realize that she's not going to speak to me anymore. I keep watching her, racking my brain and trying to think of what I can say to engage her in conversation again. I never thought I'd actually meet her, and now that she's in front of me, every single question I've ever wanted to ask her comes bubbling to the surface. How many years did she attend culinary school? What made her want to be a baker in the first place? How does it feel to be a female boss with a staff of all men? Why doesn't she use raspberries in her layer cake? Did she really throw a drink in Thomas Keller's face at last year's South Beach Wine and Food Festival?

There is only one female Certified Master Pastry Chef in the entire nation, and she's standing next to me. I have to ask her something in case I never get this opportunity again! I filter through the litany of questions and quickly decide on the most important.

"Is it cardamom? Is that what you put in the *budino*?"

Her head turns in my direction. Her mouth is outlined on all sides by wrinkles from a lifetime of smoking, and when her lips purse, I take it as permission to continue.

"There's a little hint of something under the flavor of the caramel, and I've always wanted to know what it is."

She studies me again in closer detail, and I try not to fidget while she looks me over. Finally she opens her mouth and shocks me completely.

"I'm hiring, Stork. You interested?"

Chapter Four

I'm not sure that I was able to give Avis any kind of verbal commitment, because I was too overwhelmed to reply. But surely I must have nodded or something, because here I am following her down the hallway like a dutiful puppy. We come from the main kitchen and in through the back of a smaller kitchen, where Latin music is bouncing out of surprisingly nice stereo speakers and filling the already-hot room.

Avis whirls around and looks at me. Through the lenses of her giant glasses, her eyes look twice as large as they are.

"You're here because I need a stork," she says.

I never thought my height would be any kind of job qualification, but Avis's oddball personality is as notorious as she is, and I'll take whatever help I can get.

I nod. "Yes, I—"

She waves me off with an erratic hand.

"No need to discuss it. Joey will tell you what you need to know. I'll only tell you one thing."

She takes out a pack of cigarettes and taps it against her hip. We stand there in silence for at least three minutes before I realize the cigarettes are keeping time with the music in the air. It's a little awkward—OK, more than a little awkward, but I wait patiently for her to tell me whatever it is she wants me to know. When she does finally get around to it, the words are no less ominous for having been delivered by the absent-minded professor.

"Nobody ever gave me a chance, Stork"—she points the pack of cigarettes at me—"and you're getting this. It's the only one you'll get from me."

I nod earnestly.

"Now"—Avis points a wrinkled finger at the tile below my feet—"you stand there."

I nod again, but she's already walking away. I'm standing in the exact spot she left me, dead center where four dark-orange tiles come together. *X marks the spot.* I look around, using the moment to try to calm myself enough to process what's happening. The scuffed toe of my Converse is so old and grimy that the white has long faded to gray. A plume of flour in the air dissipates and settles around my shoes, snapping me into focus, and my brain finally catches up.

I'm standing in Dolci!

I whirl around until I can see the partition of glass that separates the kitchen from the lobby, just to confirm where I am. How many times have I stood on the other side of that glass and wondered what it would be like in here? How often have I watched the first crew and wished I knew what they were working on?

I spin back in the other direction, suddenly wanting to memorize every single bit of the action I can, in case I never get back here again.

The energy isn't frenzied, unlike the restaurant kitchens I'm used to, but the handful of people working around me radiate with a kind of intense focus as they carry out the tiniest of movements over and over. In the far corner of the room, a young guy is using a long paddle to add dry ingredients into a mixer that's at least twice as big as I am. When the muscles in his back move each time he lifts one of the giant bowls, it looks as if they're going to pop through the chef coat he wears. I wonder if he needed those muscles to do this job, or if having the job gave him the muscles.

Just next to him, tall metal rolling shelves are stacked with sheet upon sheet of baked goods. Even from a distance I can spot the scones, muffins, and chocolate croissants that compose Dolci's morning offering. On the next rack over, dozens of cupcakes wait to be iced. I can't see the color of the cake they're made of, but I'd know the current menu in my sleep. I imagine I can make out the colors of black forest, raspberry red velvet, lemon ricotta, and a pumpkin spice with a cinnamon cream-cheese icing that shouldn't be on anyone's summer menu but is so popular that they serve it year round.

Next to the baked goods an older man is drizzling what looks like melted dark chocolate over long rows of biscotti. If they're the menu item I think they are, he'll finish them with a dip in crushed, toasted hazelnuts.

To my right is a tall bald man with biceps that are roughly the circumference of my head. He's working on something that bubbles and steams from a saucepot in front of him. The hum of the kitchen is blocking out the sound of whatever he's saying, but from here it looks like he's professing his love to the sauce. The action is so totally incongruous with someone who looks more like a thug than a saucier that I can't stop staring.

"It's a sonnet," someone says behind me.

I turn around, expecting to find Avis since I didn't know any other women were in this kitchen. A beautiful petite woman stands in front of me wearing an oversize chef coat that barely covers her extremely pregnant stomach. Her long dark hair is braided over one shoulder, and I can't tell if it's the heat or the pregnancy that makes her shine, but her deep golden skin absolutely glows.

"Excuse me?" I ask, confused.

"Harris." She smiles and nods her head in the direction of the saucier. "He recites Shakespeare's sonnets to his recipes. It's early in the day, so I'd guess he's still at the beginning of the list. Sixteen or seventeen, maybe."

Her speech is slightly accented, but I can't place where she might be from.

"Papi," she calls out to him.

The giant's lips stop moving instantly, and he turns in her direction with an indulgent smile.

"Which one are you on now?" she asks.

"But wherefore do not you a mightier way," he says loudly above the din, "make war upon this bloody tyrant, Time? And fortify your self in your decay with means more blessed than my barren rhyme? Now stand you on the top of happy hours, and many maiden gardens yet unset with virtuous wish would bear you living flowers." He finishes his recitation with a wink and turns back around to the stove.

She smiles and reaches out a hand to me.

"I'm Joey."

"Mackenzie Jennings," I say, shaking her hand. "Everyone calls me Max."

I blame the introduction on nerves. I haven't introduced myself with my full first name in years.

"Come on. We'll get you set up." She starts to waddle towards the back of the kitchen, rubbing her lower back with one hand. I have no idea how someone can be this pregnant and work in this heat. It can't be good for her.

It makes me anxious.

"When are you due?" I can't stop myself from asking.

Joey turns her head with another sweet smile.

"Oh, a few weeks from now," she says wistfully.

At my horrified expression she continues, "I think she hoped if she just ignored my belly, it wouldn't eventually pop and turn into a baby. Avis is excellent at ignoring things she doesn't want to deal with. Frankly, I'm shocked she hired a replacement. We all thought I'd still be in here when I went into labor. Everyone was betting on what recipe I'd be making when my water broke. My money was on the syllabub."

Joey giggles at her own joke before leading me to a cabinet in the back of the kitchen. She reaches up on tiptoes to grab one of the freshly pressed white chef coats from the inside and hands it to me. I stare down at the stark white linen in my hand, mesmerized by the large cursive "D" embroidered in silky black thread on the front.

I reverently trace my fingers back and forth over the lettering. My exchange with the jacket can't take more than a few seconds, but there must be something telling about the deferential way I'm holding it. Because when I look up again, her smile has been replaced with a grimace.

"Please, *please* tell me this isn't the first time you've held a chef coat in your hands!" She starts rubbing her lower back faster in clear agitation.

It goes against my nature, or probably anyone's nature, to actively try to piss off a woman this pregnant. I don't want to stress her out more with the truth, but she'd catch me in a lie easily. I reach down and fiddle with the bracelets on my left wrist before answering.

"It is, but—"

Joey's head snaps to the left like a hunting dog narrowing in on a small bird.

"I'm going to kill her," she says vehemently. "This time I'm actually going to kill her!" Her right hand continues to rub her lower back aggressively, and she storms off as quickly as her belly will allow.

When I catch up to her a few steps later, still clutching the coat in my hands, she's mumbling to herself in Spanish. I'm shocked at the four-letter words streaming out of this petite cherubic-looking woman. I didn't mean to upset her, and I do my best to break into her diatribe.

"I haven't worked in a kitchen before, but I've been a mixologist for the last few years."

Joey stops and glares at me.

"A bartender!" she says with disgust.

Her accent is more pronounced now, feisty and Latin in her anger. Before I can say another word, Harris, the overly muscled poem-reciting thug, steps up to us and places a hand on her back, rubbing in the exact spot she was just touching. I stare on stupidly as he uses his other hand to sweep the hair that's escaped her braid off of her face. His large, rough hands look like they could do some serious damage in a bar fight, but he touches her with utter reverence. I notice the wedding band on his finger and then the smaller matching band on hers.

Man, I did not see that coming.

"Love, what's wrong?" he asks, searching her face for the answer.

At his question Joey leans into him and looks back at me, her eyes shiny with tears.

"She's a stage." She looks up at him miserably. "She's never even worked in a kitchen before! How am I supposed to train a stage in a few weeks?" She sniffs weakly.

I've researched enough about chefs to understand the word she used now. A stage is someone who comes into a kitchen as an untrained intern and works from the bottom up. It takes months, sometimes years, to move into a better position, but it's one of the only options if you haven't been to culinary school. I don't want her to cry, and I certainly don't want to piss off the giant next to her, but given my years of experience with confrontation, I'm not about to let them stand four feet away and talk about me as if I'm not here.

"Look," I say with enough emphasis that they both turn my way. "I've never been in this kitchen before, but I've worked in and around Gander's for the last three years. I haven't been trained, but I do know the mechanics and I'm a fast learner."

"I don't have the time to teach you," Joey says miserably.

At least she's not as angry anymore. I go for broke.

"You don't have time *not* to." I lift my chin defiantly. "You said it took her all nine months to grab me, and yes, I wasn't exactly well vetted. But I'm here now, and I'm smart and hardworking, and I've studied your menu like it's the Bible."

She keeps looking back at me doubtfully while Harris, a quiet mountain at her side, rubs that spot on her back.

I can't get this close and not even get a real chance! In a flash I see myself as that little girl dreaming up a recipe for brookies with my mom, then as a bit older, doodling what the storefront of my bakery would look like. Then I am a teenager looking through the websites of culinary institutes and trying to decide which one I'd attend after I finished undergrad.

They're long-buried hopes, but they're still just as strong. The dreams of your childhood aren't easy to ignore or to leave behind. They're the most powerful because you design them without boundaries or limits. It's what makes growing up so hard, because even though life has shown you different, it's hard to forget that there was a time when you believed anything was possible.

I work hard at being stoic—aloof, even—when it comes to work, but I hope she can see that little girl in my eyes now instead of the woman I've become. The woman I've become wants to say something rude and walk out the door. But that little girl in the small apartment kitchen, who dreamed about this for so long, is the one who keeps me standing here now.

"Please," I say quietly, "just give me a chance. I promise I won't let you down."

Joey breathes in slowly through her nose and out through her mouth. She could very well be having a contraction for all I know.

"Fine. I'll show you whatever I can in whatever time I have left—"

"You have eighteen days," Harris tells us both.

She looks up at him beseechingly. "You know that's not enough time, Papi. The doctor said I could go up to two weeks over before they'd have to induce, and I'm already cutting my hours in half as it is and—"

"You have two and a half weeks, Josephine," he tells her more firmly.

"Don't you dare use my full name. You are not my mother!"

Joey attempts to stomp away, but Harris grabs her gently and frames her face with both his hands. It is such an intimate moment, especially against the heat and the chaos of the kitchen around them, that I have to look away. I can still hear him, though, speaking to her in that same gentle cadence he used to recite the poem earlier.

"Love, you promised me. More than that, you promised *yourself* that you wouldn't work past your due date. Your back hurts all the time, and it's too hot in here. It's not good for you or the baby. You promised, Joey."

I don't know how she responds because I am staring intensely at the giant ovens lining the wall in the corner, but her voice finally pulls my gaze in their direction.

"Max, there is no way this is possible. I'm not saying that to be rude; it's just a fact. But this is Avis's kitchen, and it's her choice to make. I told her I would train a replacement and I will." She lets out a long sigh. "You have eighteen days."

I can't help but smile. I didn't plan on this moment, and I never thought I'd actually try to accomplish this dream. But it's right in front of me, and I'll jump at the chance.

"I'll take it!" I say, already unbuttoning the coat to put it on.

———

"This is Ram," Joey says, gesturing to the ripped Latino kid I'd seen working the giant mixer earlier. He smiles back at us both, a cocky grin that says he expects female adoration wherever he goes. His apron is stained with several different batters, and large bowls filled with every imaginable concoction cover the high tables around him like stainless-steel sentinels.

Joey continues, "Ram is short for—"

"Just Ram," he tells us both, using his fist to emphasize the word.

Joey snorts and keeps on going. "Ram, *elle es Max. Esta en entrenamiento.*" She looks at me and continues in English. "Ram makes all our batters and mixes. From there he'll hand them off to Tomás, who does the baking. I'll take you over to meet him next," she says, turning to go.

Ram reaches a fist towards me for a bump, and after I awkwardly oblige the gesture, he turns back around to heft a bowl up and into the arms of the mixer. Between the metal, the mixture inside, and the way his muscles work to maneuver it, I'm guessing that each one of those bowls weighs forty or fifty pounds. No wonder he looks so buff.

We tour the rest of the kitchen. Tomás takes batters from Ram and turns them into cakes, tart shells, piecrusts, and cookies. Harris is still whispering sweet nothings to a berry filling when we pass by him again. Joey tells me he makes all the sauces, fillings, glazes, and icings. I am suitably impressed. There are dozens and dozens of recipes on Dolci's ever-changing menu. To continually create totally different flavor palettes with such variation and nuance must require extreme attention. Maybe reciting sonnets is a way to help him focus, sort of like white noise.

Two older men take the finished products from Tomás and Harris and combine them to create the final confections. One of them is the man I'd noticed earlier with the biscotti, but now he is icing black-and-white cookies. Each person, it seems, has a specialized skill-set. For some it involves an incredible palate, while others might not know the difference between white or brown sugar, but they can ice a cake with the dexterity of a neurosurgeon. It is a hodgepodge of people, but each of them is an imperative cog in a well-oiled machine, and at its helm is an unusual old woman in a turban.

Avis stands at a high table in the corner, hand-whipping a small batch of something and muttering to herself. As we pass by her, Joey doesn't lower her voice. Even though we are a few feet away and audibly discussing her, I don't think Avis notices. She is far too caught up in what she is doing.

"Avis is working on new items for the room-service menu. We store all our pastries here, but there's no guarantee that once they hit room-service prep, they'll keep them properly chilled or fire them just right. She's trying to create recipes that are idiot proof but still feel like Dolci originals."

"So she creates all the new recipes for the hotel?"

"The desserts, breads, and pastries, yes. Then she also handles special orders for the events that come through here. She's mostly self-sufficient, but there are days when she'll want a babysitter." Joey looks at her with equal parts adoration and annoyance.

My eyes dart to Avis, who is hunched over her mixing bowl. I'm certain that she'll bark at us now, but she still doesn't acknowledge our presence. Joey turns and I follow.

"So she comes up with the recipe, and then you—"

"I take it from there. I test it in large batches, I teach it to each member of the team for quality control, I handle everyone's hours, I deal with management." She stops and looks at me seriously. "I run the kitchen, Max. She's a genius, to be sure, but she's also an artist. Artists are flighty, irresponsible, erratic. She needs someone who can manage her and this chaos." She gestures to the kitchen around us. "She needs that person, or this all goes away. It's not just her legacy either; there are ten people on staff here, and they need to be able to count on stability. That's not something she can give them."

As if on cue Avis stands and throws her recipe—whisk, bowl, and contents—into the large industrial sink with a crash. The noise is deafening, but no one in the room reacts to it but me.

"Damn it, Joey! I told you I wanted to stop using this chocolate. It's too sweet! I can't make anything with it!"

Joey doesn't even turn around. She just calmly calls over her shoulder, "Try the Valrhona instead—the one you used in the soufflé."

Avis stands in place, tapping an angry foot. When she speaks again she is slightly calmer.

"The Caraibe?"

"No, the Guanaja," Joey calls back, her eyes never leaving my face. "It's seventy percent cacao. It will balance out better for you."

Mollified by what Joey told her, Avis walks off to the back room.

"She needs someone to manage her, and it's not an easy job. I've trained under her for the last five years. The team here is great and they'll help you, but even still, I have no idea how you think you'll accomplish all you need to in so little time."

I finger my bracelets under the edge of my left sleeve.

"I'm tougher than I look," I tell her seriously.

"You'll need to be," she says as she walks off.

When she stops short I nearly run into her back.

"You'll also need different shoes," she says, eyeballing my Converse with disdain.

"Absolutely." I nod emphatically.

"And the bracelets," she continues.

"What?" I ask in confusion.

"The bracelets—you can't wear them in here. They could get snagged on something, carry bacteria, heat up enough over the ovens to burn you. There are a ton of reasons, but the biggest is that the health department doesn't make allowances for personal jewelry. A wedding ring? Yes. A hundred dangly bracelets?" She points at my wrist. "No way."

I feel something close to panic hit me then. I always wear my bracelets. Some of them are extremely important; the rest are, well, a way to camouflage the ones that matter. But I wear all of them constantly. I never take them off for any reason.

"I need to—" I clear my throat. "One of them is for medical reasons."

Joey doesn't even bat an eyelash.

"OK, so *one* of them you can wear," she says sternly. "The rest have to go. Same goes for the dramatic nail polish."

I look down at the deep black polish that Landon always teases me about. It is far easier to have bare nails than to take off the jewelry, but I'll think about that later. Right now I need to secure this job, and I'd agree to almost anything she says at this point. I nod in agreement.

"Yes, Chef," she tells me pointedly.

"Excuse me?" I ask, ever slow on the uptake, apparently.

Joey does another one of those breaths in through her nose and out through her mouth.

"The proper response in this kitchen," she says slowly, though not unkindly, "is, 'Yes, Chef.'"

"OK, I—" I catch myself just in time. "Yes, Chef."

Placated by my answer, she continues on her way and I hurry to catch up. I'm sure my face is the usual impassive and untouchable mask that gives no indication of how I feel. On the inside, though, I am laughing and screaming and jumping up and down. I've never been this excited in my entire life, and I'll allow my inner six-year-old to feel this joy, even if no one will ever know how much this job means to me.

Chapter Five

Five hours later I stumble back to my car in a daze. I spent all afternoon with Joey learning the intricacies of her job. Managing both the prep and general staff plus keeping the kitchen in working order, all within a massive hotel, requires a level of paperwork and politics on par with the Pentagon. Seriously, there are venture capital firms that don't require this many spreadsheets.

In our time together I learned about payroll, expense reports, purchase orders, and security. I learned who to call if someone cuts off a finger, if someone comes to work drunk, or if Avis goes completely off the deep end.

Apparently all three have happened before, and when I asked Joey to clarify what exactly "going off the deep end" meant, she told me not to worry—that I'll know it when I see it. We went over inventory, seasonal menus, and the hierarchy of the staff. We talked and worked so much that my brain turned to mush, and we hadn't even baked anything yet!

The whole process was overwhelming, intense, and so, so exciting. Despite my frustration with the awkwardness of our relationship right now, there is only one person I want to tell. I pull out of the parking structure and turn my car towards home.

———

When I park in my usual spot on the far left side of the circular driveway, Mom has the front door open before I even have my seatbelt all the way off. She stands in the entryway, her blonde hair pulled up in a ponytail, wearing fancy loungewear that she likely changed into the second she walked in the door tonight. Even in casual wear with no makeup on, she's still just as beautiful to me as she was when I was little. I've been avoiding her for the past few weeks because I'm tired of her hassling me about what I plan to do with my life now that I'm finished with school. But seeing the evident joy on her face because of something as simple as my dropping by unannounced actually makes me want to cry. I can be such a jerk sometimes, and usually it's directed at the people who deserve it the least.

"Mackenzie, will you get in here? Daddy is about to take the fillets off the grill, so you're just in time for dinner!" She sounds happy, like this was always part of our plan, like I haven't been avoiding her for the last month, like our relationship hasn't been strained for the last several.

I don't even make it all the way through the door before she pulls me down for a hug and smooths my hair as if I'm six years old again.

"I'm so happy to see you," she whispers into my hair. Then because she can't seem to help herself, she adds, "You need to get in for a cut. Should I have Christy make an appointment for you?"

I can't help but roll my eyes. Leave it to my mom to notice my split ends even without her contacts in. I shake my head.

Before I can say anything, she does.

"We're not going to get into it. I'm sorry I've been pushy. You know how I am," she tells me sardonically. "But please, don't disappear like that again, OK?"

"OK," I answer.

She smiles and touches my cheek once more.

"You look dead on your feet, which means you need food and probably alcohol, and I can supply both! Let's go find your dad."

We find Dad in the kitchen slathering melted Brie onto crostini.

"Well, this an unexpected treat," he says when he sees me walk in.

"I was hungry, and you guys can always be counted on to have the good cheese," I tell them by way of explanation.

I walk around the large center island in their massive kitchen to give him a hug, then he and I both start working our way through the cheese board in front of us.

Mom pours me a glass of pinot from the bottle they've opened and then starts making me a plate of food from the lineup on the counter. There are fillets cooked just a tad over medium, new potatoes in garlic and butter, and a green salad with a hodgepodge of likely every leftover vegetable they found in the fridge. She looks up at me when she comes to the last bowl.

"Do you want some fruit salad? Maria went to the farmers' market yesterday, and the berries are incredible."

On the surface the question seems completely innocuous; she's just asking if I want fruit. But with my mother, and my condition, her questions are never so innocent. What she's really asking is whether my blood levels can handle more sugar. I shake my head lightly.

"Better not." I nod towards the wine glass, which is sugar enough, especially when I didn't eat all that healthy today to begin with.

To her credit she plasters a smile on her face and casually sets my plate down at the table in the breakfast nook. I walk over and sit down in the same chair where I've eaten hundreds of meals throughout my life. At a holiday or a dinner with our whole family, we'd be more formal, likely sitting in the dining room eating a meal of perfectly prepared courses designed by their chef. But weekends are casual, a small reprieve for these socialites after a week filled with work, charity functions, and other formal events. I smile at the picture they make at the island as they work together to fill each other's plates in a ballet choreographed over years of happy marriage. I'm too hungry to wait for them to finish, though, so I start eating before they've even finished plating their meals. I've polished off half my steak when Daddy sits down and asks me how Landon and Miko are doing. When I look up to answer him, I see my mom still at the counter, dishing up a bowl of fruit salad. It's a simple task, but she looks as if she's fighting the urge to scream at the collection of seasonal berries.

Damn it.

I thought she was doing better lately. When I first had my accident back in December, she hovered over me obsessively, wanting to know every single thing I was eating and how much sleep I'd had the night before. I had to battle with myself daily not to snap at her because of it, and several times we launched into full-on arguments that always ended with her storming off in tears and me feeling terrible. I understand how scared she must have been when Brody called her. I understand that she doesn't ever want to see any of her kids sick. I understand that I nearly died that night, and that I likely would have if Landon hadn't found me. But even knowing why she's obsessing doesn't make it OK. I can't help but feel smothered and claustrophobic when she starts looking at me as if she's trying to calculate exactly how to fix me. I'm broken in so many ways, and I wish she'd just stop trying to figure out how to mend me.

She finally sits down with us and begins making chitchat. I can see her trying to pull herself back together, and I'm sure she realizes that her tendency to hover is why I've been avoiding her in the first place. If it's a battle between knowing my current insulin levels or having the kind of relationship where I drop by unannounced, she'll choose having me in her life over playing doctor, but it's a close thing.

As Daddy launches into the plans for a new high-end outdoor shopping center Barker-Ash is about to break ground on in the valley, Mom sends me a little wink to show me just how OK she is. She's still upset about my accident, but she's trying to show me that she can be respectful of my boundaries. What's going to happen if I tell her that I just took on a second job, one that's intense and stressful with long hours and little time for rest? How will she handle it if I try to explain that I can't yet quit the job at Gander because I don't know for sure if I'll get to keep the job at Dolci? I don't need to guess at the answer. That conversation would lead us back to her favorite argument of all: why I won't just let them give me money.

I know most people would jump at the chance to exist off funds from wealthy parents, but I live perpetually in the shadows of three golden siblings. My little sister, Malin, is blonde and sweet and beautiful, a near replica of my mother. The two Ashton boys both graduated college with honors and worked their way up to run Barker-Ash alongside my father. My brothers run a multimillion-dollar business with a combined staff in the thousands, and by the time they were my age, they each owned a home and an extensive stock portfolio. The most I have to show for my early twenties is the creation of muddled drinks and a handful of bar regulars who don't even know my first name. I may fall short in a lot of ways, but just like my brothers, I've been financially independent since I was eighteen years old, and pride won't let me go back now.

I take another bite of my food, though I'm not really hungry anymore. I force a smile as my mom laughs at a story my dad is telling and reaches out to squeeze his hand. This is the woman who taught me to cook, the one who gave me a love of baking, forged over a thousand sugar cookies. This is the person who showed me exactly what to eat so that I could enjoy at least one of those cookies we'd worked so hard to create without throwing off my insulin.

As a food lover, she'd understand my excitement and celebrate any accomplishment with me. But as my mother, she'd never accept a situation where I'm knowingly choosing to do something in direct opposition to what's best for my health. It's not even up for debate. I can't tell her about Dolci.

I can't tell her, or anyone else for that matter, because they're all in cahoots with her. They'll all worry and obsess and make my life hell, and I can't handle that, because I'm going to need every ounce of energy I have to keep a job I had no business getting.

"I'm sorry, what?" I ask. I didn't realize she was addressing me.

"I said"—she smiles sweetly across the table—"Kenzie, what's new with you?"

I can't remember how long it's been since we made it through an entire meal without arguing. I don't want to ruin this new truce, and I'm definitely not ready to tell them what's really going on.

I plaster a smile on my face and let the necessary lie fall from my lips. "Oh, not much."

———

It takes about a hundred cotton balls doused in acetone to remove every trace of polish from my nails.

My hands look sad and boring without the dark paint I'm used to, but I can't give Joey another reason to call me out. Especially since I'm going to disobey a direct request she gave me. I know it's stupid to take such a risk, especially since my job is in no way guaranteed, but I just can't remove all of my bracelets. I take off all but two.

I unclasp the smaller bracelet and wrap it around the bigger one like a vine before closing it up again. Without inspecting it closely it would be impossible to tell that it's two separate pieces.

One of the bracelets is the medical badge that identifies my condition. The other is a small inscribed piece that identifies my mistakes.

I won't ever forget those mistakes, just like I won't ever forget the day I knew I needed something to remind me of them.

———

I didn't get the chance to tell her to come in, because she didn't knock or ask for permission. She just barged into my room, and even across the dimly lit space, I could see her concern through my swollen eyes. Apparently the confirmation of my tears was enough to rein her in, though, because she closed the door behind her much more quietly than she'd opened it. She crossed the space to my bed carefully, as if landmines might be hidden under the hardwood. Each step just made me more emotional. At nineteen I was far too old to be crying to my mother about my problems, but I didn't try to stop the tears; what was the point now that she'd seen them?

She sat down on the edge of my bed and reached out to turn the lamp up on my bedside table. The light wasn't much stronger, but it must have been enough for her to get a good look at how ravaged my face was from another night of sobbing. It wasn't the only time I'd cried myself to sleep since I came home; it was just the first time she'd walked in on me doing it.

"Mackenzie"—she reached out gentle fingers to push my hair back from my face— "sweetheart, I wish you'd speak to me about what's going on."

Another tear followed the well-worn track down my cheek. I didn't answer her, but for the first time in weeks, I didn't stop her from trying to comfort me.

"Did . . ." She searched my face. "Did something bad happen?"

I couldn't help it. I snorted in response.

It was a disrespectful sound, one that mocked the question and the person who asked it—a reaction I never would have considered last year. There was something in me now, something hard and dark, that hadn't existed before. I'd learned to latch onto the bitterness, the sarcasm, and even the anger. Any of those were better than the never-ending tears.

"You're right." My mother smiled sadly. "Of course something happened. You're so"—she ran her fingers through my hair again—"different."

Anger came then, flinty and swift. I sat up against the headboard to glare at her properly.

"And by 'different' you mean 'not pretty,' right?" I ran a hand roughly through my messy hair. "It must be so upsetting for you to see me like this! Because even a faded beauty queen can work her way into at least one good marriage, right, mother?" I ignored her wounded gasp. "I mean, not the first marriage, obviously, but you certainly knocked it out of the park the second time around. I doubt you can expect the same stellar results from me since this is what you're working with!"

It was the ugliest thing I'd ever said to my mother, the ugliest thing I had ever even thought about her before. I hated myself so much in that moment that I could barely breathe. I didn't look at her face, because I was too terrified to see her expression. I turned to lie on my side facing away from her and pulled my knees to my chest, waiting for her to leave. The bed shifted when she got up, but I didn't move or say anything. It was better for both of us if she left now before I hurt her more. But then the mattress shifted again, and she was lying behind me. I felt her hand on my back. When she began making slow, gentle circles just as she used to at bedtime when I was little, I started to cry again. Only this time it was out of sheer *gratitude. A deluge of emotion in response to the understanding and forgiveness in that touch.*

"Mackenzie," she finally whispered into the near darkness. "My sweet, intelligent, beautiful *girl. I don't know what this is you're going through, but you're so strong. Do you understand that? Do you remember what I used to tell you when you were little? You can do anything you set your mind to, and that includes overcoming any obstacle.* You will get through this." *We sat in silence again with her vehement statement ringing in my ears. It resonated with me. Resonated enough that for the first time in a long while, I thought there might be a day when I didn't wake up hating myself.*

"Can I set up an appointment for you with Dr. Henry? Brianne said that he's wonderful. She's been going to him for—"

"No, mom," I croaked. "I don't want to see anybody. Please stop asking me to."

I heard and felt her sigh.

"Kenzie, I need you to look at me," she said then.

I rolled around to face her and watched her quietly while she seemed to be searching for words.

"Daddy told me to stop asking you about this. He thinks you'll tell us when you're ready." She searched my eyes as if looking for confirmation, but I couldn't give her any. "And I will stop talking about meeting with a therapist, because I know that makes you uncomfortable, OK?"

This time I nodded slowly.

"But Mackenzie, I need you to tell me—no, I need you to swear *to me—that nobody did anything to hurt you. That you weren't—"*

Understanding dawned, and I realized what she was asking. This was one answer I could give her honestly, because no, nobody else had hurt me. I'd done it all on my own.

"No, Mom. I swear nobody hurt me."

She closed her eyes, looking pained. When she opened them again they were glossy with tears.

"OK," she said quietly. "OK."

I could see the relief and the unconditional love in her eyes. For a moment I thought that maybe, just maybe, she'd be able to forgive me for what I'd done. I almost told her then, almost let it tumble out around me just so that the thoughts might stop eating away at my heart.

"Thank you," I told her instead, "for always taking care of me."

"Of course." She smiled radiantly. "What kind of person would I be if I didn't take care of you? You're mine. That's my most important job."

I slammed my eyes shut, shattered by how earnest her statement was. That was my mother, someone who put everyone else's needs above her own. She was unselfish, good down to her very core—the opposite of me in every way. Because of that, my current sadness wasn't something she could absolve me of. I was responsible for my mistakes, and if there was any bright side in that at all, it was that I now understood exactly how the world worked. My own naïveté was responsible for this hurt; I wouldn't allow myself to forget that. I wouldn't allow myself to forget the biggest lesson I had learned in all of this. I'd carry it around on a sign if I had to, but I would not forget.

Chapter Six

"So these are the molds," Joey says, handing me a stack of scalloped metal tart pans. "You get that butter there"—she points to a pile of European butter stacked to one side of the high metal worktable—"and use it to grease each one like this." Her fingers reach out for a scoop of butter and quickly work it in and around each groove of the tart pan. "Then you roll out the dough that Ram made this morning. Use this cutter to make the circle and then press it down into the mold like this." Her hands move as quickly as her words, shaping the dough as if she's done this a million times before.

When I came in this morning, she announced that I'd learn prep today. It wouldn't be part of my day-to-day work, but since I'm woefully unskilled for the job I've been hired for, I need to learn anything and everything she can teach me.

"Understand?" She holds up the pan, which now contains one perfectly pressed tart ready for the oven. I'm supposed to prepare the other eleven circles, but I'm actually not that nervous since I spent all of last summer perfecting my fruit tart. I feel pretty confident.

"Yes, Chef," I answer, already starting to stamp out the circles in the rolled-out dough on the counter.

She flashes me a quick smile, amused at my eager attitude, I'm sure.

"Then I'll leave you to it," she says, sliding the pan closer to me. "You can finish off today's quota, and then we'll work on something else."

"OK, great. How many do you need?" I ask her, not taking my eyes off the dough in front of me for fear of making a mistake.

"There's a luncheon here at the hotel tomorrow, and this is the signature dessert. Why don't you do four hundred just to be safe?"

My head snaps up from my work and then back down to the tiny scallops on the individual tarts. "Four hundred?"

Each one will take several minutes for me to fill. I had no idea they'd need so many. It's not impossible, just tedious.

"OK," I say again, already trying to move my fingers as quickly as she did. The dough looks a little beat up because of my efforts, and I slow back down. I'm going to have to crawl before I can walk.

Joey turns to leave, and I look quickly around the table to make sure there's nothing else I need before she goes.

"Oh, wait! Can you tell me where to find the rest of these?" I hold up the edge of the pan with buttery fingers.

She *almost* manages not to smile when she says, "That's the only one, I'm afraid."

"Excuse me?"

"Avis swears it's the only one that works right, since she's used it for a decade. It's the only one we've got."

"But . . ." I stutter stupidly. "How am I supposed to bake off several hundred tart crusts with only one pan?"

"I'm not sure, but figure it out quickly because Harris needs to start filling those at four so they have time to set." She says this with a wink.

I look back down at the dough miserably.

Damn, this is going to suck.

———

Several hours later I've amassed only a few dozen finished tart crusts, but I try not to focus on that. I just work my way through cutting one circle after another so that at least the dough is ready for the next round as soon as the pan comes out of the oven. I shouldn't look, but I can't help glancing at the clock every few minutes. The time just keeps slipping away bit by bit, and I can't finish them any faster than I already am. It takes twenty minutes to bake them, and during that time there's nothing to do but prep the dough. I'll be done with that soon, and then I'll have nothing to do but watch the oven like an idiot.

"Come on, Mama, I'm going to show you how we pull recipes next," Joey calls from behind me.

I turn around to see her waddling over alongside Ram, who's holding a stack of nearly a dozen pans. Tart pans.

What the hell?

"Ram will help Tomás finish these up," she tells me with another wink.

The pans clatter against the metal table, and Ram looks over what I've prepped so far. I stare back at Joey in utter annoyance.

"Hazing? Are you serious?" Without the oppression of three hundred unfinished tarts weighing me down, it's much easier to be sarcastic again.

Joey and Ram both smile like little demons.

"If we had the time, it would have been so much worse than this." She laughs.

I look to Ram, who's nodding along in agreement.

"At least you got a pan! When I started here they asked me to prep the tarts, only they didn't give me a mold. It's the closest I've ever come to crying in public!" he tells me with a grin.

I mutter something inappropriate under my breath, which only serves to make Joey laugh harder. She signals me to follow her, and once I wash the butter off my hands at the back sink, we walk to the area of the kitchen that's farthest from the ovens. It's only marginally cooler here, but marginally makes a hell of a difference when you start sweating through your clothes nine minutes into a ten-hour day.

Joey reaches to grab something from a rolling rack and lumbers over to me with it.

"This," she says as she lets a binder the size of a Mini Cooper fall to the table in front of me, "is the recipe book."

The binder is smudged and dirty, no doubt from its close proximity to a recipe in process at any given time. It's just a simple three-ring option, the kind of thing you'd find in any office-supply store, but I gasp when I recognize what it is. This ordinary book is filled with all of Avis Phillips's recipes. That's got to be at least forty years' worth of creations.

Are the secrets to my favorite cakes in this thing? Does it have the directions to make the profiteroles she won the US Pastry Competition with? Are there ideas in here that I've never even dreamed of before? I reach out to touch it and have a brief flash of that moment in *Indiana Jones* when their faces melted off because they looked at something too powerful for them to understand. I mean, I get that this isn't the Ark of the Covenant, but it sort of feels that way to me.

When I hesitate to actually touch it, Joey reaches out, unaware of the level of reverence I'm swimming in, and opens it at random. She starts to flip through the pages as she speaks. I inch closer until I can see everything. Each recipe is in a clear sheet protector, but beyond that there's no organization that I can determine. Some of them are written on notebook paper, some are typed, and some are so old they're yellowed and warped.

"All of her work is here. The handwriting on some of them is a little hard to read, but most of the recipes we work with at Dolci are new, so you'll find them typed out," she says, pointing out a lemon chiffon cake.

I know from firsthand experience that that dessert is like a citrus-infused cloud; it's so light and fluffy.

"She just stores these here on a back shelf?" I ask, dumbfounded. "They're not in a vault or something? What if someone steals them?"

"Everyone who comes through here wonders the same thing." She sighs. "Avis has her own way of doing things, and she's too old to be swayed. Occasionally she looks up an older dish as a reference, and if she couldn't find the binder, she'd have a meltdown." She gives me a deadpan look. "We try to keep the Avis meltdowns to a minimum."

"OK," I say, more than a little confused.

"Also, she changes her recipes up so often that if someone did try to rip something off, they'd be outdated. Most of her competitors would hate to think of themselves as behind a trend. Plus there's security here, and surveillance." She gestures to a small camera in the corner of the room near the ceiling. "And the staff is small and incredibly loyal. So this is relatively safe."

I nod in agreement with her logic.

"You've given this some thought."

Joey lets out a self-conscious laugh. "This damn book kept me up at night for weeks after we left the old restaurant. She put it on that shelf and said she wanted it left there, and I made myself sick worrying that someone would take it. I've given myself that speech about the surveillance cameras more times than I can count."

She rolls her eyes at the story, but I totally understand the notion. I'd be pretty sick over being responsible for something so valuable too.

"Now, why don't you start with this one?" She chooses something seemingly at random. "I think it's best if we just throw you right into it, OK?"

"OK," I agree.

I look down at the recipe for caramel-apple cupcakes with a cream-cheese filling. That is simple enough; I make cupcakes all the time.

"So go ahead and just make a dozen. This one is written for"— she taps the recipe with her finger as she reads—"four times that. But it's easy enough to divide out from there."

She raises her eyebrows in question, and I nod confidently. Joey heads back to the office with the promise that she'll be back in an hour. I lean down to get a closer look at the ingredients so that I can start gathering them.

I see words I know: eggs, water, milk. But then the words start to change into some kind of odd lingo, or they are written in symbols I can't decipher or understand. CF, PF, 10X, 6X, and even a hashtag. I don't know what any of it means. *How do I—*

I roll my eyes when I understand what's happening. Joey said they'd harass me more if they had time. I guess they decided they could make time. The thing is, though, I don't want my time wasted. Joey is only here for a little while, and I need to learn as much as I can before she leaves if I have any chance of succeeding. I don't want to spend the next two weeks playing stupid games with them. I need to do real work, not screw around with riddles. I remove the sheet protector holding the recipe and wonder how long they had to mess with it to make it appear so old. I go in search of the hazing committee.

I find Joey in the small office working through a spreadsheet on the computer in front of her. She has two small fans coming at her from different directions, both of them aimed directly at her face, but she still looks miserably hot. Some of my annoyance fizzles out. Even if she has been screwing around, I'm not about to yell at a pregnant woman.

"Hey," I call to her, and she spins around in my direction.

She looks at the recipe in my hand.

"Is there an issue? Are we out of the nutmeg? I don't always have it in stock this time of year, but I'm sure there's some in—"

"Seriously?" I ask with a sigh. "I get that this is probably entertaining for you guys, but I don't think we have time to be messing around."

Joey's brow furrows, and she manages to look truly confused.

"I don't understand," she tells me.

I take the two steps necessary to cross the small office and hold the recipe out for her inspection.

"I don't either," I tell her, pointing at the symbols. "The joke's on me; I get it. The recipe is written in code, and I don't understand it. Can we skip the part where you all harass me further and just give me a real recipe so I can get to work?"

"Written in code?" Joey asks, sounding totally perplexed.

She pulls the page out of my hand and starts to look it over. I watch her face take on some kind of comprehension, but I don't know what it is. Her eyes close slowly, and when she opens them again she doesn't look up at me.

"You don't know how to read shorthand."

It isn't a question. It's a statement, but it sounds more like a death sentence.

"What?" I nearly whisper, sensing something off in her tone. She isn't joking or even angry anymore. She sounds utterly disappointed, which scares the crap out of me.

"Baker's shorthand. This means powdered sugar." She points at the nonsensical words on the page, seemingly at random. "This is refined sugar, pastry flour, and this is the symbol for a pound of something."

I feel like a total moron. I had no idea there was such a thing as baker's shorthand. I'd been baking most of my life, but it was at home, using our family recipes or those we'd found in a cookbook. There was a whole special language I'd have to learn. The realization is daunting but also totally exciting.

"OK, sorry about that," I tell her. "Do you have a summary of terms or something I can—"

"I'm sorry, Max," Joey says, putting the recipe on the desk and standing up slowly. "This isn't going to work out."

I am so startled by the words that it takes me a moment to respond.

"I might not know the language yet, but I know how to bake. I've been creating new recipes since I was—"

"Max, you don't get it," she tells me sadly. "This isn't about creating *new* recipes. I'm a sous-chef. I'm Avis's second-in-command. I take her ideas and bring them to life. I teach them to the others on staff. I configure them for large quantities or check to see if there's a more streamlined way to get the same result. There's a science in that, and the most basic necessity of this job is the ability to understand what she started with and extrapolate from there."

"But if I just—" I try desperately.

"No." She says it without raising her voice, but I hear the finality just the same. "Half the time she doesn't even remember what she wrote down, but she never forgets one of her flavor palettes. That's why it's so critical that you can read her recipes, because she only really pays attention long enough to write it down once."

I open my mouth, but she cuts me off by shaking her head.

"This was already an impossibility, but I thought maybe we could figure it out. I didn't factor in the shorthand. Even the kitchen assistants are familiar with it before they apply here. There's just too much you don't know, and I can't risk it. Thanks for trying, though. It was really nice to meet you."

She sticks her hand out, and I am too stunned to do anything but shake it.

As I grab my bag and walk slowly out of the kitchen, I am in a daze. I don't look at anyone or notice if anyone looks at me. I make it all the way to the hallway next to the underground employee parking garage before I stop moving. It is early afternoon, a time of day between shifts, so no one is around. I let myself lean against the wall. My backpack falls from my loose fingers to the floor, and it seems like such a good idea that I follow it. I slide down the wall and let my forehead drop to my bent knees.

How did I get here? How could I possibly have made it so close to this dream and then lost it all because I was too flipping stupid to keep my mouth shut until I figured out what was going on? If I'd taken thirty seconds to Google the shorthand, I would have realized what it was. It might have taken me longer, but I could have worked out that recipe. At the very least I could have been canned because I screwed up. Not even getting a chance to try was so much worse!

I know better than to get my hopes up. I know how minimal the chances of happiness are. How could I let my guard down? Why did I think that for once it would actually work out in my favor?

Disgusted with my line of thought, I close my eyes tightly and take several deep breaths. I will pull myself together. People go through way worse stuff than this. Hell, I'd been through way worse stuff than this. I open my eyes, and a hint of orange peeks out at me from my feet. The sight has me taking in a strangled breath. Excited about the new job, I'd gone out yesterday and bought Native Shoes in every color they had, since an online search informed me that they were the coolest nonslip shoes you could wear. They also sort of look like rubber Converse, so they seemed like the perfect choice. I'd worn the orange today in a dorky homage to Mario Batali, a fact that utterly ashames me now.

The color blurs before me, and damn it, I hate myself in that instant.

I didn't cry when I ended up in the hospital in December. I didn't cry when Grandma died last summer or Pop Pop the year before that. I haven't cried since that night six years ago when my mother found me in bed, and the sight of these stupid orange shoes is going to push me over the edge!

I swipe at my eyes angrily and choke on the sobs in my chest, refusing to let them out.

I don't even hear the group of guys until one of them speaks to me.

"Jennings?"

My head flies up in time to see Bennett effing Taylor walk down the hallway towards me with two other guys trailing behind him. They are all dressed in black jeans and black T-shirts. But unlike the other two, Taylor looks utterly shocked and totally concerned. About me.

Great. This is just absolutely flipping perfect!

I look away. I don't have the energy to acknowledge him right now.

"You guys finish getting that step-and-repeat signage set," he tells the other two. "I'll meet you there in a bit."

The guys walk past without another word while Taylor, who clearly can't take a hint, sits down next to me. He acts like finding some chick he barely knows in tears in the garage hallway is the most normal thing in the world.

When I don't turn my head to look his way, he tries a more direct approach.

"Are you OK?" he asks so gently that I almost start bawling again.

Jeez, I'm a mess!

"I don't want to talk to you," I finally croak.

"OK," he says slowly. "Is there someone I can call for you?"

As if there were someone who I *do* want to talk to. As if I were going to lay this all out for my family or my few friends to pick through. *Hey, you didn't know it, but I had this stupid childhood dream that I've secretly been obsessed with all my life. Oh yeah, and*

I finally got the chance to realize it, only I wasn't good enough to pull it off, and now I'm crying alone in a hallway.

I laugh, though nothing about this is funny.

Taylor must hear the irony in the sound.

"OK." He stretches his legs out in front of him and crosses them at the ankle in a deceptively casual manner. "So then talk to me. I'm right here."

I wipe my eyes again and my bracelets jangle.

A fifteen-percent chance. The memory flits through my mind, and I bat it away. I know the chances of happiness. Why did I set myself up for this?

"You said it yourself the other night," Taylor tries again. "You don't give a damn about my opinion, so why not just tell me what's going on."

He nudges my shoulder with his own playfully.

I don't respond.

"Look, I promise I'll go back to being patronizing and antagonistic when I see you next. We'll forget this ever happened. Just tell me what happened."

He is so easygoing about the whole thing, as if he is offering me a beer at a party instead of a chance to vent. But I can't actually consider it. I don't talk to anyone about anything. It's just easier not to.

"I lost my job," I utterly shock myself by saying.

"That sucks. I'm sorry," he says gently.

I watch some tension come out of his shoulders. Maybe he was expecting something more traumatic, but he doesn't understand how traumatic this is for me. No one does.

"You don't understand." I suddenly feel the need for at least one other person to understand, even if it is a near stranger.

I look up into his eyes. How had I never noticed that they are the exact color of black-forest-cake batter?

I shake my head to get rid of the thought. Rather than stare into something that prompts ridiculous analogies like that, I look down at his forearm colored in pattern and ink. I follow the lines of his tattoos in order to avoid looking at the questions in his eyes. The story comes out of my mouth without my volition. It just pours out into the quiet hallway in a near whisper.

I tell him about baking with my mom as a child and how it has always been my dream to do it professionally. I tell him about Avis Phillips and how much I admire her. How I knew she worked at the hotel and how I got a job tending bar there because even though I didn't have the courage to try for my dream, I wanted to watch others do it. I tell him about getting the job at Dolci and convincing Joey to let me keep it. I even tell him about how excited I was to buy my shoes, which makes me cry all over again. And then, because I have no pride left, I tell him about the shorthand and how I've been summarily canned without ever really getting the chance to prove myself.

When I finish I feel totally deflated. I put my forehead back down on my knees. Maybe I'll never get up from this spot. They'll find me here years from now, a fossilized memorial to epic failure.

"OK, look." Taylor's voice is overly loud in the nearly empty space. "Between my mama, my gran, and my little sister, Dee Dee, I grew up surrounded by women. So I know that you're probably not looking for a fix here. Experience tells me you're not even looking for a pep talk; you're just looking for someone to listen."

For most women he'd be dead on, but I'm not most women. I don't even really want him to listen. I can't believe I actually told him all that; it just came out.

"But even though you're not looking for it," he carries on, "I'm going to give you both."

"Both?" I ask stupidly.

"Advice and a pep talk," he answers.

"Great," I grumble.

My aggravation puts me back on steadier ground.

"Oh, hush," Taylor says, sounding as southern as Landon.

When I only raise my eyebrows, he continues.

"So you don't actually know what you're doing. Who cares? That's the same as half the people in this town. If this is your dream job, then you have to try. You can't give up without a fight."

My eyes fly to his in shock.

"I did try! They don't want me!"

He doesn't even flinch at my tone, just shakes his head slowly in response.

"They didn't say they didn't want you. They said you weren't qualified."

"I'm *not* qualified," I say viciously, because it is true and I hate to admit it.

"Yeah, but can you do the job?"

"What?" I ask, confounded. What did that have to do with anything if I didn't have the job anymore?

Taylor smiles and crosses his arms.

"When I was in the fourth grade, there was this kid named Monty Kirchner." He looks over at me. "You following me here, Jennings?"

I cross my own arms.

"I have no idea," I answer honestly.

"I'm an Okie," he tells me conspiratorially. "We tend to expound on a point, and we love to share childhood stories like they're proverbs. Just go with it, OK?"

"OK."

"So Monty—"

"Kirchner," I supply.

"The very same," Taylor agrees. "He decided he hated me. I don't know why or what I did to piss him off, but he decided he was going to beat the crap out of me. I knew this because he screamed it one day at recess. Just like that. No conversation, no chat, just those two facts screamed across the sandbox. He hated me and he was going to beat the crap out of me. Now, that might not seem like a big deal, except that I was maybe sixty pounds soaking wet, and Monty was twice my size. I know it's hard to believe that I wasn't always this glowing specimen you see before you."

He winks and I roll my eyes, but he is right. He is well over six feet tall and has a full sleeve of tattoos on each arm. Even though his arms aren't bulky, they are solid muscle, and so is the rest of him. It's hard to imagine him as a scrawny kid.

"So Monty decided he was going to murder me, only he didn't do it that day. It was so much worse, because he put the fear of God into me and then didn't act on it. Every day he'd find me in the hallway or on the playground and tell me how he was going to beat the crap out of me, and every day I went home sick to my stomach. Finally, one night at dinner my mama noticed I was off my feed and asked me what was wrong. I was so keyed up that I started crying like a baby. I told her the whole story. Even though I knew she'd tell me that violence isn't the answer and we're supposed to love our neighbor, I was sort of hoping there was a chance she'd call the principal or let me be homeschooled or something."

He smiles at the memory and shakes his head.

"But you know what she did, Jennings?" He looks over at me. "She got down on her knees and looked me right in the eye and asked, 'Bennett, can you take him?' I was so shocked I just stared at her, and so she asked again, 'Do you think you can take him?' The thing is, I didn't think I could take him, but I could see in her eyes that she did. She didn't want me to get pushed around or bullied, and she wasn't about to let me run away. So I nodded and told her that yes ma'am, I could take him. She smiled, like she expected this all along, and then she said, 'Bennett Taylor, you aren't allowed to start a fight, but if you get in one, I expect you to finish it.' You get it, Jennings? This is your fight to finish. I didn't ask if they wanted you there or if you were qualified. I asked if you could do it. Can you?"

I think about the last few days, the last few years, and the decades before that. I look at the hallway around us and then down at the chef coat I'm still wearing and the tangerine-colored rubber shoes on my feet.

"I can," I say, looking over at him, "but how do I convince them of that?"

It's the first time I've asked anyone for advice in as long as I can remember. I can't believe that he is who I am turning to, but he is here and I have no one else to ask.

Taylor doesn't say anything but jumps to his feet like motion might propel us to the right answer. He reaches a hand down to me, and I let him pull me up.

"They need someone who can recreate the recipes, and I don't understand them. It's like they're written in Greek!" I tell him helplessly.

He purses his lips in amusement. "Then I guess you'd better figure out how to speak their language."

I nod in response because my mind is spinning too fast to come up with words. He is right; Joey didn't fire me because she didn't want me there. Hell, she is desperate, which means she'd probably take a well-trained dog right now if it meant she had a replacement. She fired me because she believes understanding the shorthand is both necessary and impossible to learn quickly. I'll have to prove her wrong on that second part, and I need to do it in a hurry. She needs someone to do her job, and she has even less time now than she did when I met her.

I am so energized that I walk halfway down the hall before I realize what I'm doing. I pause midstep and turn back around. Taylor stands at the other end with both his hands shoved down deep in his pockets. He smiles like a proud parent, which is kind of mortifying, really.

"Did you finish it?" I ask him.

"What's that?"

"The fight, with Monty—did you finish it?" I clarify.

"Oh, hell no." He chuckles. "He beat the snot out of me before I could even get my fists up. But I went down swinging, Jennings. You get that?"

I nod in response. I *totally* get that.

"So you promise to go back to being a jackass the next time I see you, right?" I ask him.

He laughs once. "Absolutely."

"OK then." I fiddle with my bracelets nervously and then take a deep breath. I'm not a child; I shouldn't be nervous. "Thank you," I tell him sincerely. "Seriously, thank you so much."

Taylor grins and a single dimple catches my attention. He rubs his jaw self-consciously. It is the first time I've seen him look embarrassed.

"You're welcome," he says. "I'll see you around, Jennings."

I pull my backpack onto my shoulders as a plan already begins to form in my mind. I am heading down the hallway when Taylor's laugh catches up with me.

"Out of curiosity," he calls, "where are you headed now?"

"To learn Greek," I call back.

Chapter Seven

"Quiz me!" I demand as I slam the piece of paper down on the table in front of Joey triumphantly.

She looks at me with equal parts pity and annoyance, which might very well be the worst combination of expressions you can have aimed in your direction.

The kitchen staff members sit silently around the lunch table, looking back and forth between the two of us. I found them all here enjoying the cool air and the coffee in the break room. The audience is unavoidable.

It took me the last four hours hunched over my laptop in the hotel lobby, but I now know every possible letter, number, and code word she could throw at me. I am utterly confident in this.

"This really isn't necessary—"

"My dream." There, I say it. I lay it out there in front of all seven members of this crew. It's mortifying, but whatever. "My dream *is* necessary. You said I couldn't work here without knowing shorthand, and I know it now, so quiz me!"

She starts rubbing her back, a sure sign of agitation. Harris throws me a reprimanding glance. He doesn't want me upsetting his very pregnant wife. I get that, but I'm not going down without a fight.

"Look, Max—"

"10X?" an old voice barks from behind me.

Joey drops her face into her palm with a groan. I spin around to see Avis standing in the doorway. She holds her box of cigarettes in one hand and flicks a lighter idly in the other. I don't need to be prompted again.

"Powdered sugar," I answer.

"What's the ten stand for?" She narrows her eyes.

"It's the coarseness of the grind," I tell her. "How fine the sugar is, I mean."

Avis lets out a slightly maniacal laugh.

"Uh-oh, the Stork's been studying up," she announces to the room.

I turn back to look at the much aggrieved sous-chef.

"Quiz me," I demand again.

Joey rolls her eyes like she is dealing with a toddler.

"Do I *need* to quiz you?" she asks sarcastically.

"No," I say emphatically. "I know it all."

She mutters something in Spanish, and beside her Harris smothers laughter with his giant hand.

"Fine." She sighs. "Then go make the cupcakes and don't come to me again until they're perfect."

"I won't," I tell her.

"What's that?" she asks.

It takes me a moment to understand what she means, but I finally catch up.

"Yes, Chef."

As I walk out of the room past a table full of grinning bakers and the old woman I idolize even though she is kind of crazy, I don't even try to hide my smile. I might go down, but at least I'll go down swinging.

Four hours and five dozen cupcakes later, I leave the kitchen.

I am exhausted after all the emotional drama of the day but also running on the high of having managed to get my job back. I would love to follow the rest of the crew back to employee parking and head straight home to bed, but I am scheduled to work the eight-to-two shift at Gander. I try not to think about how tired my arms already are from hauling big trays around or how much more tired they will be after hours of making drinks. I focus instead on the new vocabulary I learned today and hurry off in the opposite direction, straight to the women's employee locker room.

My gym bag is close to bursting at the seams, but it holds everything I need for both my shifts. I have just enough time to wash my face and reapply some makeup, though the cheap florescent lighting means that the results are less than stellar. A shower isn't an option, but I guess that's why God invented Victoria's Secret body spray. Once I have *mostly* replaced the smell of the kitchen with a hearty dousing of Love Spell, I slip into the skinny jeans, black boots, tight white button-down, and suspenders that make up my uniform. Another glance in the mirror reveals that my hair is unattractively flattened to my head in random places because of wearing a bandana all day. The bandana is totally *Karate Kid*, but way better than a hairnet. I run my hands through my hair a few times to try to fix it, but it is the kind of mess that no amount of product is going to remedy. I normally don't care all that much about my hair when I'm at work, but it's pretty terrible-looking. When I say flattened I don't mean Mia Farrow in *Rosemary's Baby*; I mean Donnie Wahlberg in *The Sixth Sense*.

Not cute.

I finally give up, pull an old vintage scarf out of the bottom of my bag, and tie it around my head where the bandana had been. It looks a little more rockabilly than I would have liked, but it is the best I can do.

I use what remaining energy I have to run down the back hallway while scarfing down some almonds and chugging a bottle of water, and I make it behind the bar with no time to spare. I have a small heart attack when I realize Landon is sitting at the counter waiting for me. I have no idea how long she's been there.

"Good grief, girl, where have you been?" she calls to me as soon as I am close enough to hear it. "I've been looking forward to this drink all day, and I've been sitting here for half an hour already waiting for you."

Maybe if I focus on the second part of the sentence, she'll ignore the first.

"You could have asked someone else for a drink," I say, grabbing a lowball glass for her. "Jack rocks isn't hard to accomplish; any one of the other geniuses here could have figured it out for you."

"Yes, but it's so much more fun to be served by you," she says, slipping her phone into her black Cole Haan.

I can't help but smile, remembering the intervention Miko and I staged to get her to move on from the pink-and-gold monstrosity of a purse she came to LA with. Our argument that no high-end client would take her seriously was finally enough to persuade her to buy a classier handbag.

I place her drink on the cocktail napkin in front of her, then casually lean my elbows on the bar. It is a Monday night and relatively slow, so it is easy enough to stop to chat. And truthfully, I am exhausted and not really interested in running from one end of the bar to the other. Landon takes a little sip, then reaches back to fluff up her hair. God forbid it should lose any volume in the eight minutes since the last time she fluffed it.

"So why weren't you around today?" She raises her eyebrows dramatically. "Don't tell me you have a secret boyfriend who took you on a day-long date."

I snort in response.

"No secret boyfriend to speak of. How about you?"

As soon as I ask it, I regret my question. I want to change the subject, but I don't really want to initiate a heart-to-heart about her and Brody's relationship. I love both of them, and I worry about how close they are getting. If—or really when—they break up, it is going to seriously screw us all, so it is probably better if I don't get too invested in their relationship now.

Landon gasps, her typical response to any given situation. "Are you actually interested in how things are going with us?" she asks excitedly.

"Actually, I—"

An older businessman sits down a few chairs away from us, and I have to take care of his request for wine before I can finish my sentence. When I come back to Landon, I pick up where I left off.

"Actually, I can think of several things I'd rather do than hear about you and my brother," I tell her. "Off the top of my head, I'd say, oh, watching an obscure Polish film without the use of subtitles, or getting a bikini wax from a one-armed clown, or—"

Landon screeches with laughter. "A one-armed clown?"

The businessman scowls at us over his glass of cabernet.

"Well," I tell her, "I was trying to think of the worst thing I could. Bikini waxes and sad-faced clowns are at the top of my list."

"Just below hearing about Brody and me?"

"Exactly," I say, but now I've opened some kind of door, and it's only polite to ask, "But if you must, how are things with him?"

Landon smiles and takes another drink. "Oh, he's fine. Granted, it's harder to apply the wax now with only the one arm, but—"

I laugh loud enough to startle the businessman again. He picks up his glass and moves to a seat outside of my section. I grin over at Landon.

"You're becoming quite the smart-ass, Landon Brinkley," I tell her happily.

She shoots me a cheeky grin. "Yes, well, I'm learning from the best, aren't I?"

———

"Pay attention or I'll let you scorch the caramel at least twenty times before I show you how to make it properly," Joey tells me the next day.

It's not like I'd ever ignore her on purpose, but Avis is across the room making a profiterole tower with a spun-sugar overlay. Watching her stretch out the hot sugar strands like spun gold is kind of mesmerizing, and since I've never seen anyone do it before, I keep getting distracted. Joey's threat works perfectly, though, because (a) I don't doubt that she'd let me burn twenty cups of sugar if she thought it might teach me a lesson, and (b) I've never made caramel before and I am dying to learn how to do it properly. Joey reaches for a small saucepot, but I grab it before she has to struggle on tiptoes with a belly that is constantly getting in her way.

She pulls out sugar and water and then surprises me by getting a lemon.

"What's the citrus for?" I ask curiously.

"It keeps the caramel from seizing up," she says while cutting the fruit in half with a paring knife.

She puts water, sugar, and a squeeze of lemon into the saucepot and brings the heat up high. I reach for a whisk so she won't have to make the grab, but she shakes her head.

"You don't want to whisk caramel in the beginning." She reaches for the handle of the pot and swirls it over the flame. "Just move it around gently over the heat."

As we watch the pot, the water and sugar begin to boil, creating what looks like white foam.

"Isn't there a way to make caramel without water?" I ask without removing my eyes from the boiling pot.

"There is, and it's much faster, but it's also easier to scorch that way. Since we make this in larger batches, it's best to take the extra time rather than risk the quality."

As she speaks she slides the handle in my direction, and I take over the swirling motion. We both watch the mixture boil with rapt attention.

"See there." She points to the edge of the pot, where the sugar is just starting to turn brown.

As the amber color slowly permeates the bottom of the pot, she uses a spoon to pull out the tiniest bit. She drops a dollop of the light-brown liquid onto a plate, then gestures for me to try it.

I gingerly stick a fingertip in and bring it to my mouth. The flavor is sweet, with just the barest hint of the deep caramel flavor I'm used to.

"This is a medium caramel. You'd use this for a caramel sauce or to flavor an icing or a filling. Understand?" I nod and look back to the caramel in the pot, which continues to deepen in color. A few seconds later, she sticks the spoon in again and removes a bit of dark-amber liquid that smells like heaven.

"This," she says, blowing on the spoon, "is what we use for the *budino*." Joey slips the entire spoonful into her mouth and shivers a little in response to the flavor. With a blissful smile she starts to gather ingredients that I quickly recognize are for the pudding. As I watch her work I recognize in her a total focus and love for what she's doing. I'm not typically one to make conversation, but I'm curious.

"Where did you learn to cook?" I ask.

A small smile plays around her mouth at some memory.

"I started washing dishes in a kitchen where Avis was pastry chef, and she pulled me up the ranks to assist her."

"You were a stage!" I gasp. "Why did you give me so much grief about it, then?" I ask, handing her a whisk when she points to it.

Joey stops cracking eggs for a moment and looks at me.

"Because I know how hard this is," she answers. "I worked under Avis for two years before I was able to manage independently. You've set yourself an impossible goal, and you're going to kill yourself to do this job you're not trained for. In all likelihood she's going to fire you before you get the chance to do anything other than waste your time."

"So why did you stick it out, then?" I challenge.

"Because I—"

She stops what she is doing, and a smile flashes across her face for no apparent reason. Then she takes a step back from the worktable and looks down at her swollen stomach. Even through her shirt and the chef coat, I can see her belly jumping wildly with every baby kick.

"You like the caramel too, I think," she says to her belly.

My heart lurches, and I bite my tongue to keep the emotion from showing on my face.

She looks up happily and reaches for my hand.

"Do you want to feel it?"

"No!" I bark in a completely irrational reaction and tuck my hands behind my back.

Joey's brows furrow, and she studies me quietly for a moment. When I don't say anything else, she resumes her work with the eggs. Eventually she answers the question I asked, and we both pretend the moment didn't happen.

"I stuck it out because she was the first person who took me seriously. Avis taught me so many things, and it was entirely different from the life I'd grown up with. The kitchen was the first place I ever felt totally in control." She holds up an egg. "One less egg and the pudding won't set; one too many and the consistency is like paste. There's an equation here, and when you know what you're doing, it's actually easier to execute it perfectly than it is to mess something up." She smiles ironically. "I'm probably too type A, but I like the order in that."

"Having a personality like yours must make you an interesting partner for someone like her," I say, handing her the milk.

"Actually, having a personality like mine is what makes me a perfect fit for someone like Avis. It's like adding sugar to your tomato sauce or citrus to your alfredo. It's usually our opposites who complement us best, because they're the only ones who can balance us out."

Chapter Eight

"Max!"

My head snaps up from the kitchen counter. I don't even remember falling asleep, but the gelatinous cereal floating in my bowl tells me I've been passed out for a while. I look up at Landon through bleary eyes, but I can make out her confusion just the same. I'm still wearing last night's uniform from my shift at the bar, but it's rumpled and stale with random liquor that splashed on me while I worked. I probably look even more like a degenerate than usual, which, believe me, is saying a lot since my at-home attire tends to lean pretty far in that direction. Pulling double shifts for the last several days is kicking my butt. This is the third time this week that I've knocked out in a random place.

"What's going on with you?" she asks accusingly.

"How much time do you have?" I rub my hands back and forth over my face, trying to wake up.

"Don't talk about yourself so flippantly." She frowns. "You're not nearly as tortured and damaged as you'd like us all to believe."

I don't bother responding.

"Your nails, on the other hand." She eyeballs my hands where they rest on the countertop. "What's going on here?"

She points at my bare nails with disdain. I should have realized she'd notice any change in my beauty regimen right away, especially since we usually get our manicures done together.

"Just changing things up," I hedge and tuck my hands into my lap.

Her face twists in disbelief, but she moves on.

"So anyway, we've—" She turns a full circle as if she's looking for something in the kitchen. "Do you want some coffee?"

"Always," I answer emphatically.

She starts pulling out the necessary ingredients and then continues as if she didn't interrupt herself.

"We've started a company team."

"Who?" I ask, confused.

"Chic. We've started a company team."

"You have exactly two employees."

"I know," she says, filling up the coffeepot with water.

"And you and Miko aren't exactly sportsmen," I inform her, although this shouldn't be news to anyone.

"You don't know that! I was captain of the varsity team."

"Cheerleading is not a sport," I point out.

She whirls around, gasping in indignation.

Here we go.

"Just so we're clear, three members of my squad went all-American! And we trained year round. That includes weight training every morning and long runs in the afternoon, and then we had practice for games and performances every day for two hours!" She presses the start button on the machine in agitation. "But your limited knowledge of cheer is beside the point here. It doesn't matter if you have one employee or a thousand; corporate culture starts from the beginning."

I motion for her to pour me coffee, even though it hasn't finished brewing yet, and drop my head down on my hand. If she's going to lecture me, I need caffeine or booze, and coffee is the most readily available option.

She pours us each an inch of coffee and hands me a cup, all the while continuing on her tirade. When she starts in on the positive effects of team sports on group morale, I have to stop her.

"Landon, why don't you just tell me what you want?"

"Why would you assume I want anything?" she asks innocently.

"Because this is way too much buildup." I sigh into my coffee cup.

"Well, it's just that . . . um . . . We need at least eight people for our team. And it's all girls, and our first game is against a boys' team, and I don't want us to fail our first time up. It's bad for morale."

"Bad for morale for the two-person company?" I qualify.

"Exactly." She smiles like I've agreed with her, though who could follow her logic is beyond me.

"So you'll do it?" she asks nervously.

"Do what?"

"Play on our team. It's this Saturday at eleven, which is late enough in the day for you. It'll be so fun, and afterwards we can go to brunch."

I stare at her over the countertop, actually debating this idiotic plan. A year ago I wouldn't even bother to respond, but nowadays, as long as they don't want to braid each other's hair or do trust falls, I'll usually allow Landon and Miko to drag me into any number of things.

"Come on! It's an entire team of men to take your aggression out on."

"Fine," I tell her as I stand up.

I need to take a shower, because the smell of old alcohol is starting to make me nauseous.

Landon jumps up and down and claps her hands.

"This is so perfect! I'll make your team T-shirt today. You don't have your own tiara, do you?" she asks curiously.

I stop and turn around to face her.

"What?"

"A tiara. Or maybe costume jewelry or opera gloves? We're calling ourselves the Ball Gowns. Miko chose it. You know how she feels about regency-era romance," she says seriously.

"What kind of—"

"Dodgeball. Didn't I mention that? Oh well, too late to take it back now. I'll see you later. I'm late for a meeting." She singsongs the entire thing, slowly backing out of the kitchen before practically running straight out the front door.

———

Saturday morning at ten forty-five I find myself trudging into a rec center on the outskirts of Santa Monica with Liam in tow. I didn't actually set out to acquire an escort to the game, but since I forgot that we were supposed to have brunch today and I'd already canceled on him twice, here we are. I glance at him through my overly long bangs. In my brother's typical fashion, he takes the unexpected outing all in stride. His hands are thrust down into the pockets of his shorts, and he smiles like he is headed out on vacation, instead of being dragged to the Westside to watch some hipsters play ironic sports. That is totally Liam, though. Where Brody is brooding and contemplative, Liam is charming and gregarious. They'd both been that way once upon a time; wealthy children with kind, supportive parents are rarely anything but happy with the world. But Brody lost his shiny outlook during his senior year of college. Which makes Liam the only one of us who hasn't been destroyed in some way by the opposite sex.

"So you're actually going to play today?" he asks with a grin.

"I get to throw balls at other people's heads." I shrug. "Seems like just as good a form of cardio as any other."

"I'd never count you as such a hipster, Mack." He pulls out his phone to ignore an incoming call before slipping it back into his pocket. "Are you going to expand on this lifestyle in any way I should prepare myself for? Maybe start playing the ukulele or become a ramp farmer or something?" He smirks as he opens the door to the gymnasium for me.

"What are ramps?"

"Now see, I thought a newbie chef like you would know all about the hottest 'it' vegetable. Ramps are the new black."

I whirl around to face him.

I don't attempt to deny it. Brody might try to coerce information out of me, but Liam is smart enough to know I won't give him anything willingly. He is wealthy, well connected, and unconcerned with scruples—probably incredible assets in a businessman, but a total pain in the ass in a big brother. The only reason his keeping tabs on me has never negatively affected our relationship is because he never shares the information.

"How did you know about Dolci?"

"That's a silly question now, isn't it, Mack? You know I'm all powerful; I've been telling you that since you were little," he says to me, all charm. "The more important question, though, is why you haven't told anyone about this."

Behind me the gymnasium is alive with the activity of several different recreational sports. The squeak of sneakers on hardwood, the echo of conversations, and the sound of balls bouncing off the backboard all scramble with the whirl of implications in my head.

"Now who's asking silly questions?" I finally answer.

My hands suddenly feel sweaty, and I rub them over the outside of my workout shorts. I'm not sure if it's the fear of him telling our parents that's making me so nervous, or just the fact that any member of my family knows at all. Monday is my last day of working under Joey, and all of her training has only served to high-light how much I *don't* know. I recognize now what an impossible task I've set for myself. Failing is still a very real possibility, and I learned a long time ago that failing is much easier to go through if no one is there to see it.

Liam looks me up and down.

"I won't start an argument about this, kid; I can't stand to piss off a woman in any capacity. But you and I both know anyone else in this family would flip out if they knew you were working around the clock. All I ask is that you take care of yourself."

I start to answer but he cuts me off, his face suddenly stern.

"I don't mean that in the generic sense, Mack. I mean that you eat, sleep, drink water, take vitamins, and check your levels like it's your part-time job. You're setting an unbelievable schedule for yourself, and I'm not hypocritical enough to tell someone else not to work too much. But you damn well better take it seriously. If you want to try to pull off something impossible, you'd better look for every chance to increase the odds in your favor, and that means taking total care of your body so it can take care of you. All right?"

I nod.

"All right." He grins and hooks an arm around my shoulders. "Let's play some damn dodgeball!"

———

I walk with Liam over to the far side of the gymnasium, and once we pass a handful of half-court basketball games and some old men playing indoor shuffleboard, we find Landon. She stands with Miko and several other random chicks who are all wearing the bright-pink T-shirts they spent last night tie-dyeing. I'm also wearing the ridiculous shirt, but only because it's easier than the backlash if I don't.

"Oh, good. You're here," Landon calls when she sees us approaching. When she sees who is with me, her smile brightens. "Are you playing too?" she asks Liam.

"Nah, I usually do my girls-against-boys activities in more intimate settings." He winks as he says it, and Landon's face turns almost entirely red. She makes up an excuse about checking in with the ref and hurries away. Liam turns to me.

"She *is* the one dating our very worldly brother, correct?" he asks.

"Believe me," I tell him, "the irony isn't lost on me either."

Liam laughs loudly in response, and as if on cue Miko turns in our direction. She had her T-shirt altered to fall off one shoulder and reveal the straps of a neon-green sports bra. Her little black boy-shorts are easily as tiny as Landon's, but Miko lacks the curves necessary to make them look quite so scandalous. Her jet-black hair has grown out past her shoulders but is still the wild, choppy mess it always has been. She walks over to us casually with an odd smile on her face. Liam is focused on the screen of his phone, so I pull his attention back to us.

"Liam, have you met my friend Miko?"

Liam looks up and reaches out a hand. "At Max's birthday party, I think," he tells her with a flirtatious grin. "You had on a great dress that night."

Miko tilts her head to the side and studies him for a moment too long.

"I had on jeans and a pineapple-themed muscle tee that night." She smiles. "But that was an admirable try just the same."

As always, Liam is unrepentant. Getting caught in the lie only makes his smile bigger.

"It was worth a shot," he tells her unapologetically.

"Out of curiosity, what's the success rate on that line?" Miko asks him, looking for all the world as if this is totally fascinating.

"Better than you'd think," he answers.

She tilts her head back to the other side, contemplating his answer.

"Do you assume that all the women you hit on are truly dress-wearers, or do you ever consider that they're just agreeing with you to be amiable?" she asks, surprising us both.

Liam barks out a laugh and looks Miko over as if sizing her up for the first time. She doesn't even come up to his shoulders, but she packs a world of weird into one tiny package.

"Honestly"—he flashes her another grin—"it's never been a concern of mine, no."

Miko nods, a small smile playing at her lips. Then, with apparently nothing else to say, she gives us both a jaunty salute and walks away.

Liam watches her go and then turns back to me.

"She's . . ." He searches for the word and finally comes up with "interesting."

"Yep. I think you can sit over there on those bleachers." I point the way. "The sooner we finish this, the sooner you can buy me eggs."

Liam does a little salute of his own and heads off to find a seat.

When I turn around to find Landon, I nearly slam into the person behind me. Dark-brown eyes twinkle with amusement.

"Oh, the day just gets better and better," Taylor drawls.

It is exactly like the way he normally speaks to me. No pity or judgment. He is just going to pretend that day in the hallway didn't happen. I grudgingly let him rise a few notches in my estimation.

He is wearing workout shorts slung low on his hips and a faded blue T-shirt with the words "Dodge Chargers" screen-printed on the front. He has a seventies-style sweatband around his forehead, and some small, twisted part of me tips her hat to anyone who can wear something so ridiculous and make it look good.

"I had no idea you were in on this thing." I point to the room around us. "I would have joined up ages ago if I knew it would mean embarrassing you over recreational sports."

"Don't set yourself up now," he teases. "I helped raise a little sister, but I never once took it easy on Dee Dee because she's a girl. I'd hate to have to prove you wrong, especially since I can't imagine you've honed a great deal of athletic prowess working the register at Hot Topic."

He is an idiot, and I'm not about to validate his severely out-dated comeback with one of my own. I'm not even going to bother responding.

"Hot Topic?" The words fly out of my mouth. "What is this, 2001?"

He starts to chuckle.

"And as far as athletic prowess goes . . ." My mind races with images from another lifetime: varsity teams and tournaments, the scholarship I'd been so proud to earn even if I hadn't needed it. I look at his sweatband with mock disdain. "You're about to get schooled, Prefontaine."

This time I really do walk away, towards the two teams that are assembling to play. As much as I hate to admit it, arguing with him is entertaining. He isn't intimidated by me, and he is quick witted. Now that I know he is actually a good guy, I worry that I might have to stop being so openly hostile towards him.

"Wanna make a bet?"

His words stop me midstep, and I swing around to face him.

Oh hell yes.

His smile grows, and only then do I realize I've said the words out loud.

I walk back over and get in his face.

"A hundred bucks says our team murders yours, Monty Kirchner–style," I tell him with a cocky grin of my own.

His eyes flare in amusement, and he is already nodding before I finish the sentence.

"Done. But when we win, my spoils are a bit different." He looks down at me in a way that suddenly makes me feel uneasy. I take a step back and then immediately want to punch myself in the face for showing him that weakness.

"What do you mean?" I ask warily.

"I want a date," he says matter-of-factly.

"No way!" It comes out as a snarl.

Isn't he smart enough to know he is barking up the wrong tree?

"Why not?" he asks, stepping closer to me. "If you're so sure you'll win, what difference does it make anyway?"

He is baiting me; I know it, and damn it, I so want to wipe that stupid smirk off his face! But a date? There is almost nothing worse he could have asked me for. Dating isn't something I do, and the list of reasons why is too long to even contemplate. I already agreed to the bet, though, and if I ask him to pick something else, he'll know he found a sore spot. Let's face it: this guy has already seen me at a pretty low point, and I don't need to give him any more ammo.

Man, I so want to gain a little pride back.

I look behind me to where Landon is gathering the Ball Gowns to pep them up before the game. A ref is setting a bunch of red rubber balls down on the line separating the two teams. Despite the tie-dye, the women Landon is talking to all look in shape. By contrast, Taylor's team looks like a mix of overweight truckers and a handful of skinny kids who are probably PAs. Taylor might be all muscle and tattoos, but I seriously doubt he can make up the difference for a team that appears to be sweating out last night's bender. I look back at the ladies in pink, and one of the taller girls is twirling the ball on her finger like a pro. Miko pops the knuckles on each hand like she is preparing for battle.

"You're on, Bennett," I call over my shoulder without looking back.

We are going to kill these guys.

———

"But you were popping your knuckles like you were about to fight someone!" I glare at Miko across the table as the waitress deposits everyone's order.

Miko looks up from her eggs, confused.

"Oh, I do that when I'm nervous," she tells me with a helpless shrug. "It's a filthy habit, really."

"And what about that girl who was spinning the ball?" I turn to growl at Landon, "She seemed totally competent."

Landon looks up from her phone. "Who, Lorelei?" she asks, dumbfounded. Understanding dawns on her face. "Oh gosh, no. She's my librarian. I invited her because she doesn't get out very much. I think that trick was something she works on in her free time."

"Lorelei is the best," Miko says around a bite of toast. "She's the one who turned me on to Nalini Singh."

Liam looks up at her. "Is that some kind of drink?"

"No," Miko chides. "She's an author." She gestures emphatically with her butter knife. "Imagine cyborgs falling in love with animal shape-shifters."

Liam looks genuinely alarmed. "Why would I want to do that?"

"Because it's the best!" she answers happily. "One can't feel emotion; the other feels too much."

When everyone stares at her in various levels of confusion, she rolls her eyes and changes the subject.

"Anyway, back to Lorelei. Did you see that ball hit her in the face?" she asks solemnly. "I've never seen anyone's ear swell up that much. It looked just like Sloth from *The Goonies*."

Landon nods soberly. Next to me Liam tries to hide his laughter with a bite of omelet and only succeeds in choking himself.

He invited the two of them to brunch with us, and the group chatted and laughed all the way here like they didn't have a care in the world—like we hadn't just had our asses handed to us by a bunch of teamsters.

"We lost, like chumps," I tell my teammates.

"Nah." Landon waves me off with the piece of pancake at the end of her fork. "We were just having fun, Max. It doesn't matter if we won or not. It doesn't mean anything."

"What doesn't mean anything?" Brody says, arriving at the table and taking the empty seat next to Landon.

"That we lost at dodgeball," she answers him, eating the bite off the end of her fork.

"Are those pancakes?" Brody asks her with a wink.

Landon giggles as if he just made a clever joke, and Brody responds to the giggle by leaning down and kissing her sweetly on the shoulder. Why anyone might get so worked up over breakfast food is beyond me. I look over at Liam to see if he is paying attention to the interaction, but he seems momentarily distracted by watching Miko add a spoonful of grape jelly to her scrambled eggs. He shakes his head slowly, either in denial or disgust, and then continues the conversation where it halted.

"Some people—not me, obviously, but some people—might suggest that you were already losers for spending any time on dodgeball in the first place," Liam tells us cheerfully.

"Well, now you're just being rude," Miko announces just as the waitress comes over to refill her cup.

The older woman pauses with the coffeepot suspended in midair.

"I'm sorry?" she asks Miko.

"Not you, Janice," Miko answers the waitress with a smile.

I have no idea at what point she caught the woman's name.

Janice nods awkwardly but dutifully refills everyone's cup and takes down Brody's order. The conversation turns to the topic of work, and I choose to act terribly interested in my frittata rather than engage in a chat that might lead us anywhere near my own work life.

"I heard Malin is coming in for the Fourth," Liam says, apropos of nothing.

"So it's going to be a thing," Brody says with a smile.

"It always is with her," I agree.

Landon and Miko both look at us, waiting for an explanation, and I guess you'd need one if you'd never met my little sister. Malin can increase the energy in the room tenfold just by stepping into it. She is the first one in the water, the last one off the dance floor, and the life of every party. She has horrible taste in guys and at least five years of poor decisions behind her. She'd be a total nightmare of a sibling, except that it is actually kind of impossible not to love Malin.

She is the girl who could talk you into stealing your mom's car and driving to Tijuana when you were still in high school, or convince a room full of socialites to do a Jäger bomb, or get you to climb a billboard in the middle of the night just to see if you are strong enough to do it. She is wild and unpredictable, and she'd be the black sheep of our family if she wasn't everyone's favorite pet.

"We go to Santa Barbara every year for the Fourth," Brody starts to explain.

"Your parents have a vacation house there, right?" Landon asks.

"Right. They've had it forever, and the Fourth is a big tradition. The whole extended family comes in for the day," he tells them.

"And Malin doesn't always get to come into town," I continue. "So if she's traveling all the way over for it, she'll demand some kind of fanfare. She's a lot like you in that way." I smirk at Landon, who rolls her eyes.

"Where does she go again?" Miko asks.

"Georgetown," Liam answers. "She starts her senior year in the fall, but she has an internship in the city this summer."

I snort.

"Allegedly," I tell them.

"In any event, she's coming in," Liam goes on, "so it'll be a thing."

"You guys should come," Brody says suddenly.

It surprises me so much that I swallow my coffee too fast and it burns my throat. I know he likes Landon a lot—anyone with functional eyes knows that—but he has never brought anyone on a family vacation, even before.

"Really?" Landon asks with a squeak.

"Are we doing *this* now? Going on group vacations together?" I ask the table.

Landon, Brody, and Miko are already talking about logistics, and nobody pays any attention to my dismay. I look over at Liam, who takes it all in stride as usual.

"Apparently we are," he says only to me. "This is what happens when you try new things. First it's dodgeball, then it's family vacations en masse, and before you know it you're posing for awkward engagement photos where you're giving her a piggyback ride at the beach. This is just another reason I avoid attachment of any kind."

"You and me both," I grumble.

The mention of dodgeball lowers my mood again. It reminds me of our game earlier and our subsequent loss, which reminds me that I agreed to a stupid bet. Now I've locked myself into a date with Taylor, and I definitely can't handle hours with him acting smug over his victory.

He didn't come to talk to me after the game. I'm sure he could see that I'd have murdered him if the possibility presented itself.

He just winked at me from across the gym and mouthed the words *Monty Kirchner*.

The response I mouthed back isn't fit to be repeated in polite company.

Chapter Nine

"Oh, and don't forget that butterscotch sauce has to sit in the fridge for exactly thirty-seven minutes to hit the right consistency. And éclairs are coming back on the menu soon, so you should probably start testing out that recipe."

Joey looks around erratically, trying to remember every last detail before Harris forcibly removes her from the room. Half of the tiny office is filled with a desk, papers, files, and stacks of bottled water. The other half is filled with Joey's swollen belly.

It is her last day in the kitchen, and we've spent several hours of it with her spouting off random pronouncements and me taking feverish notes. With each new page I filled, I felt more and more nervous. It wasn't the management of the kitchen that threw me off. I had a bit more confidence after I'd given my two weeks' notice at the bar. The GM looked like he might be sick when I told him the news. He offered a significant salary increase if I stayed on, and he looked even sicker when I told him there was no possibility of me taking it.

It was an uncomfortable conversation to have, but a good reminder that I've been overseeing the revolving line of employees at Gander for years and Dolci's crew is way more talented and hardworking than that one. I am not freaked out about managing this kitchen; what freaks me out are the recipes. Joey has shown me everything she could, but we've barely gone through the current menu. Even with detailed notes I'm not entirely sure I could recreate all of the signature dishes perfectly. I secretly hope Avis is too self-indulgent to take notice of me until I have several more weeks under my belt.

"I showed you where the payroll info is, right?" Joey asks as if it were a life-or-death question.

"You did, yes," I tell her.

She'd actually shown me where it was three times today alone.

"And the contact information for that French butter company? You know she won't use anything domestic," she says, worrying her lip with her front teeth.

Harris walks into the room with us, crowding the already-full space.

"It's time to go, Joey," he tells her.

I pull my feet up onto the seat of the chair to make room for him to get to her.

"I just need half an hour more," Joey says, shaking her head.

She's already told him that four times today, but he looks resolute. He chances another step towards her.

Joey grabs the desk behind her with both hands. Something like panic fills her eyes.

Harris takes a deep breath and then gently reaches out to her as if she is a wild animal he's set out to tame.

"Love," he tells her gently, "it'll be OK."

Joey responds by mutely shaking her head. I notice the look in her eyes, and I finally understand why she's been acting so erratic all day.

Trapped in this kitchen with me all week, she's been able to focus solely on the job, in a place where she feels totally in control.

But when she leaves here she is going to have a baby. Everything after she walks out the door today is a nonstop list of unknowns. No perfect equation or recipe to follow, no way to know exactly what's on the other side. I know that look on her face. I know how it feels to be terrified of something so big.

The urge to leave the room is overwhelming. I want to get as far away as possible from that look on her face, but Harris is blocking the door. I don't know how to remove myself without making it more awkward for them both. I stare down at the notebook propped on my knees so I don't have to see them.

"Joey, baby, you've got this," he whispers to her. "You're the strongest woman I know."

A broken little whimper is her only response.

"You *can* do this," he tells her emphatically.

"You don't know!" she finally cries. "You don't know that for sure. You don't know how hard it will be!"

She starts crying then, in long sobs that are quickly muffled by his chest. It is physically painful for me to sit in this room, with the sound of her breaking apart echoing off the walls.

"You don't know what it will be like," she sobs again.

"You're right. I don't," Harris says, trying to console her. "But—"

Joey's crying gets louder still. I can only imagine what fear and nearly ten months of hormone buildup must be making her feel, but it can't be good for her or the baby. Harris swears loudly.

It seems like the only thing he can think to say. When I glance up at them from under my lashes, he looks totally at a loss for what to do next.

"You don't know what it's like," she cries again.

It becomes a nonsensical litany she says over and over.

I can't stand it anymore.

"I do."

My voice comes out whisper-soft, but it shocks all three of us into silence. They both look at me in surprise. I finger the bracelets on my wrist and force myself to continue.

"I know how hard it will be." I shake off the memory that fills my head. "Becoming a mother will hurt and it's scary, but you'll have a beautiful baby when you're done, Joey." I force myself to look up into her eyes. "A little—" I clear my throat. "A little boy, right?"

She nods in response.

"Then you need to get ahold of yourself. You're his mommy, and you have to be the grown-up here. It's your job to take care of him, even if that's scary. Even if you're not sure how. You'll hate yourself if you let him down."

My gaze holds on to hers until she nods in agreement.

I stand, not sure my legs will hold my weight, but they do.

I leave the room.

The next day I get a text from Joey with a picture of their beautiful baby and two words.

Thank you.

———

The traffic passes in a blur outside the car window, but I don't really notice it. I haven't noticed much of anything in the past couple of weeks. Ever since that moment with Joey, I've been deep inside my head and unable to pull myself out of a funk. I do little more than work at Dolci and cover my last few shifts at the bar. I don't even have the energy to put up a proper fight when Taylor calls to set up his victory date.

Which is why I find myself inside his massive black SUV now, unsure where we are headed. I did little more than put on some mostly clean clothes and wash my face to get ready for our date, and I haven't said more than two words to him since he picked me up. My fingers trace random shapes on his leather seats, and my mind is a thousand miles away.

"I never anticipated this form of retaliation." His words cut through the air between us.

I look over. His thumbs drum absently on the steering wheel along with the classic rock on the radio.

"Excuse me?" I ask, confused.

"The silent treatment." He glances my way before changing lanes. "I figured you for a sore loser, but I at least thought you'd make it interesting."

I know he is trying to bait me because he aims a grin my way. I turn and look back out the window.

"Don't you worry, though," he tells me gallantly. "I've got it all planned out. There's not a chance you can hold onto your stoicism when you see where I'm taking you."

"And where is that, exactly?" I ask as we merge onto yet another freeway.

We drove through Pasadena fifteen minutes ago. I'm not even sure what could possibly be this far east.

"To the worst date ever," he says happily.

I look at him in surprise.

"Excuse me?" I ask again.

"Well, Landon and Brody went on a non-date." His eyes dart to mine. "Have you heard this story?"

"I guess, yeah," I tell him, confused.

"Well, they went on a non-date, which was essentially the worst first date ever. I thought it was sort of clever, and well, I'm nothing if not competitive."

That is the understatement of the year. The sting of the dodge-ball hitting my lower back with a snap is still a fresh memory. He grins happily when he sees me scowl.

"And so I thought I'd see if I could do better. Or worse, I guess," he finishes up.

"With a bad date?"

"The worst ever," he tells me emphatically.

"For anyone or just for me?" I ask, my curiosity creeping out of the numb place where I've been hiding all my feelings for the last two weeks.

Taylor clutches his heart as if I've wounded him.

"Now what kind of gentleman would I be if I'd planned out something generic. No way, Jennings! This day was built specifically with you in mind."

He flips on his blinker and exits the freeway. We seem to be in the middle of nowhere, except for all the traffic around us. I look back out my window again. I don't want him to see the curiosity on my face as I try to figure out where we are going. We crawl along several roads in a long line of traffic before I see the first sign. I gasp in genuine horror.

"A Renaissance faire?" I scream at him.

He doesn't even try to play it cool. He starts to laugh so hard at my outburst that he can't talk. He is wiping away tears by the time he gets enough air to reply.

"Ah Lord, Jennings, that was worth the drive just to see your face." He chuckles again.

"So we're not really going there?" I ask hopefully.

"Hell yes, we're going! I won that bet fair and square. You agreed to spend four hours in my company however I see fit, and this is how I choose."

"Do you"—I gesture emphatically at a group of teenagers who walk by his SUV dressed like gothic princesses—"*like* this kind of thing?"

"Of course not." He starts laughing again. "But even with our limited interaction, I figured this would be your worst nightmare, so here we are!" he says grandly.

We pull up to a stoplight to wait, and an obese couple waddles by dressed as fairies. I run my hand back and forth through my hair in agitation, and Taylor follows the movement with his eyes.

"Why would you actively try to piss me off?" I growl at him. "Do you have a death wish or something?"

"Your problem is that people don't mess with you nearly enough." He points an accusing finger at me. "You need someone to ruffle your feathers."

"And you've appointed yourself to the task."

"I find it entertaining." He gives me a boyish grin, dimple and all.

"Well, I find it—" I stop short at the sight of a small photo propped on the dash behind his steering wheel. "Is that a cat?" I demand, too shocked to do anything but ask the question.

"Don't worry about the cat," he says, gesturing to my side of the car. "Roll down your window and ask that pirate where we're supposed to park."

———

"Gramercy, my lord!" a pleather-clad idiot announces merrily as we pass through the gates of the Renaissance faire.

I scowl at Taylor through my oversize Wayfarers, which only makes his smile grow bigger. We are both wearing jeans and T-shirts, which means we are in a very small minority of people not swarming this dusty crap pile in full costume. Honestly, who knew there were this many freaks in Los Angeles County who would show up for something like this? There have to be five thousand people here, given the number of cars parked in the field next door.

Pop-up stands of various heights line the makeshift streets, and costumed freaks and geeks of every shape and size stand around drinking out of giant metal cups and yelling obscure, vaguely

Renaissance-sounding things into the chaos around them. Down the way a group of people are dancing around a flipping maypole, for freak's sake!

"My lady," calls a woman old enough to be my grandmother. Her boobs defy the laws of both gravity and nature, piled so high in her corset that they nearly touch her chin. "Care ye for proper English garb? We rent them here for but a tuppence."

"The tuppence is from an entirely different century," I tell Taylor in annoyance. "You'd think they'd give them a CliffsNotes or something before they throw them out here to pedal dirty-wench costumes to kids from Northridge!"

Taylor bumps me with his shoulder, directing me farther into the crowd.

"Come on, killer, there's a jousting tourney starting in twenty minutes. Let's get a turkey leg to gnaw on before we head that way."

"You're a nightmare," I tell him honestly.

Before he can answer, his eyes light up at something behind me.

"Don't look now," he tells me, fighting a smile, "but there's a warrior fairy heading straight for you."

"What. The. Hell?" I sputter as Miko comes to a stop in front of us in all her shining, shimmering splendor.

She is like a Disney movie gone horribly wrong. She smiles at us both, totally unashamed that she is dressed from head to toe in gold leather, with wicked-looking wings and a pretty realistic-looking sword hanging from her hip.

"I didn't know you guys came to these things," she says happily. "In fact, I didn't know you guys came to *anything* together."

"We don't," I grumble. "This is a one-time thing, and the result of my losing a bet. But way more importantly, what are you doing here?"

"Oh, we're about to go watch the hypnotist. Then later we're gonna meet up with some friends from the IE for lunch. They have a really good food court, actually," she tells us.

I can only stare at her in shock.

If I only have two friends and one of them is a fairy on the weekends, shouldn't I have known that?

"We?" Taylor asks curiously just as a few other people walk up and come to a stop next to Miko. They look like the unwashed extras from Medieval Times.

"These are my friends." She points out each one in turn. "Sara, Gretchen, Michael, and Lonny."

Lonny, a mutant of a man in an ill-fitting purple tunic, clears his throat pointedly.

"Sorry, er, this is Lord Dilston, the ninth Earl of Canterbury," she announces grandly.

Lonny seems mollified and goes back to the Droid in his hand.

"I need a drink," I announce to no one in particular.

Lonny glances up from his phone at the suggestion.

"Not from you, Dilston." I look pointedly at Taylor, who smiles and pulls me away.

"There's a beer garden past that band of jugglers," Miko calls after us. "If you hit the Dragon's Lair, you've gone too far!"

It is all too ridiculous, and Taylor must agree, because he starts laughing harder with every step we take. Before I know it I am joining him.

I laugh because Miko has no sense of irony. I laugh because somewhere in Van Nuys, Lonny's parents are wondering if he'll ever actually move out of the basement. But mostly, I laugh because it feels so good to do it. It is the first time I can remember smiling in a while.

———

"OK, just one more stop before I take you home," Taylor says as he pulls into a small lot and parks in front of a nondescript building.

We'd walked around the faire for a couple more hours, sipping beers and people-watching. Once I got over the initial shock of being in such a ridiculous place, it actually became a really interesting way to spend an afternoon, if for no other reason than it was fun to walk around and silently judge others.

I look at the lot around us, which is mostly empty. There isn't a sign announcing our location, and I have no idea where he's taken me now.

"Are you going to up the ante?" I ask, fighting a smile. "Maybe push me into the middle of a bum fight or sell my organs on the black market?"

I mean, seriously, he actually succeeded in taking me on the worst date ever. He purposely picked something horrible, which ironically at least garnered him some of my respect.

"Something like that," he says, pulling the key out of the ignition and getting out of the car. He is already opening my door for me before I've even taken my seatbelt off. I forget occasionally that he is southern, since his accent rarely makes an appearance, but he has impeccable manners.

I follow him up to an unmarked door and into a small lobby. The smell of vanilla hits me before I've even taken three steps into the room. All around us are wedding cakes of every shape and size, each one more impressive than the one beside it. A small old woman comes out of the back room, and my mouth falls open when I see her hurrying towards us.

"Bennett Taylor, I don't never see you no more," she chides while reaching out to pinch his cheek with her weathered old hand. Her southern accent is much deeper and richer than either Taylor's or Landon's.

"That's not true," he tells her sweetly. "You know I just saw you two weeks ago at the McCarthy wedding." He nearly yells the words at her, reminding me that of the few stories I'd read about this woman, one of them said she must be nearly ninety.

"Jennings, I'd like you to meet my friend—"

"Edith Marshall," I say in wonder.

She is the most famous wedding-cake designer. Ever.

Celebrities from presidents to kings vie for her work. She costs a small fortune and is very choosy about who she'll actually take on as a client. Rumor has it, she doesn't even take directions from the bride or groom. You get whatever she wants to give you, and it is always epic.

She shakes my hand with a hearty "Speak up, girl, I can barely hear you!"

"I'm so flattered to meet you, ma'am." I raise my voice to match her volume level, and she nods in agreement.

"Ben says you're a baker." She smiles at Taylor indulgently. I panic for a heartbeat, remembering the day I told him everything and thinking for one crazy moment that he might have mentioned it to someone else. But then I realize that regardless of my initial opinions about him, he has never been anything but totally cool about the whole breaking-down-in-the-hallway thing. I couldn't imagine him sharing that information with anyone else.

Edith keeps speaking. "He thought you might like to try some of my creations."

I look over at Taylor in surprise. He smiles sheepishly, like he is embarrassed by whatever he sees on my face.

Edith shuffles along ahead of us to a small but pristine kitchen, where a handful of apron-clad worker bees carry out their tasks. Tucked into a back corner is a small table covered with several tiny layer cakes. The cakes are covered on top and between sections with icing, but the sides are bare, so I can tell what flavors they are. Chocolate, vanilla, lemon, red velvet, and either carrot or maybe spice cake sit on the table, and next to them are a ton of little dishes holding fillings. Edith points them out as we take our seats.

"That there's lemon curd, then strawberry preserves, chocolate ganache, a pistachio cream, raspberry jam, caramel cream cheese, huckleberry preserves, some kumquat preserves, and a maple buttercream which I like to pair with the carrot cake there."

"This is incredible," I tell Edith honestly.

"Nah." She shoos my comment away with her hand. "It's just a little baking. Some good ingredients, along with a little of this and a dash of that. You mix it up till it's yummy. If it don't come off quite right, you try it another way. It ain't supposed to be scientific; it's just supposed to taste good. Simple as that."

I smile at her summation. Most classically trained pastry chefs *would* call this science, and they take it quite seriously. She makes it sound so simple.

"Y'all want some coffee to go with them sweets?" Edith asks.

When we both tell her yes, she shuffles away.

The smell alone is wonderful, and I try to map out which cake would taste best and how I can sample the most options without taking more than a few bites. I checked my levels in the restroom before we left the faire and they were OK, but more than a couple bites of this much sugar is dangerous for me.

Taylor picks up a fork without hesitation and takes a bite of the red velvet. His eyes close as he manages to chew and smile at the same time.

"That one"—he points at the red velvet with his fork—"is my favorite."

I look around the options before us, struggling to choose. Finally I take the smallest bit of carrot cake and top it with the maple buttercream. Edith was dead on about the combination. It hits my taste buds in an explosion of flavor: nutmeg, cinnamon, apples, walnuts, and even a little allspice, paired perfectly with the creamy icing with hints of pure maple syrup. Taylor follows my lead and tries the same combination just as a young woman sets down two cups of coffee for us. Taylor hums as he closes his lips over his fork.

"Oh Lord, I change my mind," he chokes out. "This one is my favorite."

I can't help but smile at him.

"What next?" he asks me.

I look around at the options before picking up a clean fork from the pile on the table. I spear a bite of the vanilla cake with buttercream icing and top it with strawberry preserves and the pistachio cream. I reach out the fork to him, and he grins before taking a bite, instead of taking the fork from me as I'd intended. I roll my eyes at his attempt to be cute before he slams his own shut in bliss.

"No, *that* one. That one is my favorite," he says before taking another bite of the same.

I hide my smile behind the rim of my coffee cup.

He goes after the lemon cake next.

"Which one?" he asks before choosing a filling.

I point to the lemon curd and the raspberry jam in answer, and he complies, dipping his fork into each one.

"Don't tell me you're not going to have more," he tells me between mouthfuls.

"I shouldn't have too much," I answer vaguely.

"Come on, Jennings, I never figured you for a girl who was afraid of calories," he says in confusion.

If you'd have told me a week ago, or even this morning, that I'd be sitting here with any man, let alone this one, considering sharing even more personal information, I'd have laughed outright. But it somehow feels wrong to hide something he could easily find out from anyone else, especially when he knows so many other embarrassing details about me, and he'd been perceptive enough to bring me here in the first place. I take a deep breath.

"Not the calories," I tell him, "just the sugar. I have to be really careful with my diet. I'm pretty severely hypoglycemic, which isn't as difficult as being diabetic, but it can be really dangerous."

I say it all in a rush, and when I look up Taylor appears to be trying to figure out the best response to my confession. He lays his fork down slowly in front of him on the table.

"But you're training to be a pastry chef," he says, sounding confused, "and even before that, Landon said you're always baking."

I wonder what else Landon has told him about me.

"Just because I can't eat it, doesn't mean I don't want to. I like to make things for other people to try."

I am embarrassed at how small my voice sounds. We are hitting pretty close to a nerve.

He must be able to tell that it makes me uncomfortable to talk about this, and he has to be perceptive enough to know that I'd hate pity of any kind.

"So you're telling me that I managed to bring a woman who can't eat sugar on a date to a cake tasting?" he asks slowly.

I nod in reply.

His head falls backwards in laughter. He sits up straighter and rubs a hand over his jaw. The tattoos on his forearms twist in response.

"Damn, I really did take you on the worst date ever," he tells me with a chuckle. "This has got to be a record or something."

Suddenly his smile falters.

"You were OK having the one bite, right?" he asks seriously. "I hope you didn't do it just to be polite."

I snort in response.

"You think I'd risk my health to save your vanity?" I ask him.

It comes out harsher than I'd intended, because it is easy for me to revert to type.

He looks away.

I have a small, absurd moment of panic. My family is used to my moods, and even Landon and Miko put up with them now. But this man has no reason to deal with me for longer than it takes to get me back home.

"It was the nicest date I've been on in a while," I tell him.

I don't tell him it is the only date I've been on in a while. That is beside the point.

Some of the tension comes out of his shoulders, and he smiles again.

"Can you have any more, or are you tapped out?" he asks.

I look at the options dubiously.

"One more bite won't kill me," I tell him, stabbing a piece of chocolate cake.

I have no idea where the flippancy came from. I have never, not once, joked about my condition, because my family takes it so seriously. It actually feels kind of great to mock it for once.

"Not funny," he says sternly.

"Kind of funny," I answer with a childish smile.

I dip my cake in the chocolate ganache and the caramel cream cheese and take a bite. I have to force myself not to groan as the incredible flavors explode on my tongue.

"That one"—I point at the chocolate cake—"that one is your favorite. You just don't know it yet."

Taylor's answering smile is boyish once again, and he starts to create his own bite that is twice the size of my own. I happily sip my coffee as he proceeds to eat the rest of the chocolate cake.

I can't make sense of where I find myself. This morning he'd set out to ruffle my feathers or just out-and-out piss me off. But he picked up on the one thing I loved most, something almost nobody would have chosen for me to do, and figured out a way to work it into our day. I'm not sure what to think about someone who forced me into this day against my will but then tried his best to make it nice for me. When I combine that with his kindness when I was upset, the whole thing makes me feel uncomfortable.

"What is it you want?" I demand.

"What?" he asks, his fork paused halfway between his plate and his mouth.

"What do you want from me here? Why all the effort?" The anger in my voice grows with each sentence. "There's not a chance in hell we'd ever go on a real date; you get that, right? I'm here because I lost a bet, not because I'm attracted to you."

Taylor puts both his hands up in surrender, which looks ridiculous since one of them is holding a fork with a piece of carrot cake stuck to the end.

"Are you serious?" he asks.

The look I give him would have sent most men screaming in the other direction.

"OK." He drops his hands. "I was kind of purposely a jerk to you the first couple of times we met."

"You don't say," I answer sarcastically.

"I do." He struggles to hide a smile. "I know it makes me a terrible person to admit this, but it's just that you're so easy to rile up. It's actually really entertaining."

I stare at him in surprise, but he just keeps speaking. "I don't know why, exactly, but it is. I made the bet because I thought it would get us back on neutral ground after our chat. I knew it would piss you off even more, but I didn't count on just how annoyed you'd be if you lost. Afterwards I felt badly about it."

"Not enough to cancel," I point out.

"Oh hell no. I'd already thought up the Renaissance faire, and I wasn't letting that go." He smiles again. "But at least enough that I tried to end it on a high note." He looked around us meaningfully.

He shocks me again by saying, "I'd like us to be friends, Jennings."

It is my turn to ask "What?"

"Friends. We hang out with a lot of the same people. I don't want to bicker every time we do."

Bicker, he said. Like we are eleven-year-olds.

"So you want to be friends?" I say it slowly, as the concept is so alien to me.

Nobody ever tries to seek out my friendship. Landon was forced into it by proximity, and Miko just came along for the ride.

"I do." He nods.

"I don't," I answer too quickly.

"And why not?" He feigns insult. "I make an excellent friend. And you said it yourself, you're not attracted to me. So there's no excuse."

"You annoy me," I point out.

"I entertain you. It's a fine distinction," he answers happily.

"We have nothing in common," I try again, unsure why I feel like I am grasping at straws.

He finishes chewing the bite in his mouth and his smile grows bigger.

"We have chocolate in common—that's enough."

Chapter Ten

"Stork!" Avis screams over the hum of the mixers Ram is running in the other room.

I look up from an invoice I am holding for insanely overpriced cheese. In the last eight days alone, Avis has run through nineteen pounds of mascarpone as she's been working her way through a new galette recipe. I jump up from the desk and hurry to find her. In the three weeks since Joey left, I've actually worked with the food very little and Avis even less. Running the kitchen occupies most of my time, and the rest of the team is efficient. In my off hours I work on the different recipes Joey taught me. I'm hoping I won't be called upon to make anything until I've perfected each one.

I find Avis hunched over a pile of dough like a scavenger hiding its food from others who might pick it off.

"It's done," she says without looking up at me.

I look at the blob of dough beneath her hands, confused.

"The, uh—"

"The galette recipe!"

One of her hands shoots out to grab a crumpled-up paper towel, which she throws in my direction. I catch it and unfurl the edges to find it covered with her chicken scratch, written in at least three different colors of ink. There is no discernable order to any of it.

"You want me to—"

She cuts me off with a look.

"What Joey did. I want it on the menu by this weekend."

When I don't respond, as I'm too stunned to say anything, she waves a flour-covered hand in my direction.

"Can you find me an Orangina? I'm thirsty."

I walk back through the kitchen in a daze, and I don't know how long I stand in front of the drink refrigerator trying to decipher her recipe before Ram walks up behind me.

"Damn," he says, looking over my shoulder. "Is that even in English?"

"I'm not entirely sure," I tell him honestly.

I know I shouldn't show any weakness since I am, technically, supposed to know what I am doing, but I look over at him in something close to panic. There is no way I can figure this out. I know from countless hours with Joey that Avis refuses to be questioned. In fact, Joey wasn't even sure Avis knew what she wrote down on her recipes, but she definitely knew if they weren't followed. This is my first test in this new role, and I cannot fail.

Ram bumps me with his shoulder. "Why don't you come in early tomorrow? Before first shift? You could try to figure it out before everyone gets here, and then you won't have an audience."

I nod stupidly and head back to bring Avis her drink. I keep glancing down at the hieroglyphs in my hand, but no matter how long I stare at them, they never make any more sense.

———

The next morning I come in at four, and since I fell asleep around midnight, I am kind of a wreck. I don't know much about this recipe or how I'll pull it off, but even if it means sacrificing sleep, I know I don't want an audience while I try. The hour is late enough that the A crew has already arrived, so the kitchen is unlocked, but early enough that no one on B shift will get wind of what I am up to.

I find an empty workspace and spread the crumpled paper towel out gingerly. Next to the towel I place my notebook, which holds my notes from the hours I spent last night trying to decipher ingredients into some kind of discernable order. A deep hip-hop beat makes its way across the kitchen, which means that Pauly must have gotten to work first today. I learned early on about the battle of wills that is the damn radio. Everyone wants to choose the station, and the crew fight constantly for their own tastes. Classical, country, banda, rap, pop, and the occasional soccer game all battle for supremacy. The house rule is that whoever arrives first picks the day's choice, but people are forever changing channels just to piss one another off. I put my earbuds in and turn on Hall & Oates radio on Pandora. It is going to take a miracle and a snappy eighties beat to get me through this day.

I look again at my list and start gathering items. I have at least a fairly good idea of what most of the ingredients are because a lot of it is in shorthand. The issue is that even though I can identify some things, I don't know their order or quantities, or a good portion of the other words. They could be ingredients, or they could just as easily be doodles she added in her spare time. I stayed up most of the night trying to figure this out, and I don't feel any closer than I did when she first handed it to me.

How the hell am I going to pull this off? Not just the recipe, but any of this at all? I have no business being here. Just because you once dream up something doesn't give you the right to try to make it your own. Especially when other people's careers are on the line. I'm such an idiot!

The words on the paper below me distort with my tears, and I swipe at them with an angry hand. So apparently I'm going to cry over everything now!

I reach down for the recipe, wildly debating tearing it to pieces before forcing myself to drop it. While Avis might be crazy, this is probably some totally genius recipe, and just because I am too unskilled to recreate it for her doesn't mean someone else might not be able to. It is a hard thing to accept, because I'd so wanted to be that person for her. Her unique flavor pairings are her specialty. She thinks of combinations very few people would even try, but somehow they always work in perfect harmony in her dishes. *What would it be like to have a palate like that? Or to—*

A small idea forms before I can stop it. I have her ingredients, at least, and I have her pairings. The only thing I don't have is her measurements. *Maybe I could . . .* I know how to bake, and galettes aren't that difficult to pull off. It is totally insane to think I could reproduce a recipe for a chef at her level, but maybe I could get close enough?

I think of Edith's words again: *You mix it up till it's yummy. If it don't come off quite right, you try it another way.*

That decides it for me. If I am going to lose this job, it won't be because I offer up something inedible. I'll attempt to recreate her recipe, and if it isn't right, well, at least I can say I tried.

———

When Avis appears without warning six hours later, I have one hand propped on my hip as I stare dubiously at the berry galette with a mascarpone filling on the table in front of me. It is the fifth one I've baked, and I've struggled to get the crust just right. The filling itself is a mix of strawberry, blueberry, lemon zest, and a vanilla-bean mascarpone. Ram and Harris both tried the fourth version and declared it perfect. I baked this one just so Avis will have it fresh from the oven when she comes in. She looks at it along with me, neither of us saying a word.

Without waiting for me to say something, she cuts herself a slice. In the absence of a plate, she drops the piece of pastry into the palm of her hand. I don't even have time to prep her before it is in her mouth.

She'll be able to tell immediately that it isn't her exact recipe, because even though I used her ingredients, there is no way I made it precisely as she did. In the end, I decided to make it as good as I possibly could, knowing it'd never get anywhere near her level.

She looks down at the slice in her hand and then back up at me, the confusion evident on her face. She takes another bite. When she finally opens her mouth, I am ready to hear the words. I prepared myself all morning to be fired again, and I am going to accept it this time.

"This is exactly right, Stork. Well done," she adds, almost as an afterthought. "Now, can you get me a Perrier? I'm thirsty."

———

"So you pulled it off," Taylor says as he keeps pace beside me.

"It took me all night and five tries, but yeah, I guess I did. Nobody is more surprised than me," I say as we round a bend in the road and jog past some old women who are meandering along the trail with their small dogs.

"And what was in it, again?" he asks, pulling the brim of his well-worn OU hat lower to escape the glare of the late-afternoon sun.

I haven't run while carrying on a conversation since the long-distance track team in high school. But over the last couple of weeks we've been texting each other stupid YouTube videos and arguing over which Pandora stations are the best. It feels remarkable, but somehow Taylor has wormed his way in just like Landon and Miko. As hard as it is to believe, we are becoming friends. So when he sent a text asking me if I wanted to jog the Rose Bowl with him, I didn't immediately hate the idea.

The Rose Bowl, like all good sporting venues, houses big football games, epic concerts, and a monthly flea market famous throughout the state. The other three hundred days of the year, it is a sort of mecca for runners who live on the Eastside of Los Angeles. At any given time of day, the loop around the outside of the bowl is covered with hundreds of joggers, sprinters, walkers, and humans involved in any kind of activity involving lower body strength and a set of wheels. One time around the outside is a three-mile trek, so it is a favorite for runners, since they can easily calculate distance based on their laps. I'd always liked the space because it is surrounded by hillsides and trees, and the affluent neighborhood makes it fairly safe to run here alone, which is not something I can say about living in Hollywood.

On the first lap around I tell Taylor how things have been going since Joey left. On the second lap I tell him about the saga with the galette. I should feel ridiculous about talking basically nonstop since I got out of my car, but I sort of feel too good to care. No one else knows nearly as much about my job at Dolci, and it is really nice to tell the stories to someone who seems excited for me. His reaction might have more to do with the food itself, since he's asked me to describe each recipe in detail, but I'm not complaining.

"Mascarpone, strawberries, blueberries, lemon zest, and vanilla bean," I answer him, ticking the items off on my fingers. My Wayfarers slide lower on my nose, and I push them back up again.

"That sounds incredible," he says emphatically. "Next time feel free to use my place as a prep kitchen. Someone should be testing your attempts for you."

"I test them, just in very small amounts. But it's enough that I can check the flavor."

"Well, use me for quality control, then." He laughs. "It's the least I can do if you're going to taunt me with recipes."

"You act like you never eat, when that's all I've ever seen you do."

"I love all food, of every kind. That's why I'm always out here running it off." He pats his entirely rock-hard stomach as if it is a beer belly. "Got to keep up my girlish figure."

Several moms with strollers jog by going the opposite way, each one of them staring at his "girlish figure" as if it were her last meal.

"Are you going to that bar thing on Thursday?" he asks.

I pop a bubble in my gum before answering.

"Ugh, no, I hate bingo! I don't know why Landon thinks it's so clever just because they're hosting it at a dive bar."

"Come on, Jennings, don't let me down. I was counting on you to make acerbic comments about the other patrons." I noticed recently that his southern accent grows thicker whenever he is trying to wheedle something out of me.

"Not interested," I answer.

I am totally immune to that accent.

"I'll race you for it," he says, purposely bumping me with his shoulder.

"I said I'm not interested. I have no reason to race you for anything." I roll my eyes behind my sunglasses.

"You nervous about getting beat again?" he challenges.

"Please," I say sarcastically. "I ran track for seven years. I could beat you without even trying."

"Wanna bet?" he asks gleefully.

I eye the remaining distance between us and our cars, then look back over at him jogging next to me. I switch pace, immediately bounding into a full-out sprint.

"Cheaters never win, Jennings!" he yells after me.

I throw a peace sign over my shoulder in response.

The sound of his laughter chases after me as he works to catch up.

———

"Where were you last night?" Landon asks when I walk back into the apartment, sweaty and still smarting from losing to Taylor yet again. She sits on our sofa working on her laptop, with spreadsheets fanned out as far as the eye can see. There are at least three different kinds of caffeine sitting on the coffee table, and her yoga pants mean she probably hasn't left the apartment yet today.

"Work. Why?" I answer before I think better of it.

"I thought you were there too. Brody and I stopped by for a drink, but they said you were off."

I walk over to the fridge for a bottle of water in an effort to buy myself some time. I don't want to lie to her, but I also am not ready to tell her what is going on. She worries about me nearly as much as my family does, and I don't want to hear it, especially when I feel so close to having a permanent place with Avis. There is also a small part of me that worries I can't pull off my dream, especially after I bullied Landon into following her own. I decide to go with something vague.

"I was at the hotel. Maybe whoever you talked to just didn't see me," I say, turning around.

"Well, it was pretty chaotic in there. Maybe you were in the back or something," she agrees.

"Did you guys have a nice time?" I ask in an attempt to change the subject.

"We did." She blushes. "We went to the Hollywood Bowl to see the LA Philharmonic. We brought a picnic, and we sat in one of those little booths down front. It was so much fun."

I grab my own computer and fall into the overstuffed chair across from her.

"Did you decide about Thursday?" she asks cheerfully.

My shoulders fall as I sigh.

"I'm in," I say, annoyed.

"Really?" she asks in surprise. "To what do we owe this honor?"

"Lost a bet," I say without looking up.

"Honestly, Max, you don't have to be so sarcastic. It'll be fun. Everyone is going."

I don't correct her or explain that I did in fact lose a bet, which forced me into this group outing. I'm not really sure why I haven't mentioned it yet, but hanging out with Taylor is just another line in a long list of things I don't want to tell her about yet.

Chapter Eleven

"Another one for you, Stork," Avis says as an empty cracker box falls on the table next to the cupcakes I am icing.

Icing cupcakes is a task, like so many others in this job, that I do because it needs to be done. Joey was the MVP, given that she worked with Avis for so long, but I feel more like a pinch hitter. I tend to jump in wherever we need an extra set of hands. Since the cupcakes in front of me are designed to look rustic instead of stylized, it is a job I can easily take on. I set down a finished cupcake, which threatens to implode given the amount of chocolate buttercream it is topped with, and look at the box on the table next to me. It is covered with so many swirls and Sharpie marks that it actually takes me a minute to realize it is another recipe. I look at Avis warily.

"This one is a . . ." I leave it open, hoping she'll at least give me some clue.

Avis looks at me curiously before answering.

"Dulce de leche cheesecake." She nods slowly as if making up her mind. "Let's serve it in individual portions."

She starts to walk away but stops suddenly and reaches inside the box. She pulls her tiny hand back out, revealing half a graham cracker, which she pops in her mouth like a squirrel.

"I want to try it tomorrow morning," she says, talking around her bite.

As she walks away my mind starts to spin. Cheesecake is hard, really hard; anyone who's ever seen a cooking show can tell you that. It takes hours to get the consistency right, and when you add in the additional flavors she wants in this one *and* the fact that I can't decipher her notes—ugh!

Why did I think this job would get easier instead of harder?

She needs it tomorrow morning, which means I needed to start trying to make it about three hours ago. I'll have to pull another late night, and I have no idea how many batches I'll have to make, which means I am going to need someone else to try it. I already had sugar this morning when I worked out the galette recipe for large batches. I've been extremely careful with my diet lately, since working here means I have to taste some of what I make. I combat the extra sugar by eating totally clean. Vegetables, protein, water, and coffee. Not the most exciting of menus but necessary to counteract the sweets. Unfortunately I didn't plan on testing two recipes in one day, and I am nervous about pushing my levels further.

I send a quick text to one of the two people aware of my job, asking him if I can borrow his kitchen and his taste-testing abilities. I start to clean the workstation around me when Liam writes back, reminding me that he is in New York this week on business.

Damn.

He tells me to use my key to his house to borrow his kitchen, but that defeats the purpose of having someone else there who can try the recipe out. For half a minute I consider fessing up to Landon or even my parents, but I just don't have the energy to battle either of them, especially on a night when I have so much work to do.

The sigh I let out is as defeated as my posture. I type out a quick text to my most recent volunteer: *Do you actually have a working oven?*

His response pops up a few minutes later: *Is that a euphemism?*

You wish. I have to make about 49 caramel cheesecakes tonight, and I need a location and a tester. You in?

49 cheesecakes is better than an innuendo any day. What time?

I respond with a time, and he writes back with his address. Now I just have to transport everything I might possibly need over Laurel Canyon in rush-hour traffic. It is a total pain, but it can't be helped. At least I won't spend another early morning trapped in this kitchen. Whatever crappy apartment Taylor lives in has to be better than stressing out here alone.

———

I check the address on my phone again and then look up at the house in front of me in confusion. I didn't expect to be coming to this quaint little neighborhood off Ventura. I thought I was headed for a grubby apartment, not unlike mine. The Spanish-style house at the address Taylor gave me is small, but it fairly preened in the late summer twilight. Nobody would ever call it grubby. It is pristine and well kept, and the front yard suggests a gardener with a green thumb and a love of succulents. Maybe Taylor shares rent with a kindly septuagenarian or a retired gay uncle?

I pull my reusable shopping bag higher on my shoulder and grab the other two off the ground at my feet. The pans in the bag clank together with every step. I sound like a wandering tinker. *Where is the Renaissance faire now when I actually have a period-appropriate descriptor?*

I ring the doorbell.

When no one answers I set my bags down and try the knocker.

Still nothing.

I pull out my phone and send Taylor a text: *Are you here? Or is this some elaborate ruse?*

He writes right back: *Sorry! Just finishing up. Come around back to the shop and I'll let you in.*

I slip my phone into my bag and follow the little flagstone path around to the side of the house. Once I make it through a gate, the pathway opens up, revealing a backyard as manicured as the front. The door to the single-car garage is wide open, revealing a workshop filled with every kind of tool imaginable. The walls themselves are lined with plywood so that everything in the space is accented by raw wood grain. In the center of the back wall hangs a large framed portrait of an old man rendered in colorful chalk. It is either worth a lot of money or something you buy at a garage sale for a dollar; I can't tell which. Shelves and tall workbenches edge up against the walls, and hand tools hang above them in straight lines of descending size. In the midst of it all, Taylor is working on a huge square piece of timber that looks like it was ripped off the broad side of a barn.

"Give me two seconds," he calls over the sound of Guns N' Roses coming from an iPod dock behind him.

I nod stupidly and he goes back to work. I should look away or occupy myself somehow, but my attention is totally skewered on the scene before me.

Since he's been doing physical work in the heat of the summer, Taylor must have removed his shirt to cool off. But now he is covered with a fine sheen that does *everything* to highlight his hard torso, which is covered completely in tattoos.

He doesn't have just sleeves like I originally thought. His chest, abs, arms, and shoulders are all inked. There isn't a single area above his waistline or below his collarbone not covered with words, pictures, and symbols.

How many years must that have taken him?

How many hours over the course of his life did he sit in a chair and let someone carve the images into his body?

It is a mess of color with no discernable order.

It is utterly beautiful.

It is staggering in its effect on me. I want to reach out and trace the lines with my fingers.

Mortification hits me, followed swiftly by anger. I know better.

"OK, all done," he calls, totally unaware of the trip I've just gone on.

The sound of the music dies and is replaced by shuffling and scraping as he puts some tools away. I pretend to be extremely interested in the papyrus lining the back fence.

"Here, let me take those." He grabs my bags, and I am too overwhelmed to do anything but let him. When I finally look his way, I discover that he has, thankfully, found his shirt again.

"I'm sorry I wasn't finished working when you got here," he calls over his shoulder while nudging the back door to the house open with his hip. "That piece has ended up being a lot more difficult than I anticipated, and I lost track of time."

I follow him through a back bedroom and down a hallway to a kitchen. Like the front of the house, the inside is small but perfectly maintained and shockingly clean for a man's home. The floors are dark hardwood, the walls are a bright white, and everything I see, from carved niches to exposed wooden beams, speaks to a celebration of the historical aspects of the home.

"This house is beautiful," I say, because it is true, and also because I can't stop thinking about the tattoos on his abs, and I want my brain to focus on something else.

"Thanks," he says as he sets the bags down on the marble countertop. "You should have seen it when I first bought the place. It was a disaster, and the only reason I got it so cheap was that nobody else was willing to take it on." He looks around the little

kitchen, pride evident on his face. "But I knew there was something special hidden underneath all the mess."

I am flabbergasted.

"You own this house?" I ask stupidly.

"Well, it'd be mighty awkward if I didn't, since I just knocked a
wall out in the back bedroom yesterday." He grins and runs a hand
through his sweaty hair absentmindedly. "Let me take a quick
shower and I'll give you the nickel tour, OK?"

"OK?" I don't know why it comes out as a question.

Except that I am totally confused by this version of him. I don't
know him at all, I now realize.

"You need anything before I leave you here?" he asks, grabbing
two bottles of water from the fridge. He sets a Perrier down on the
counter in front of me before starting on the other, a Fiji, himself.
I'm not sure when he noticed I like sparkling water.

"I have everything I need," I tell him, twisting the cap of my
water bottle just to give myself something to do with my hands.

"Ahh, I doubt that's true, Jennings," he says with a wink before
leaving the kitchen.

I squeeze the cap between my fingers until my knuckles turn
white.

A kitchen towel flies across my field of vision before landing on
the other side of me. I pull out a single earbud and turn to look at
the culprit.

"I *said*," Taylor announces, holding a frying pan in one hand
and several brown eggs in the other, "would you like some eggs?"

His hair is still wet from the shower. He is wearing long gym
shorts, a faded blue T-shirt so thin from a lifetime of use that it is
nearly transparent, and flip-flops in a similar state of distress.

"No, thank you," I answer, and turn back to my batter. I don't put the earbud back in, so I hear him when he starts talking again.

"So this isn't what you expected, huh?" he asks.

His back is to me as he starts to crack the eggs against the countertop. I turn to answer him.

"I didn't expect anything," I say, though truthfully I am dying to know how someone who works in event production can afford his own home in Los Angeles.

Landon, Miko, and Taylor met while working for Selah Smith Events, and even though Taylor played an important role, I knew the owner, Selah (the aforementioned soul-sucking nightmare), wasn't overly generous with her employees. A tiny bungalow like this, even if he'd purchased it in crappy shape, would have still been well over half a million dollars. LA is not a cheap place to own property.

I crack an egg and use a whisk to beat it against the side of the mixing bowl.

"Come on; admit it," he says. "You think I'm a degenerate, and you were looking for further proof." I can hear the smile in his voice.

"Honestly," I say with a practiced shrug, "I don't give you much thought at all."

I pour the latest version of the batter into the pan holding the graham cracker and walnut crust. I am making four mini versions at once, each with a different variation on the recipe. The mini cheesecakes go into a water bath and into the oven. It will take almost an hour to bake them, so I have nothing to do but talk to him while he makes his eggs.

"I am surprised by the carpentry, though. Did you restore the house by yourself?"

"What I could." He opens the refrigerator and returns to douse his eggs liberally with Tabasco sauce. "The woodwork I can handle. Managed a lot of the plumbing and the tile too. The electrical, though, seemed like a dangerous thing to attempt myself. Luckily the wiring wasn't as bad as it could have been." He reaches up to open a cabinet for a plate and then dumps the contents of the pan onto it in one heaping pile. He grabs a fork from a drawer and leans up against the countertop behind him before taking a big bite.

"How long have you lived here?"

His chewing slows while he considers the question.

"Three years, I think. It was back when it was a buyer's market, and I could still swing a 4.2 interest rate."

"Kind of young to take on so much responsibility, aren't you?" I can't help but ask.

He shakes his head and spears a last bite of egg. I am shocked to realize he devoured the whole plate in under four minutes.

"Honestly, it's been a long time since I felt young," he answers.

"I totally understand the sentiment," I agree.

"How long for those to bake?" He points at the oven, where the cheesecakes are baking away.

I look at the timer on my phone.

"About forty more minutes," I answer.

"Well then, follow me."

He leaves the room, and then I have no choice but to do what he says or stand there awkwardly in the empty kitchen.

———

His big living room is dominated by overstuffed couches in taupe, and the only color in the room comes from an oversize framed Warhol print of a large smoking gun. My dad would approve; he loves Warhol. Across from the print is a flat-panel TV nearly as big as the picture, held aloft by a giant vintage-looking easel. Beyond the living room is a dining room totally dominated by a gorgeous lacquered table. I reach out a hand to run along the top when I realize what it is.

"Is this a door?" I ask, surprised.

The lacquer makes it shine, and the metal base makes it feel industrial and so cool, but beneath the varnish you can clearly see the weathered effect of years spent outdoors.

"It used to be," he answers, looking down at the table along with me.

"It's gorgeous," I whisper, because it is.

It must take incredible skills to preserve the patina of the wood, not to mention a design aesthetic that would imagine juxtaposing a modern-looking base that shouldn't complement it so well.

"Where did you find this?" I ask, running my fingertips along a groove.

"My granddad's barn," he answers sheepishly.

I look up in surprise at his tone. The piles of wood in the garage make sense.

"You made this," I say in wonder.

"I did." His mouth quirks up to one side.

"You should sell your work," I tell him sincerely.

A piece like this would go for thousands of dollars. With the right exposure he could make a fortune.

The other side of his mouth joins the party, and soon there is a massive grin splitting his face in two.

"Jennings, not to put too fine a point on this, but how do you think I bought the house in the first place?"

"You do sell your work."

He nods.

"A lot of it?" I ask.

I know it is just barely not rude, but I have a thousand questions about him now. He is totally different than what I'd first expected, and I can't help but wonder. Before he can open his mouth to answer, a gray ball of fur lands on the table in front of me with a hiss.

I jump backwards a full two feet to escape a wild claw swung in my direction.

"What is *that*?" I demand as the thing curls a giant tail around its front paws like visiting royalty.

"This," Taylor says, reaching out to rub a hand affectionately over the thing's head, "is Holden, and he's far more interesting than my work."

A single golden eye blinks at me in disdain—single because there is only a puckered scar where his other eye should be.

"He's basically the greatest cat on the planet," Taylor says, giving his ears a good scratch.

I scrunch up my nose, meeting the cat's dislike with a gaze of my own.

"If you say so," I tell them both.

———

"It's perfect," Avis says in utter surprise.

The tension of the last eighteen hours leaves my body in a rush. I'd never made cheesecake before last night, and it took eleven tries before I found a recipe I thought was good enough. Taylor, to his credit, never complained once but sat at the small table in his breakfast nook working on a laptop and dutifully sampling each option I brought to him. He pronounced each one better than the one before, but when I added an extra ingredient to the last batch, he nearly melted to the floor in a puddle after the first bite.

Even with that response, though, I still hadn't known if I could get Avis's recipe right a second time, and I'd been sick with nerves. Hearing the word "perfect" makes me feel incredible.

"Really?" I squeak.

"Why, weren't you sure about my recipe?" she demands.

"I . . . uh . . . no. I just wasn't . . ." I decide for a little honesty. ". . . totally sure about the chili powder. I didn't know if I was reading that ingredient right."

"Chili powder," she says, and I can't place her tone.

"Yes, it was surprising to me, but then I don't have your palate. It ended up making all the difference."

A small smile plays around the edge of her lips.

"It sure did." She smiles grandly before leaving me there with a half-eaten mini cheesecake. I pick up a clean fork and take a bite from the untouched half. Last night I only let myself have the tiniest taste to make sure the flavors were right, but now the full impact hits me in a riot of creamy decadence. Caramel and chocolate mix with the filling and play off the crunch the walnuts add to the crust. The barest hint of heat from the chili powder is incredible.

Avis is utterly full of herself, but I guess when you are a creative genius, you earn that right.

Chapter Twelve

"B-17!" a drag queen dressed like Miley Cyrus in her famous VMA costume calls from the front of the bar.

I take another sip of my drink, and Miko reaches between us to stamp the spot on my card.

"Honestly, why would you come and not even play the game?" she asks in a huff.

She's been filling in my card for me for the last half an hour.

At a table nearby a couple is apparently having some kind of fight. It becomes very audible as the girl slur-screams something unintelligible, slams her drink on the table, and dramatically huffs her way to the door. The Miley impersonator watches her under lashes that are longer than a standard-size ruler. Miley can't seem to resist commenting as the woman stumbles by.

"Oh, honey," he calls after her, "emotions are for ugly people."

I snort before taking a sip of my drink.

"I came for the booze, obviously," I tell Miko without taking my eyes off the drag queen.

The face of the teddy bear on his one-piece bathing suit distorts each time he rolls the bingo ball around in the cage, and when

he sticks out his tongue in exaggeration after each pronounce-
ment, you can see his dental work. It is grotesque and therefore
mesmerizing.

"I-32!" he hollers again.

"Y'all are no fun. At least get into the spirit of it!" Landon calls
across the high bar table at me.

Brody looks up in response, his lips pursed in barely concealed
disdain.

"I'm at a bar in Hollywood on a Thursday. I'm drinking
domestic beer while a man in a furry leotard screams directions to
a room filled with college students. Sweetheart, I'm not sure how
much further I can get into the spirit without requiring a tetanus
shot," Brody tells her pointedly.

Landon just smiles in response and gives him a kiss on the
cheek. She must have realized long ago what a snob Brody is and
what kind of fuss he'll put up if forced to come to a place this far
east of Cahuenga. The fact that he is here at all just shows what he
is willing to put up with in order to hang out with her.

A group of guys walk by our table holding a third round of
beers, and one of them slides his gaze slowly up and down my
leather leggings.

"I like those pants." He starts in on the pickup line that nobody
has used since '98 and that no one had *ever* pulled off successfully.
"They'd look way better on my—"

Before I can even open my mouth or move to block Brody
from jumping to my defense, an angry voice cuts through the buzz
around us.

"If you value your teeth, you won't even finish the line," a deep
voice rumbles from behind me.

The creeper smirks in typical douchey male bravado, but it
totally loses the effect when he trips and his friends have to catch
him. They stagger back to whatever corner of the bar they came
from without looking back again.

I spin around in shock.

Taylor stands behind me, close enough that I can feel the anger radiating off him in waves. His right hand flexes menacingly at his side, and the map of artwork curves around his hard biceps. I recognize what he must look like to another man: trouble.

Beside him my brother appears equally tense as he looks back and forth between Taylor and me. There isn't any love lost between the two of them and hasn't been for months. Taylor and Landon are close friends, which means Brody knows he has to play nice. That doesn't mean he has to like it. He looks at Taylor now like he is appraising him for the first time.

"Bennett," Brody says, reaching a hand out.

Taylor looks off over my shoulder, staring after the group of guys, his jaw still clenched. Honestly, I appreciate the anger on my behalf, but that wasn't anything I couldn't have handled. He finally reaches out to shake the hand in front of him.

"Hey, man. How's it going?" he finally asks civilly.

"Well . . ." Brody looks around us as if the mass of bodies and neon lighting is explanation enough. "I'm going to need another drink," he announces. "Who else needs a refill?"

"Me!" Miko says, shaking an empty bottle in the air.

"Ditto," Landon calls.

I shake my head since I've barely touched my drink.

"I'll help you carry," Taylor tells him, and they walk away to the bar together.

I fiddle with my bracelets nervously, feeling suddenly stupid to have worn leather pants in the first place. I rarely put any effort into going out, but I felt like putting some in tonight. The leather pants fit like a second skin, and while the white T-shirt isn't tight, it still hugs my curves. I'd finally found the time to have my hair cut, so my pixie cut is back in a perfectly styled fauxhawk. With the smokiest of smoky eyes and a deep-plum lip stain, I am actively trying to look hot for the first time in years. I don't want to peer too closely at why that is.

"Unlike you to be so quiet," Miko throws out conversationally.

I snort, feeling more like myself with the disdainful response.

"Hardly. I'm rarely talkative. That's Landon's area of expertise," I tell her.

"You're right. You are typically quiet unless challenged or pissed off or dealing with a jag bag," she tells me, all the while never taking her eyes off the six bingo cards laid out in front of her. She watches them with childlike glee as if willing them to possess each new number Manly Cyrus calls out.

"Jag bag?" I can't help but ask.

"It's a perfect word for guys like that, trust me." She points a thumb behind her in the direction of the drunk guys and stabs her stamp down on O-73.

"Ah," I answer, taking a sip of my drink.

"The point being that you don't ever hold your tongue in situations like that. Makes one wonder what's got you so flustered and introspective."

"They didn't have Perrier," Taylor says, setting a bottle down in front of me. "I got you a Pellegrino instead. I know you like lemon, but I don't trust anything not from a hermetically sealed container in this place."

"Thanks," I mumble.

The tension is gone from him now, and he takes a long pull of his beer while sliding my card closer so he can have a look.

I don't have to look Miko's way to know her head is cocked to one side, studying us both. I keep playing with the straw from my drink while Taylor turns to talk to Brody. I studiously avoid turning in Miko's direction, so she finally leans close and whispers so only I can hear.

"One can't help but remember a lost bet that resulted in a day trip, a trip you still haven't told Landon about for some reason.

That makes one wonder why he nearly rammed his fist down some guy's throat for half a pickup line. Or when, in your limited acquaintance, he started to care so much about how you take your water."

I don't have the nerve to look back at her or play dumb, because I am wondering the same thing myself.

"Max," she sings my name with wicked glee, "are you keeping secrets?"

"Bingo!" Landon screams above the crowd, clapping happily.

All eyes swing to her as she jumps into Brody's arms, laughing like she just won a new car instead of a free drink ticket.

Around us everyone smiles along with her because her joy is infectious, and I am saved from having to face a question I don't have a good answer to.

———

"Oh, Kenzie, isn't this just divine?" my mother coos to me.

I look at her over the top of a rack of summer scarves as she holds up a long-sleeved top the same color as the sign out front. Only in Los Angeles are there such things as summer scarves, and only at Fred Segal do they cost more than a small fishing boat.

"Mom, you already have, like, several hundred tunics, and I'm sure you have more than one in that color," I say, walking over for a closer inspection.

She sticks her tongue out at me playfully. "Well, you're no fun as a shopping buddy today."

"Which makes sense because I came for the chicken paillard," I say while looking idly through a line of leather shorts.

"Ooh, what about these peasant tops?" she asks, making her way over to the next line of clothing. "But then, you don't like an empire waist, do you?"

"Makes me look like my torso is nine feet long," I tease over my shoulder.

"Some people might love to have a nine-foot torso." She waves the peasant top in my direction.

"Name one."

"Um . . ." She fights a smile. "Someone with a twelve-foot inseam?"

I laugh loud enough that I'm sure they hear it all the way back in men's shoes. We haven't hung out like this for a while, not because she didn't ask, but because so many unresolved arguments between us made wandering through an overpriced department store more than tedious. When she suggested the outing earlier in the week, I internally balked at the idea since I would have to fit it in during the only hours I'd had off in several weeks. But I still have some pretty epic guilt about all of the secrets I've been keeping, and some part of me loves afternoons like this for the same reason she does: they remind us both of better days.

Fred Segal, with its all-American signage and its leaf-covered façade, is the epitome of Southern California shopping. Everything inside it is unique and hand-picked, and has the price tag to keep out the riffraff. We'd been having lunch at the café together since I was a teenager.

"All right, miss. I promised you lunch," she says, linking her arm through mine. "Let's head out there before it gets too crowded."

As we sit down at a small table on the patio, I push my sunglasses up on my head to see the menu better. I know what I will order; I always get the same thing here, but I love reading through a restaurant's description of its food. Now that I work on recipes regularly, I know how hard it is to sell a dish based on a single flowery description.

"What are you going to have?" I ask, looking up at her.

Rather than respond, she knits her eyebrows in a frown. She reaches out her hand to run a thumb along the top of my cheek.

"Mackenzie, you look so tired," she says, sounding sincerely worried. "Look at these bags under your eyes."

I pull my face away, and her hand drops back down to the table.

"Thanks, Mom. That's just what every woman wants to hear."

I try to deflect her attention with my annoyed tone, but I know she is right. The weeks of double shifts are still evident in the dark circles under my eyes. Even with only one job, I am still working too many hours to catch up on the sleep. I keep telling myself that once I know the menu better, I won't have to work so many extra hours to perfect every dish. But it seems like each time I figure out something new, Avis has another challenge to throw my way.

"I'm serious, Mackenzie," Mom tells me.

"So am I, Mother." I raise my eyebrows. "The waiter would like to take our order. What are you going to have?"

She smiles sweetly at the waiter she only just noticed.

"Oh, Matthew," she tells the guy standing next to our table. "I'm so sorry. I didn't even see you there."

"No problem, Mrs. Ashton. Should I give you both a moment to decide?" he inquires.

"Oh, of course not." She looks over the menu in front of her. "Kenzie, do you want your usual?"

I nod in response to her raised eyebrows and sit farther back in my chair to watch the show. My mother makes ordering from a menu into some kind of art form. She rarely chooses one entrée but rather selects three or four things so she can have a couple bites of each. It is a complete indulgence, and she spares no expense in her selections or her requests to alter those selections to suit her ideals. Her love of food combined with the fact that she tips exceptionally well makes her a favorite of waitstaff on both coasts.

"First we'll have the quinoa salad without the peas. And Matty, can we get just a dash of that Italian truffle oil on top?" she asks, knowing full well she'll never be denied anything despite the fact that the menu clearly states there can be no substitutions.

"Of course." He smiles grandly.

"You're an angel." She beams at him. "Next, I'm dying for the *vongole*. What wine should I have today?"

"We just opened a gorgeous Sancerre," he tells her, nearly giddy as he writes down each new addition to the order.

"Divine! Two glasses, please. Then we want the chicken paillard, but can you ask them to sauté the potatoes in butter instead of olive oil?"

"Absolutely," he agrees again.

"Ooh, what's the pizza today?" she says, apparently coming to that line on the menu.

"Mother, where are we putting all of this?" I have to ask.

She dismisses my question with a wave. "You know Daddy will eat whatever we bring home." She looks up at the server expectantly.

"Margherita, with heirloom tomatoes. Would you like to add that as well?" he asks.

She wrinkles her nose in distaste. Apparently the choice isn't exciting enough to warrant the calorie count.

"No, let's just start with the first three, and if we need to add on we can later."

"Perfect." He takes the menus from us. "The wine will be right out."

She turns to me with a huge smile on her face.

"I can't wait to try that *vongole*," she says happily.

I shake my head, amused at her obvious excitement. "You've had it at least a thousand times before," I tell her.

"Exactly. I know it's good."

When the waiter drops off our wine, she takes a sip and closes her eyes in bliss. When she opens them again, she snaps her fingers and points a well-manicured finger at me.

"Did I tell you about the event I'm chairing for Elysium?"

"Is that the one next month?" I ask, taking a sip from my own glass.

The waiter might be obsequious, but his taste in wine is stellar. The Sancerre is, in fact, just as gorgeous as he predicted.

"No, this is set for the fall. Let me give you the details. I'm thinking of asking the girls to help."

At some point over the last couple of months, my mom started to refer to Landon and Miko as "the girls." She does her best to adopt them in everything but name, and they return the adoration with the kind of devotion little girls reserve for their favorite Barbie.

I listen attentively as she tells me the details of her event and marvel, not for the first time, at her ability to keep so many of them straight in her mind. Her favorite saying is "To whom much is given, much is expected," and that belief is evident in the way she lives her life. My mother sits on the board of at least five charities, all of which have something to do with art (which is my dad's second great love) or helping single mothers in struggling economic conditions (which is particularly close to her heart since she had once been one). She and my father have given millions over the course of my lifetime to causes important to them. Beyond financial support she is totally involved with each cause, donating as much time with her hands as she does with her wallet. She might drive me crazy at times, but they don't make women any better than the one sitting in front of me.

They bring the salad to our table, and she chats on while we start to eat, pausing only long enough to praise the flavor of the truffle oil she added. I smile as we nosh, and I am once again reminded that she is the reason I love food so much. Maybe it is the wine or the gorgeous summer day or heck, maybe it is the truffle oil, but for one split second I almost tell her everything about Dolci.

"Sweetheart, please drink some more water," she says, sounding concerned again. "You don't drink enough of it, and you know you need to stay hydrated. If you don't stay hydrated, you run the risk of wearing yourself out and having another accident. You have to be responsible about this."

I smile tightly and reach for my glass. All thoughts of baring my soul wash back down my throat along with the Perrier.

Chapter Thirteen

"What's on the menu tonight?" Taylor asks as he walks into his kitchen. He runs a hand back and forth through his hair, and sawdust flies out in every direction, but he doesn't seem to notice.

"It's some sort of black forest cake"—I tap the Post-it notes in front of me—"which doesn't really make sense because I don't see anything that might be chocolate on here. But that's what she said, so here I am."

Taylor looks over my shoulder at the mess of baking ingredients on the counter in front of me. He reaches around and taps a bag of chocolate chips with his finger in silent demand.

"It seems like you're figuring these out faster each time. Last week it only took you three tries to get the trifle right."

I fill a quarter cup halfway up with the chips from the bag and then turn to pour some into his waiting hand. He shifts to lean back against the counter, tossing some of the chocolate into his mouth.

"I think I'm just getting better at deciphering her handwriting," I say, combining the dry ingredients into the batter.

"I don't see how," he says as he leans down closer to inspect the notes in front of me. "It looks like a toddler wrote this."

His shirt moves the slightest bit, and I see a quick flash of black script on skin. I should not be so curious about all the different words inked underneath his clothes.

I force my eyes back to the whisk in my hand as I move it slowly in circles around the bowl.

Whisk, whisk, scrape the sides, whisk, whisk, turn the bowl a quarter to the right. If I just keep watching my hands work, then I won't be tempted to look at him, or to notice how that white T-shirt clings to his chest or how good he looks in worn jeans or how the jeans are covered in varnish and dust or how he smells like sweat and the Douglas fir he just spent the last hour sanding down into someone's conference table.

I don't realize I've dropped my whisk until it crashes to the floor, flinging chocolate against the cabinet next to me.

"Hey," Taylor says, reaching for me.

I crouch down to grab the whisk before he can touch me.

"Are you OK? Do you need to eat something?"

"No." I shake my head.

I need to get a grip—and not just on the utensil in my hand.

I toss it in the sink with the other dirty dishes and grab a new one to work with. Taylor still looks concerned, but I wave him away.

"I'm fine. Go take your shower. I promise to still be upright when you come back."

Taylor's lips twist in annoyance.

"You know I hate it when you joke about your health," he tells me seriously.

I nod, only slightly chagrined.

"You know, it used to just be this thing I had. But since the accident it's overshadowed every conversation I have with my family." I start in before I can think better about revealing even more information to him. "It's really nice to treat it irreverently. You're the only one I've joked about it with. Ever."

I roll my eyes at how moronic I sound.

"Man, I don't know what it is about you. I keep telling you all of these ridiculous things!" I start combining the wet ingredients into the mixing bowl in agitation. "I am the least expressive person I know, and every time I get around you, the word-vomit just won't stop."

I am annoyed with myself now, because even the diatribe about word-vomit is just more word-vomit. Ugh!

Taylor doesn't say anything in response, and when I can't stand the silence anymore, I look up at him.

I can't read the expression on his face.

"I get what you're doing. Making fun of it, I mean," he says, referring to my earlier joke. "I still don't think it's funny, but I get why you need to make light of it."

He pushes off the counter and starts to leave the kitchen. I look back down at my recipe and exhale, releasing the tension of the unexpected serious moment with him. Taylor is always great about not bringing up my seemingly compulsive need to overshare with him.

I look up again when he calls my name.

He stands in the archway of the kitchen. I can tell he is searching for the right words to say, which is rare, since Taylor typically runs his mouth at ninety miles an hour.

"I'm—" He rubs his hand over the stubble on his jaw. "I'm really happy it's me."

"What?" I ask to save face.

But I know exactly what he means even before he clarifies.

"I'm happy I'm the one that you talk to."

He holds my gaze for a second longer and then walks out. It would be easier if he'd wink or make a joke as he'd done a dozen times before, but he doesn't. He leaves the weight of the moment to hang in the air around me, so I can't excuse it away. It is a subtle shift, totally outside the parameters of our friendship, and so minute that no one else would have noticed. But I notice it, and it scares the hell out of me.

———

"Explain to me why we need an audience for this?" I ask as I spray the kitchen counter down to clean it.

Landon looks up from polishing our yard-sale coffee table. Miko is perched on the counter, working on her laptop.

"It's not an audience," Landon tells me cheerfully. "It's just Miko. She came over to hang out with us."

"You insisted we clean the apartment today and insisted we do it as a team—" I start to point out the obvious.

"Because cleaning is so much more fun in a group!" Landon interrupts me.

"You think everything is more fun in a group. Regardless, I can't very well tackle the kitchen if someone is parked on the countertop designing an ice sculpture," I gripe.

"It's a martini luge," Miko says, affronted. "As if we'd allow one of our clients to incorporate an ice sculpture."

"And it's a *Frozen*-themed party, so we had to incorporate ice in some way," Landon agrees from the underside of a side table. She is clearly into thorough cleaning.

"You're serving martinis at a little girl's birthday party?" I ask them both.

"Who said it was for a little girl?" Miko asks, genuinely confused. "It's a gay wedding reception. Rob and Martin have worked for Disney on Ice for ten years."

"Oh, well, good theme then, actually," I tell them both.

"We thought so," Landon calls from behind the TV.

I toss my sponge down into the sink, having zero desire to clean the apartment in my rare time off.

"I need more caffeine if you expect me to commit to this," I tell them.

Landon looks up from the rag in her hand.

"But you've had coffee already."

"Not enough. I need something stronger. Either of you want to walk down to The Bean with me?"

"Road trip!" Miko announces with the slam of her laptop.

"If it's across the street, it's not really a—" I start to tell her.

"Don't be unnecessarily confrontational. That line is in at least four of my all-time favorite movies," Miko admonishes.

I grab my keys, sunglasses, and credit card off the counter with a roll of my eyes.

"This isn't actually a movie, though," I tell her.

"This is," she says, running her neon-tipped fingernails through her messy hair, "whatever I want it to be."

"You are—"

"Children," Landon interrupts us both, "shall we?"

She gestures to the front door, and Miko and I both take the direction and head out to the hallway and then downstairs. The three of us trudge over the dirty streets and up to Sunset Boulevard, where our favorite coffee place is located.

Hollywood and the surrounding area are a study in juxtaposition. Fifteen years ago you couldn't walk around here after dark; now it houses some of the nicest clubs and restaurants in town. It's undergone a big revitalization, but the grime is still there, mixed in among the freshly painted walls and high-end hotels. Homeless men camp out in front of posh eateries, which butt up next to stores that cater primarily to strippers and slutty coeds looking for risqué Halloween costumes. No matter how hard it tries, Hollywood will always be a little bit of a mess—this city and I have that in common.

Once we've ordered coffee we find a table in the corner, sharing an unspoken understanding that we aren't headed back to the apartment to clean anytime in the near future. I tuck one leg under the other and take a sip of my coffee just as Miko asks, "So how is everything with Brody?"

"Oh, because this won't be awkward at all." I scowl at them both.

I *so* do not want to hear the BTS of Landon's and Brody's relationship.

My tablemates are splitting what appears to be the largest blueberry muffin known to man, and Miko pops a bite into her mouth and looks at me sternly.

"Dude, you're going to have to get over it. They're dating and you're Landon's friend. I didn't ask her to describe him in the sack—"

I make a gagging sound that doesn't require any acting at all, at the same time that Landon squeals, "You know we haven't—"

"My head will actually explode—right now—all over this table. You can't seriously consider having this conversation in front of me," I say in total annoyance.

"I'm not. Of course I'm not," Landon says, reaching over to pat my hand like I am a little old lady. "I won't tell you anything that will freak you out." She looks back at Miko. "But things are really, really good," she says wistfully.

Miko turns to look at me, the picture of practiced innocence.

"And what about you, Maxy-Poo? How's your love life?" she asks me, grinning.

"Nonexistent," I tell her pointedly.

I wondered how long it would take her to openly start insinuating things about me and Taylor in front of Landon. The answer, apparently, is eleven days. Truth be told, I'm shocked she lasted this long.

"Really? No one of particular interest? No special new friendships to speak of?" Her eyes twinkle with evil joy.

Landon looks back and forth between the two of us as if she was just clued into the possibility of the statement.

"What's she talking about, Max?" she asks, leaning down to whisper across the table like we are sharing state secrets.

Miko is only barely not smiling in challenge, daring me to have the balls to admit what is going on.

To hell with it. Landon will find out eventually anyway.

"I've been hanging out with Taylor," I say with a casual shrug.

Landon flies back against her chair with a gasp as if I physically pushed her. Her perfect French-manicured nails grasp at her T-shirt. If she were wearing pearls, she'd be clutching them.

"*What?*" she screeches so loudly that everyone else in the small coffee place turns towards us, likely to see if she has Tourette's.

Her shock is such a tangible thing that I feel sort of ridiculously embarrassed for the first time in years.

"It's not a big deal. We're just friends," I tell her calmly.

Beside her, Miko takes half the muffin without looking away from the spectacle Landon is making. She starts to nibble the piece like a hamster.

"I can't believe this!" Landon says, looking from me to Miko. "I just can't believe this."

"Seriously, we just hang out," I insist, a little more desperately.

They are my friends, so surely they know me well enough to know I'm not actually doing anything serious with Taylor.

"We hang out. I, um . . . I bake for him sometimes."

Miko nearly chokes on her muffin, and I start talking faster in an effort to cut off their thoughts at the pass. Our whole table is the center of attention now: the hamster, the drama queen, and an overemotional stork. We are like sideshow freaks.

"We go run together sometimes. Look, it's just . . . we're just friends!" I bark.

"I can't believe this," Landon says again in wonder.

"What is so flipping hard to believe?" I demand.

Landon looks from me to Miko in total chagrin. "It's just . . . now I owe Miko a hundred bucks. She called the two of you, like, *last year.*"

———

The rhythmic tapping of fingers announces Avis's arrival before her voice does. She carries a box of cigarettes around with her at all times, and even when she isn't smoking, she'll hold onto the box like a security blanket. Her fingers drumming against the edge of the cardboard is a familiar sound now, but that doesn't mean it has any less of an effect on me than it did in the beginning. That harmless beat always makes my stomach drop because I am never sure what kind of mood she'll be in when I hear it headed in my direction.

I turn my chair completely around to face her, my back now to the mountain of payroll paperwork I am working through. Avis is leaning up against the doorjamb, peering at me through her giant glasses. Today, instead of her usual turban she is wearing a vintage-looking bandana around her topknot like a 1950s housewife.

"The dulce cheesecakes sold out again yesterday. That makes three weeks in a row," she says.

I smile in response.

"I know. I've asked the team to increase the quantity by twenty percent again this week."

Avis grunts in what I assume is agreement.

"You know, this might just become one of the new signature dishes. Everyone is saying it's one of your best in years," I tell her with more than a little fangirl in my voice.

"So I've heard," she agrees.

Her fingers still tap, tap, tap on that box. She looks down at her shoes for several long minutes. She could just be thinking or in some other place entirely. I never really know with her, and I've learned it is best to wait it out. Either she'll start speaking again or she'll eventually wander away. I study my manicure while I wait. This color is called Bubble Bath. I know that because I have a weird fascination with nail polish names, and this particular one stuck out because it was the first time I'd had anything other than Black Satin on my nails in years. Since my first day here I'd had bare nails, and because this polish is light pink, and therefore kind of girly, it is the equivalent of a bold new choice for me.

"We need something special," Avis says to her shoes.

My head comes up with a small smile already in place. I know she'll get around to her point eventually.

"What did you have in mind?" I ask, having no idea what she is talking about. But I've learned from the very beginning that if I can keep her talking, I have a better chance of getting more information—or at least enough information to have some idea of what she wants.

"Marcus is hosting a dinner." My ears perk up at the mention of the famous celebrity chef who put this hotel on the map. I've seen him a few times in passing, but he seems aloof and unapproachable to me, not the type to host a gathering of any kind.

"The owners, several VIPs, other chefs." She looks up at me. "When I say chefs I'm talking Teague, Dutton, and Birdwell." She names a few of the world's greatest chefs as if she is throwing items at me for a grocery list. I suppose those names might not be a big deal to her because she's part of the same crowd, but hearing them bandied about so casually makes my eyes want to pop out of my head.

"Marcus wants something special," she continues. "A dessert sampler. Three options served in miniature for twenty-two guests.

I've written them out here," she says, pulling a crumpled piece of paper from her pocket and handing it over.

On closer inspection it is a copy of her cable bill with her usual chicken scratch covering both sides. As usual, I can pull out just enough ingredients to have a basic idea of what she wants.

"Looks like a . . . sticky toffee pudding"—I squint at the sheet—"a buttermilk *panna cotta* . . . and a banana custard." I stare harder, shocked when I identify the ingredients for the accompaniment.

"Is this a bitter-chocolate sorbet? To set off the custard?" I look up at her in awe. "That's genius!"

"Sure," Avis answers noncommittally.

I wonder, not for the first time, what it would be like to be such a prodigy that you can't even recognize how special your work is. I hold the crumpled bill with a bit more reverence.

"You want me to help you with this?" I ask her.

"I want you to make it completely."

I am more than a little taken aback. The idea of making these creations, even if I am just recreating her recipes, is more than a little disconcerting, given who'll be eating them.

"But should you . . . I mean, you typically handle the special orders," I say, grasping the paper a bit harder.

"Stork," she says, sounding slightly exasperated, "I'm a guest at the dinner, which makes it a little hard to fire the dessert in a timely manner."

Of course she'd be invited to the dinner. Avis is easily as famous as the other chefs she mentioned, and Marcus Balmain is her boss, even if I'd never seen them interact with each other.

"Um, OK," I answer, fighting the sudden need to throw up my breakfast. "When is this dinner?"

Please be next month, please be next month, please be next month.

"It's on the first," she answers, shoving the cigarettes into her pocket, a sure sign that she's grown tired of the conversation and is about to walk away.

"Of August?" I ask hopefully.

"Of July," she answers with a roll of her eyes.

"As in . . ." I choke on the words.

"As in Thursday of this week. Stork, you better get on it."

With that, Avis turns and leaves me staring at the empty space she just occupied. Three days to figure out three new recipes and their plating. Then I'll need to prep and serve them to twenty-two VIPs for a dinner hosted by one of the biggest chefs in the nation, who also happens to be my boss's boss.

I start manically making a shopping list: eggs, milk, butter, cocoa.

And oh yeah, some crack, because surely I'll need to be smoking some in order to believe I have a flipping prayer of pulling this off!

———

"OK, so this is the final plated version," I explain, placing the rectangular plate down in front of Taylor on the table with the same reverence you'd give an operational nuclear warhead.

"It looks unbelievable," he says, looking down at the food before him.

All the tension falls out of my shoulders.

"Really?" I squeak.

Chocolate-brown eyes catch mine.

"Really." He picks up a fork and waves it at me. "Now do the thing."

"I don't want to. It's stupid. I'm not a real—"

"Do. The. Thing," Taylor demands.

I roll my eyes, fighting embarrassment and a ridiculous urge to giggle.

"OK." A sigh falls from my lips. I point to the first dainty dessert on his plate. "This is a sticky toffee pudding made with dates from an organic farm just outside of Palm Springs. It's finished with a caramel whiskey sauce and some Baileys-infused whipped cream."

Taylor makes a sound deep in his throat. I laugh and keep going.

"Next is a buttermilk *panna cotta* finished with a Meyer lemon zest and fresh seasonal berry compote. Last is a caramelized banana custard topped with a bitter-chocolate sorbet, which you need to eat before it starts to melt," I admonish.

Taylor digs into the custard first as I knew he would. I learned a while ago what a sucker he is for anything with chocolate. He moans into his spoon, and I roll my eyes again rather than admit how ridiculously happy it makes me that he likes what I've created. He reaches out to try the next dessert and asks, "Will you give that little speech tomorrow night at the dinner?"

The slide of fur against my bare foot stops me from answering for a moment. I reach down and rub one hand over Holden's hideous face. He deigns to accept the caress. It is just like the ridiculous cat to ask for attention and then receive it like a magnanimous sheikh. He flips over onto his back as I stand up again, but I use my foot to rub his belly. Sometime over the last month this thing and I have come to a truce. He isn't allowed in the kitchen with me, but if I step out of it, I will pet him. Most of the time he allows it.

"I don't know," I tell Taylor honestly. "I'm not sure if she'll want to do it herself. Also, Harris and Ram are staying to help me, so it's not like I'm the one to take the credit."

"You deserve some kind of credit," Taylor says, spooning up another bite, "or an award or something. The fact that you can make heads or tails of her recipes is a sign of divinity or a special power at the very least."

I shrug at Taylor, more than a little uncomfortable with his praise. When I remove my foot from the soft belly below it, Holden hisses in annoyance and bounds away.

"Ingrate," I call after him.

I head back into the kitchen to clean up the disaster I left in my wake. I haven't been in there for more than five minutes when Taylor comes up next to me and starts loading the dishes I am rinsing into the dishwasher next to him.

"You don't have to help," I say while scrubbing a particularly difficult bit of caramel off a bowl.

"I know," he answers, picking up another plate.

"You didn't make the mess, though, and you've already helped me clean up every night this week." I hand him the now-rinsed bowl.

"Because you're the least tidy person I know." He bumps my shoulder. "If I didn't help, this would take hours. Besides, this is a good workout."

He makes a show of using a whisk as a dumbbell before putting it into the proper receptacle in front of him. Taylor has a weird OCD thing about the precise way to load a dishwasher. I'm not about to fight it, though, because it means less work for me.

"And you have to keep your girlish figure," I say, throwing one of his favorite lines back at him.

"Exactly," he says with a wink.

We continue to clean up while Mumford & Sons croons out of an iPod dock in the corner of the room, and my mind starts to wander. It still amazes me that I find myself here. That I am working with Avis Phillips is shocking enough, but the fact that Taylor has been my biggest cheerleader is even more unbelievable. In all the weeks I've been coming here to borrow his kitchen, he's been here every single time, ready and available to taste-test or cheer me on or make me super-spicy eggs (which I am beginning to suspect is the only recipe in his arsenal). I know from Landon that he never lacks for female companionship, so it strikes me as odd that he never has other plans when I ask to come over. No matter what I do, he ignores my grouchiness and sidesteps my bad moods, and I am utterly shocked to realize that Taylor has become one of my best friends.

Taylor has become one of my best friends?

It's true. He has become one of my best friends—*the* best friend, if confessing my secrets to him counts for anything. And honestly, there is almost no one I'd rather hang out with now than him.

Oh, how the mighty have fallen.

I let out a maniacal laugh, which makes him look at me in confusion.

I'm sure I sound like a psychopath, but seriously, *when did this happen?*

"Something funny, Jennings?" Taylor says as he divides the silverware up by type.

"Yes. No, not funny, just . . ." I look for something to say that will sound less crazy. What comes out only reaffirms the loss of my mental capacity. "You should go away with us this weekend."

It probably would have been better as a question, but somehow it comes out as a command.

He doesn't turn in my direction, but I can see him fighting a grin.

"To your parents' house? For the Fourth?" he asks casually.

Wait . . . should I not have asked that?

Maybe I shouldn't assume that he doesn't have plans already. I mean, just because he's been hanging out with me constantly doesn't mean he is without a life. Taylor is a social butterfly, and I'm sure there is a long list of parties he could attend this weekend.

"Yeah, I mean, there's plenty of room and everyone is going." I scrub at the whisk in my hand hard enough to take the top layer of stainless steel off. "Landon, Miko, my siblings, my parents—"

"You want me to meet your parents?" he teases. "Jennings, that's so junior-year prom night of you."

There is no way he could know what a big deal it is for me to even have a male friend, let alone invite one to go away for the weekend. But his dismissal stings just the same.

"Never mind." I reach for a bowl. "It was just an idea."

Taylor grabs the other edge of the mixing bowl and holds it suspended between us. When I won't look at him or release the bowl, he shakes it gently, forcing me to pay attention to him.

"It's a great idea," he says softly. "I'd love to come."

"You don't have other plans?"

"I don't have anywhere else I'd rather be," he replies.

It isn't really the answer to my question, but it is a good answer just the same. I have worked nearly seven days a week since I started at Dolci, and since I am working even harder on the menu for the Balmain party, Avis is letting me take a few days off. I am already excited about getting the time off for the holiday weekend, but knowing Taylor will be with us makes it more exciting. Now I just have to figure out how to tell my parents he is coming without everyone being weird about it.

Forty-five minutes later the kitchen is pristine once again, and all my odds and ends are packed back up. Taylor insists on escorting me to my car, which is ridiculous since it is just a short walk across the lawn in one of the safest neighborhoods in Los Angeles. I argued with him over it the first few times I came to his house, but his chivalry is deeply ingrained and he won't be budged. Now I secretly look forward to that short walk. He never does anything other than load my bags into the trunk and wait until I drive off to head back inside. What he doesn't know is that this simple act is the most I've let someone take care of me in years.

I watch as he drops the two bags inside my trunk and closes it. When he turns back my way, I freeze in place. Even with just the distant porch light illuminating his face, I can see that he wants to say something. I touch my bracelet nervously.

"You nervous?" he surprises me by asking.

My stomach flips over.

Good grief, what had I expected him to say?

"Honestly?"

He nods.

"Of course." I push a hand through my hair. "I'm out-of-my-mind terrified of screwing this up."

His eyes fill with understanding and he smiles kindly, a look that completely sums up his character. That's the thing I've learned in the last couple of months, something I think few people realize because they focus on his humor or his big personality, or the fact that he is sort of stupidly, ridiculously handsome. But I know that Bennett Taylor is utterly kind.

That gaze continues to hold mine for one breath, then two, and then I am in his arms with no knowledge of how I got there.

I am completely overwhelmed.

Besides an occasional playful shoulder bump, Taylor and I haven't touched at all. It's like he could sense that I couldn't handle even so much as a handshake from him, and he would have been totally right. I haven't embraced any man other than those I am related to in more than five years. So when I find myself enfolded in his arms, my brain shuts off.

It has been so, *so* long since I let someone hold me. I'd forgotten that it gives you a ridiculous sense of safety. I'd forgotten how it could nearly overwhelm you and make you believe that the arms around you would hold you up, even hold you together, if that's what you needed.

I drop my forehead to his shoulder. I breathe in clean laundry and sawdust, a smell that never really leaves him.

"It's your fight to win, Jennings, right?" he whispers into my hair.

I nod without really moving my forehead from his shoulder.

It feels too good to stand there. I have to make myself turn around and get in the car. At the end of the block I look into my rearview mirror.

Taylor is still standing where I left him, watching me drive away.

Chapter Fourteen

In the end, I do have to do "the thing" for Marcus Balmain and the other food deities at his table. I am pretty proud of myself for the confidence in my voice as I explain each dish, especially as the famous young chef looks on without even a hint of a smile.

After I finish explaining the creations, Avis nods at me, which I take as my cue to leave. I walk back to Dolci's kitchen in the kind of mindless fog that only comes on the other side of finishing a really stressful task.

"Well?" Ram asks as soon as they see me in the doorway.

He and Harris are leaning against a counter drinking beers they pilfered from who knows where.

"I think they liked it?" I say, fully aware that shouldn't sound like a question.

"Well, that's probably the most you can hope for," Ram says good-naturedly.

"Exactly," I agree with him, and reach out to grab the bottle he waves in my direction.

Pedestrian or not, nothing has ever sounded as good as a beer does right at this moment.

"On the contrary, they more than liked it," a deep voice says from the doorway behind me. "It was exceptional."

I turn around to see Marcus Balmain walking towards us. His deep-hazel eyes seem to scrutinize everything in the room, including, and maybe especially, me. But when he reaches out a hand to introduce himself, he doesn't seem quite as intimidating as that hard gaze initially made him appear. Not that he seems friendly, mind you. Even with the overly long auburn hair that curls around his face and the lashes that are so long that they would seem feminine if they weren't attached to chiseled, almost harsh features.

I shake his hand by rote.

"Thank you"—I swallow—"for coming over to tell us."

Balmain nods once and lets go of my hand.

"Avis mentioned you were a rare talent." He looks me over again. "I look forward to seeing what you'll work on next."

This moment just gets weirder and weirder. The fact that Avis mentioned me to him at all is only barely eclipsed by the fact that he's left his party to give me a compliment. Since when did a fledgling sous-chef rank high enough to garner the attention of someone like him?

Whatever the answer is, he won't be sticking around long enough to give it. He nods to the two men behind me, gives me a tight smile, and then leaves the kitchen.

"What the—" Ram starts.

"Exactly," I agree.

———

It isn't until I am walking to my car an hour later, bone tired but so grateful to have made it through the dinner party in one piece, that I remember what Balmain said.

Avis told him I am a rare talent? Avis thinks I am talented?

I am so elated that I don't notice the man propped against the hood of my car until I am right next to him. Oddly enough, discovering him there doesn't even startle me, as if on some level I knew I'd find him waiting for me.

I smile, and it's not a little smile or a shy one or even a smirk. This is a big, Holden-ate-the-canary, all-is-right-with-the-world, ear-to-ear grin.

Taylor's answering grin is just as big.

"Did you do the thing, Jennings?"

"I sure did," I say, opening the passenger door to toss my bag inside. "What are you doing here?"

He covers the short distance to where I stand.

"I wanted to see how it went," he answers.

"You could have texted."

"But then I wouldn't have been able to take you out to celebrate," he says, pushing both hands down into the pocket of his jeans.

"And you'd like to?"

"Yes ma'am." He nods. "Anywhere you'd like to go."

"Anywhere?" I ask.

"As long as they serve alcohol," he agrees.

I am tired and elated and wound up and emotionally spent, and there is only one place I want to be. But before I can take him there, I need some dinner.

"I have two places in mind," I tell him.

"Lead on, lady," he says.

———

"This was a perfect choice," Taylor declares between bites of his chicken taco.

I nod happily and grab for another chip.

"I know, right? Hugo's is my all-time favorite," I agree.

I smile up at the tiny taco stand we're sitting next to. Latin music drifts into the hot summer air around us, and people from all walks of life sit enjoying the Mexican food. The seating area has a mix of groups who are either just starting or just ending their night, and the line of cars clogging up Coldwater Canyon out front just adds to the ambiance.

"Really?" He sounds surprised.

"Really." I nod. "We used to live not too far from here. Well, actually, it was Van Nuys, but the food is so good that my mom would make the trip on special occasions."

His raises his brows.

"Wait, when did you live in Van Nuys? I thought you grew up in Beverly Hills."

I take a big bite of my taquito and have to finish it before I can answer him.

"We moved to BH when I was nine, right after my mom married my dad. Before that we lived in different places in the valley. Deep in the valley," I say dramatically. "But most of them were in and around Van Nuys. Mom was a flight attendant for the private airport there. It's how they met."

Taylor reaches across the table and swipes a chip from my container.

"She was working on his flight?" he asks before popping it into his mouth.

"Yep." I grin. "So cliché, right?"

He grins too and takes a sip of his soda.

"Ah, I bet they're not cliché at all."

I shake my head and wipe my greasy fingers on a paper napkin before I answer.

"They're not, no," I tell him. "They're pretty great, actually."

"And what about your biological father?"

What started out as an easy conversation is quickly drifting into a heavier territory than I can handle after the day I've had.

"Oh, that's the most cliché tale of all." I try for nonchalance. "Ran out on us when my sister was born and I never saw him again. It's OK, though," I say when I see his face fall. "It really is. I mean, it's embarrassing to admit that your parent ran away from home, but Charlie is truly the only dad I've ever known. I don't think we could be any closer, even if we were really related."

Taylor looks chagrined.

"I'm sorry," he tells me after a minute. "I didn't mean to pry."

I make sure he sees it when I elaborately roll my eyes.

"Yes, you did." I smile at him.

He chuckles. I love that sound. It makes me as happy as if I'd made it myself.

"You're right. I did," he tells me. "Not because I wanted to talk about anything uncomfortable or upsetting; I just want to know more about you."

I straighten up and take a sip of water.

"OK, what else do you want to know? Astrological sign? Birthday? Hobbies?"

He leans back in his plastic chair and folds his arms across his chest. The kaleidoscope of artwork on his skin is no less dazzling even in the dim light.

"I know all those things already," he says finally. "Tell me about your mom."

I consider him for a moment. He probably does know little details like my sign and my birthday. Taylor isn't the kind of person who treats people casually. He pays attention, he asks questions, and he always seems to remember the littlest detail, even if it is something I only mentioned in passing. He remembers it all, but he also guards my secrets as well as I do. For all those reasons, I once again find myself telling him more than I should.

"My mother is wonderful and kind and supportive"—I play with the cap of my water bottle—"and a fixer."

I look up into his dark-brown eyes. He nods for me to continue.

"I love her more than anyone I know." I shake my head rue-fully. "And she also drives me insane a good majority of the time."

"She worries about you?" he asks.

"Constantly," I agree. "And I don't remember if she was always this way, or if it was just something that happened after I was diag-nosed. But she's been hyperfocused on my health for as long as I can remember."

"And that's why you still don't feel like you can tell her about your job?" he asks gingerly. "Even after all this time?"

His face is carefully blank, and it occurs to me what he's doing.

"Is that where this whole conversation is leading? You're get-ting around to telling me that I need to fess up to everyone."

I don't know why I expect him to deny it. Taylor is always up-front with me.

"Well, yeah," he says with a gentle smile.

It feels a little too much like something one of my brothers would tell me, and that pisses me off in more ways than I can count.

"Are you trying to manage me now too?" I demand.

"Jennings, calm down. No, don't look away from me; listen to what I'm trying to say."

I sigh and force my face to relax out of a scowl.

"You have worked so hard for months, and you killed it tonight. Do you realize that? Do you know how incredible you are, or how few people could have actually pulled this off?" He's so sin-cere that it makes my heart hurt. "I'm so proud of you, Jennings. I just thought that they'd be so proud of you too, if they knew. I just want you to have that."

I have to put both hands down in my lap to keep from reach-ing for him. It's one of the kindest things anyone has ever said to me, and I'm not sure how to handle all of the things it's making me feel. If we keep this up I am either going to cry a little, or cry a lot. Either option would officially ruin the buzz from my night's achievements and the calorie-fest from my favorite taco stand. Time to segue into something new.

"Are you ready to hit up that awesome bar I told you about?" I ask him.

He grins and lets me change the subject.

"That's where we're going for drinks, right?" He stands up and dumps our plates and napkins into a trash can nearby.

"Yes, sir," I tell him. "It's my favorite place to have a cocktail lately, and you promised to buy me a drink anywhere I wanted."

He smiles and pulls his keys out of his pocket.

"Just tell me where I'm headed, Jennings."

———

"This isn't exactly what I had in mind," Taylor says as he hands me a vodka soda with lime *and* lemon inside a small mason jar.

I toss him a wink and grab the drink gratefully to take a sip. On the carpet below me Holden rubs his head back and forth over my legs in a play for attention until I reach out with bare toes and scratch his belly.

The gigantic flat-panel TV is set to some show with an obstacle course where contestants compete to—I think—become a ninja. It is the exact kind of mindless entertainment my brain can handle right now.

"This is *exactly* what I had in mind," I tell him honestly. "I can't imagine fighting our way into a bar right now. It requires energy I just don't have."

I take another sip and let my head fall back on the sofa behind me as Taylor sits down at the other end while simultaneously pushing a lime wedge down into his Corona. I shoot him a look, telling him exactly what I think of his choice in beer.

"Is this really the hill you want to die on, Jennings?" He salutes me with the beer before taking a sip.

My only response is the roll of my eyes. Taylor and I have been arguing over his drink choices for weeks. Mostly because, while his liquor cabinet is top shelf and totally respectable, he has a bad habit of drinking from an embarrassing selection of beer.

On the TV a contestant face-plants, and we both laugh loudly. The combined decibels must freak out Holden, because he scampers off into the other room.

I feel the slightest touch on my left wrist, and before I can even comprehend its meaning, Taylor asks, "Fifteen percent—what does that mean to you?"

My heart, lungs, hands, and everything else go utterly still in response to the question. Then I blink once, twice. I know he isn't done with the twenty questions tonight, but out of all the things he could ask about, it's my bracelet.

There is absolutely no way I can explain that number to him, or to anyone else for that matter. No one knows its meaning because the number is only valuable to me. I can't do this right now. I don't have the energy to be evasive. I choose deflection instead.

"What do your tattoos mean to you?" I ask harshly.

I refuse to look away while Taylor stares at me, doing his best to strip past the outer layer, as if the truth is just below the surface.

"*That* personal, huh?" he finally asks.

"Too personal," I answer, and turn back to the wannabe ninjas on the screen in front of us.

I take a drink and then another, trying to chase away the anxiety brought on by his question. I have figured out his Achilles' heel. There is no way he'd cover every available surface with tattoos if they weren't a symbol of something for him too, though I suppose it makes me a bit of a scumbag to use it against him.

"My father hated tattoos," he shocks me by saying.

My head swings around to stare at him, surprised that he is going to talk about them after all. When he doesn't say anything else but continues to stare absently at the bottle in his hands, I prompt him.

"And?" I ask softly.

Dark-brown eyes find mine.

"And I hated my father."

He runs a hand along his jaw in agitation and takes a deep breath. "He was all about appearances. Perfect little family, same pew at church every Sunday; he did everything to protect the truth. Truth was that he'd get drunk, slap my mom around, hit her harder if she got in between him and me." He clenches his fist repeatedly as he did that night in the bar. I am pretty sure he wants to hit something. Without thinking I fit my hand into his. He doesn't look at me, but he holds onto it. "He ended up running off before my seventh birthday, before I was old enough to stand up to him. It's stupid, really, how much I wanted"—he laughs, but there is no joy in the sound—"or *still* want to beat the hell out of him. When I was seventeen I got a fake ID and had my first ink done." He pulls up a sleeve to show me the inner biceps of his left arm. A solar system of colorful planets spreads out down his arm and (I knew from a brief peek one day in the shop) runs down his ribs. The planet he points to now is blue with white striation throughout. Whoever did the work on his body is an artist in the truest sense of the word.

"Is that—"

"Uranus," he says.

His grin is self-deprecating, but at this point I am relieved to see any kind of smile on his face. So relieved, in fact, that it takes me a minute to get the implication.

"As in god of the sky, father of the Titans—" I start to ask.

"As in, I was seventeen and thought I was esoteric and deep. How did you get that reference, though? It's pretty obscure."

"I got my degree in English," I answer him.

"Why did you pick English?"

"To keep my mom off my back." I sigh. "It's incredibly immature, I know, but the master's bought me a bit more time before she started questioning my life choices."

"You call grad school immature? I had a ball tattooed on my arm! Can you imagine the field day the guys on the football team had with that? The color only added to their fun."

I nearly do a spit take as I catch his implication.

"Oh man, I bet." I chuckle into the mason jar as I take a drink. "It clearly looks like a planet, just to give you an unbiased third opinion."

"It'd better! I've had it recolored twice." He smiles and drinks too.

"And the others?" I gesture with my glass at the expanse of artwork I know is hidden under his shirt.

Taylor kicks off his flip-flops and props his feet on the coffee table, settling in. I do the same.

"At first I just wanted to add on and turn it into a sleeve. I was twenty-two and almost entirely covered with ink from the waist up when I realized what I was doing."

"And what was that?" I ask, genuinely curious.

"Still letting him affect my decisions. On some level I was doing it because I knew he'd hate it. I couldn't have been more than five at the time, but he made some comment about the type of people who get tattoos. The memory stuck with me. I hadn't seen him in fifteen years, and I was still a seven-year-old trying to fight back. I haven't gotten one since."

"I'm sorry." I can't think of what else to say.

"Don't be." He grins and winks. "Women totally dig it."

I laugh and turn my attention back to the TV. I feel the slightest pressure on my wrist, a single fingertip running back and forth along the chain. I look back at him. He is closer now, leaning over onto the cushion between us and looking at me with a question in his eyes.

I know the implication. I showed you mine, now you show me yours. He has laid it all out between us and honestly answered my questions. He is hoping I will do the same. The problem is, he doesn't understand how impossible it is for me to speak the words out loud.

Not improbable.

Impossible.

I've never talked about it and done my best not to think about it at all costs. The only reason I wear the bracelet now is as a reminder. A reminder of the thing I shouldn't be allowed to forget.

A small penance in the grand scheme of things.

Neither of us speaks as we both watch that single finger rub back and forth. Back and forth.

His eyes don't look into mine; they are staring intensely at the bracelets on my wrist, as if he can't quite believe he is touching me at all.

My eyes follow the line of tattoos that starts at his wrist, symbols that create a map of his life.

A vintage clock held aloft by an angel.

Music notes climbing the scale to turn into a poem.

Forearm, biceps, shoulder, jaw. My eyes finally fall on his lips.

I won't, *can't* answer his questions, but I know I can give him something, something I haven't given anyone else in so long that it isn't worth thinking about.

The idea takes root and begins to grow, my heartbeat clambering along behind it. It isn't liquor that hums in my veins, because my drink is only half-finished on the coffee table. It is anticipation. My fingertips tingle, and energy rushes from the top of my head all the way down to my toes. I am going to do this stupid, crazy thing, even knowing what an absolutely terrible idea it is. I am going to follow my instincts instead of the little voice in the back of my head, which is reciting a litany of past mistakes as a reminder not to make another one. I can't listen to that voice, though, because I am too busy staring at his mouth.

If I don't do this now, *right this second*, I am going to talk myself out of it, and then I'll never know what it is to feel his lips on mine.

The lips I can't stop staring at part slightly as he inhales a sharp breath. My eyes shoot to his. He must see some of my thoughts written all over my face, because he starts to speak. I don't let him get the words out. I don't give either of us time to contemplate.

The feel of his lips on mine is electric, a sensation that is so good and perfect and *right* that I whimper. The sound of his drink hitting the hardwood floor only vaguely registers, because the feel of his hands holding my face consumes every rational thought. Those hands are infinitely sweet, just like our lips dancing against each other, and it isn't enough. Sensations I have gone too long without course through every inch of my body. *It isn't enough.* I climb over to straddle him, demanding without words. The kiss deepens, becomes something else. *I* become something else.

Lips, tongues, and teeth clash. My fingers claw at his shirt, desperate for more of him and this feeling between us.

It isn't until he pulls back and catches my hands that I realize he's calling my name.

"Jennings, slow down," he says softly.

I shake my head.

"I don't want to." I reach up to pull his head closer to mine, but he captures my hand again and holds both of them between us. I stare at him in shock as he leans in to kiss my cheek.

"Baby," he whispers into my ear, "you're shaking."

His words bring me out of my daze, and I recognize the truth. My entire body trembles in his arms. It's too much adrenaline, way too fast, and his stopping it and not wanting to kiss me back is like being doused in ice water. As quickly as my body was lit up, the fire is extinguished. I pull my hands free and start to get up.

"Wait. What are you doing?" he asks, trying to get me to look him in the eye.

I look anywhere but at him, because my mortification is bad enough without seeing it reflected back at me in his eyes.

"I'm sorry." I nearly choke on the words. "I shouldn't have thrown myself at you. I just thought—"

My words are unceremoniously cut off as Taylor grabs me around the waist and hauls me back onto his lap. This time he cradles my chin and forces me to meet his gaze.

"You thought what? That I might want to kiss you? That I've wanted to kiss you since the very first time I saw you?" he says. "That I've thought about it so many times already that I could almost convince myself it had already happened? That I tricked myself into thinking that I actually knew what your lip gloss tastes like or what it feels like to have your fingers in my hair? Or that the actual reality of any of those things is so much more fucking perfect than anything I dreamed of that it actually physically hurts to stop doing it?"

I blink at him in shock.

Taylor's smile is almost shy. He leans down to kiss my shoulder, then my neck, then the spot just below my ear. His voice is a physical caress across every single one of my nerve endings.

"Baby, you thought exactly right. But you're not ready to move so fast. I'm not going anywhere, OK?"

I am so overwhelmed by his speech, by our kiss, by the feel of his lips still rubbing back and forth along my ear that I can't speak. I let my forehead fall on his shoulder and I nod. His lips stop moving and he takes a deep breath.

"Do you want another drink?" he asks.

I shake my head.

"Something to eat?"

Another shake.

"Do you want to stay the night?"

I sit back and look at him in question.

"To—" I start to ask.

"To sleep," he says with a slight grin. "It's almost two, and you've got to be dead tired. Do you want to crash here? Or I can drive you home."

Ever the gentleman.

I smile at him, feeling suddenly younger than I have in ages.

"Yes, I'd like to stay."

I don't say anything as Taylor leads me down the hall to his bedroom. He leaves me there with one of his clean T-shirts, some pajama bottoms, and his toothbrush in the bathroom if I'm not too weirded out to use it. When he comes back into the room fifteen minutes later, I am sitting at the end of his huge fluffy bed, unsure what to do next. He stands in the doorway, dressed in running shorts and a white T-shirt, and rubs a hand over his jaw, seemingly unsure what to do.

"I can sleep on the couch . . ." His voice trails off along with his eyes.

"But?" I prompt.

Brown eyes find mine again.

"But I don't really want to," he answers.

I take a deep breath and blow it out.

"I sleep on the left side," I say, already turning to crawl to that spot.

Taylor laughs and flips off the light. "I can live with that."

I pull back the duvet and slip under sheets that smell like him. I hear him walk to the other side of the bed and then the sound of his shirt hitting the floor. I feel suddenly nervous, unsure what is going to happen and still not entirely recovered from all the adrenaline from earlier. When Taylor finally slides under the covers, he doesn't make any move to get closer. He stays on his side of the bed, and I stay on mine. It makes me feel antsy.

Even though I am beyond tired after the long day, the knowledge that he is lying next to me keeps me from falling asleep. I turn onto my back, then my side, then my stomach. Nothing seems to work. I flip onto my right side again, and he curses, reaches a hand around my waist, and slides me back into the wall of his chest.

"Go to sleep, Jennings," he whispers into that place on my neck.

I blame whatever vodka is left in my bloodstream for the ridiculous sigh that leaves my lips. I am asleep a moment later.

————

My bare foot rubs over something soft. Back and forth, back and forth. I have rubbed my feet together in my sleep ever since I was little, but today there is something warm and silky to rub against. My feet slide against it before I am even fully awake. Realization comes in short waves. The bed is fluffier than normal. My bedroom smells different. I am warm. Wrapped up in warm heat that is way too heavy to be a blanket. My foot stops sliding against the foot next to it.

A man's foot.

Taylor's foot!

My eyes fly open, but I don't move a muscle. Behind me Taylor is still, so I guess he must be sleeping. Memories of the night before come back to me in a flash. Taylor is sleeping with me in his arms, wrapped up tight the same way we fell asleep last night! Like this is the most natural thing in the world, which is totally overwhelming, because some weird part of me *does* think this feels natural. His arms are around me, I am wearing his pajamas and sleeping in his bed, and I've been tangling my feet with his.

And then it is another morning from another time, and I am reminded of the mistakes I let myself make, just like this one.

Suddenly I can't breathe.

I have to get out of here.

I slip out of bed as quickly as possible and thank every god I know when Taylor doesn't wake up. Holden lifts his head up from his bed in the corner to throw me a reproachful look I try to ignore.

I find last night's clothes and hurry out of the room. I change quickly, grab my bag and my phone, and hurry out to my car. I know it is a coward's way out, but I can't handle anything else right now.

If playing footsie is enough to send me over the edge, how in the hell did I think I might have handled anything more? It is a glaring reminder that I am too far gone to actually be with anybody. I finger the bracelet on my wrist, pinching the little gold disk with the percent etched into it until my fingertips turn white.

I will not forget again.

Chapter Fifteen

"You're awfully quiet this afternoon." Landon turns to look at me from the passenger seat.

Her hair is as buoyant as ever, and her outfit is yuppie personified: a chambray button-down tucked into navy-blue shorts with little anchors on them. She is also wearing wedge sandals in coordinating colors. It is the kind of ensemble you'd only find at J. Crew or the Kennedy Compound. I, on the other hand, barely found the energy to shower and am dressed in cutoffs, flip-flops, and an old tank top with bleach stains lining the seam.

Beside Landon, Brody pulls his eyes from the road to look at me in the rearview mirror. He raises an eyebrow in question.

I shrug in response and look away from the golden picture they make in the front seats.

Landon and Brody intertwined their fingers as soon as we got in his car, and I'm not sure they've broken physical contact since we left Hollywood. They aren't overly affectionate, probably because they know it would wig me out, but their constant touches and whispered conversation are nearly impossible to be around, especially today.

"You are kind of sedate, Max," Brody calls back to me.

"No more so than usual," I answer.

My voice sounds weird and monotone. Miko looks up from the book she is reading in defiance of every carsickness law I know.

"You cool?" she whispers.

I nod quickly and look back out the window to avoid seeing Taylor's name flash on my phone for the umpteenth time. He's sent a thousand texts and keeps calling. I turned my phone on silent after the first ring this morning, unable to answer the calls but not willing to ignore them either. I don't want to have to explain to him why I freaked out and ran away. I don't want to tell him that I am too broken to be fixed. I just keep the phone clutched in my hand and watch the Pacific fly by as we drive up the 101.

———

"We're almost there," Brody announces a short while later. "House first, or store?" he asks the three of us.

"What do you think?" Landon asks me with more than a little concern in her eyes.

That look is all the warning I need. I had better suck it up, or I am going to have to deal with an inquisition of mammoth proportions. I clear my throat.

"Let's go to the house. Mom spent days stocking up, and she can't really play hostess properly if we walk in with our own food."

Brody nods in agreement. "You're right. Besides, Malin should be there by now, right?"

He smiles and I join in with him, feeling the tiniest bit lighter. There is nothing like my little sister's vibrancy to help me shake off a dark mood.

As if to spite me, my phone lights up again, making my stomach churn. I just need to stop thinking about it.

I am good at not thinking about things.

I am going to have to force myself to have fun this weekend and to ignore what is happening with Taylor. Even if that means that I will lose him as a friend. In fact, there is no way I won't lose him as a friend. Because even if we could go back from this morning, how could he ever forget about last night?

Brody turns his Rover off the main road and winds higher and higher up the hills towards our destination.

"Holy—" Landon yelps, and then covers her mouth either because she realizes she sounds naive or because she is about to curse.

"—crap balls!" Miko finishes for her.

They both stare in wonder at the home at the end of the long driveway.

My parents have owned the beach house almost as long as they've been married, so I guess I've never really thought about how it must look to someone who's never seen it before.

"It's not that dramatic, you guys," I say, feeling sort of embarrassed.

My parents live in a mansion in Beverly Hills, but it is tasteful and almost modest by LA standards. The beach house isn't modest at all. Even though they purchased it in bad shape and had it refurbished, it still stands as a stark display of their net worth, which is, well, a hell of a lot of money.

The house sits perched on three acres on the side of a mountain that is the kind of lush green you only find next to the ocean. It has a panoramic view of the Pacific stretching out in every direction and Santa Barbara below. It is done in a Cape Cod style with white walls, a gray roof, and a wraparound porch, complete with a long line of rocking chairs. It is also massive, with ten bedrooms, a guesthouse, and an infinity pool out back. I guess if you were seeing it for the first time, it might be a lot to take in; but it is easy to forget the grandeur, because to our family it is just home.

Brody parks the car in the driveway. Landon and Miko jump out and openly gawk at the view before I can even unfold myself from the backseat. Landon turns in a full circle, taking in the setting with wide-eyed wonder.

"This looks like a Nancy Meyers movie!" she says, clapping her hands.

"Well, that's fitting, because Jack Nicholson lives next door!" someone calls from the porch.

I turn, feeling my first bit of happiness all day, just as a blonde ball of energy throws herself into my arms.

"Mali." I smile at my little sister.

She looks like the poster child for a California girl, even though she's been back in the state for less than twenty-four hours. She is almost as tall as I am, with long legs and the same golden hair as our mother. She has always been stunning, but at twenty-two she's finally matured enough that she's stopped being so vain about it. I have a sneaking suspicion that one too many failed relationships have made her question the value of those looks and whether they attract only the wrong kind of man. She kisses my cheek and then hugs Brody with the same kind of enthusiasm.

He releases her from a bear hug and tries to introduce Landon, but Malin cuts him off.

"You must be Landon!" she says, giving Landon a big hug.

Landon, I'm sure, senses a kindred spirit in another bubbly blonde who isn't aware of personal-space issues and enthusiastically hugs her back.

"I am," Landon says. "It's so nice to finally meet you, Malin."

"And you're Miko." Malin turns and repeats the process with the final member of our entourage.

Next she hooks arms with them both and hustles them into the house before they can protest.

"We've just opened the crispest bottle of sauvignon blanc, and Liam and I have decided to use it for wine pong," she tells them as

Brody and I follow them up the steps. "You *have* to play with us; it's tradition."

"Wine pong?" Landon asks.

"Same rules as you'd expect, but we guzzle wine instead of beer," Malin explains. "Oh, and we use clear plastic tumblers because Mommy won't allow red Solo cups into the house."

"A woman after my own heart." Landon giggles.

"There you are!" my mom calls from the other side of the house. I can't see her yet, but she can always be identified by the racket her shoes make hurrying across the hardwood. And if you listen carefully, you can probably make out the sound of the ice bouncing around in her wine glass as she walks.

"We're so glad you all could come!" she squeals when she rounds the corner and sees us in the entryway.

She hugs everyone in turn, being careful to hold her wine glass out to the side, and then launches into hostess mode like a commanding general.

"Now, we've just opened the most *divine* bottle of white, and there's some Dubliner on the cheese board that will make your toes curl—it's so good! Brody, take their bags up. And Kenzie, will you show the girls to their rooms?"

I nod and pull my backpack higher up on my shoulder. Against my volition my eyes dart to the screen of my phone long enough to see that another text has come in. I shove it into my back pocket before I am tempted to read it.

After I show Landon and Miko their rooms and drop my stuff off in my own, I have to fight the urge to crawl under the covers on my bed and hide from everyone. But I know there is no way I'd make it half an hour before my mom would check me for fever, and her behavior makes everyone else worry, so I take a deep breath and leave the room. I find everyone in the backyard, where an intense game of wine pong is already underway. Landon and Malin have teamed up against Brody and Liam, and the girls' team sinks a ball and celebrates while Liam pounds a tumbler of wine that probably costs more than my phone.

Daddy, as usual, is working his way through the cheese board and ignoring the gross abuse of his wine cellar. I hug him before taking a bottle of water from the fridge and making myself a little plate. I sit down at the long wooden table beside my parents and force myself to take some bites. Every time I think about my phone, I think I might be sick, but skipping meals isn't an option for me. I pop some prosciutto into my mouth and force myself to chew. As if my thoughts are conjured into life, my mom looks in my direction and asks, "What time does your friend Taylor arrive, Kenzie?"

I fight the urge to choke on the food in my mouth.

"Yeah, when is he getting here?" Miko asks. "I thought he was riding up with us."

"He . . ." I clear my throat. "He couldn't—"

"Couldn't give her a definitive time, because I thought I had some work to finish up," a very familiar voice says from the doorway behind me. "But it turns out I wrapped up early. I must have left not too long after you guys did."

For a second I think I might actually be sick. I sit frozen, unable to peel my eyes from the table in front of me while everyone jumps up to shake Taylor's hand, and he thanks our housekeeper for showing him outside.

A sharp pain rushes through my shin, pulling me out of my daze. My eyes fly to Miko, who has just purposely kicked me under the table. She gives me a look that reminds me, once again, how perceptive she is. I need to pull myself together, because I am about to go full-on Marie Osmond and pass out in front of everyone. If Miko notices, then everyone else will clue in here soon.

"Kenzie," my mom calls to me, "will you show Bennett to a room?"

I stand and turn around, and I try to act casual—I really do. But there is Taylor in those jeans he wears low on his hips and that faded blue T-shirt that is secretly my favorite and those stupid flip-flops that are way too beat up but that he refuses to trade in. And no matter what is going on in my head, right then I am so happy to see him that I nearly cry.

"I'll help her!" Miko jumps up cheerfully to shuffle both Taylor and me into the house before anyone can question it. Thank God for her interference, because otherwise I might have just stood on the patio like a deer in headlights for several long minutes. As soon as she closes the patio door behind her, she hisses at us both.

"What's going on with you two?" she demands.

"Nothing," I say, looking away.

"Everything," he says, looking right at me.

"What happened?" I can hear the accusation in her voice.

I don't answer this time.

"She spent the night," he tells her.

My eyes snap up in surprise.

"Why don't you make an announcement?" I growl petulantly. "Maybe go tell my parents or my brothers? I'm sure they'd love to hear!"

They both ignore my ire.

"Just to sleep," Taylor continues. "But it freaked her out, and she ran away this morning before I woke up."

I expect Miko to give me grief in response to this information, but she lets out a very Landon-like gasp in outrage.

"You realize this makes two of my friends you've run out of your bed, Taylor?" she demands.

"Now that's not fair," he says, fighting a smile. "You know that time with Landon was alcohol related and nothing happened." He runs a hand along his jaw. "This was the only instance where I was actively trying to get one of you three into bed with me."

"Yeah, well," she grumbles, "the buck stops here. Try hosting a slumber party that doesn't send her careening in the opposite direction next time."

"Yes ma'am," he tells her seriously.

This is ridiculous! I am not going to stand here and listen to them discuss me like I am a problem to be fixed. Or worse, have them compare what happened last night to that time Landon got drunk and passed out in Taylor's bed like a hobo. That pisses me off most of all.

"Come on," I say briskly as I pass by him to head upstairs. I sound rude, and I know I am walking way too fast; but I have to, or else I'll scream at them both and admit to being pissed off for all the wrong reasons.

"Godspeed," I hear Miko whisper to Taylor.

I am up the stairs and opening a guest room door before I turn to see if he is behind me. Taylor walks right by me, and when I follow him into the room, he reaches over my head and slams the door, shutting both of us into the room.

"What are you doing here?" I demand.

Anger is good. Anger I know how to do. This thing with him, that's where I am completely in the dark.

"You invited me." He smiles, but for the first time since I met him, his smile seems forced.

"Don't be obtuse," I say, stepping away from the door—away from the close proximity to him.

"Don't be a coward," he counters vehemently.

I am momentarily stunned. I look away, at a loss for words for the first time in as long as I can remember.

"Max," he says softly, but I feel the word like a caress.

It is the first time he's ever used my first name.

He reaches out for my hand before I can pull it back. His touch is light, barely there at all, but I feel it all the way down to my toes.

"I told you I wasn't going anywhere, and I'm not"—his finger-tips brush my wrist—"but you can't just disappear on me."

I take a deep breath.

"Last night was a mistake."

I'd meant for it to come out defiant. It sounded pitiful and unsure.

His fingers slide higher, running the length of my forearm and back down again.

"Last night was a long time coming," he says gently, "and you know it as well as I do."

His fingertips are playing havoc with my emotions. I want to throw myself into his arms, because I know how safe I'd feel in them. But the part of me that wants to do that battles with the long-ingrained belief that I need to guard myself. It is the only way to avoid being hurt again, or even worse, hurting someone else.

I pull my hand away and step towards the door.

"I don't think I can do this," I whisper, unable to produce any more volume than that.

He catches my hand again before I can get away.

"What if you don't think?" he asks with a grin. I can actually see him forcing himself back into a familiar role. "Let's just go downstairs and play in that monstrosity of a beer-pong tourna-ment. And we won't think about it. OK?" He leads me out into the hallway without stopping his monologue. "We'll eat some cheese. I'll charm your family. We won't talk about kissing or sleepovers, or how soft that spot is just behind your ear—"

"Taylor!" I yelp when he runs his nose along the spot in question.

I hurry out of reach, unable to stop a smile. It is hard to hold on to an emotional shank spiral when he is here teasing me, pre-tending like nothing happened. He follows along at my heels.

"And we won't talk about desserts or secret jobs, or that little sound you make in the back of your throat when I—"

He trails off just as we step out onto the veranda, and everybody looks up at us.

"Well, well, well. I don't think I've ever seen Mackenzie blush!" Malin calls from the Ping-Pong table. "Quick, somebody snap a photo for posterity!"

———

I sit quietly at the table for most of the afternoon, watching Taylor doing exactly what he said he would. My parents are ready to adopt him by the time everyone leaves to go change for dinner. He's thrown me quick smiles and winks, and everyone tries to include me in conversation, but I can't make myself join in.

I am relieved. Every single part of me is relieved that he is sitting here making jokes, deflecting everyone's attention away from how weird I am acting. But feeling relief comes with the ever-increasing anxiety about what that relief says about me. This morning I ran out, and I told myself that I was upset because of how far I'd let things go and how easily I slipped into intimacy with him when I never allow that with anybody. But if that is true, if I was only upset about slipping up and not about being at odds with Taylor, why am I so grateful to have him here now?

I hurry back to my room and go through the motions of taking a shower. Since I spent the entire day dressed like a meth addict, I think I should put in at least a little effort for dinner.

We aren't headed anywhere fancy, just following another long-standing tradition of visiting our favorite Mexican restaurant on the night before the Fourth. I don't even know when it started, but we've been going to the same place every year for as long as I can remember.

I start to grab a pair of skinny jeans from my closet when Malin bursts into the room without knocking. She is wearing a white linen baby-doll dress that does everything for her long legs, and she has some sort of coral fabric wrapped around her throat like a scarf. She closes the door behind her and launches herself onto my bed just as she used to when we were little.

I start to slip a foot into the jeans when she scoffs.

"Holy Moses, not those!" She stares daggers at my pants. "I brought something better!"

She sits up abruptly and starts to unwind the material from around her neck. When it comes loose she lays the maxi dress on the bed next to her.

"I'm not really a dress kind of girl," I say, stating the obvious.

"Don't be such a bum!" She flashes me a grin. "A maxi dress is the equivalent of wearing a muumuu in public, and you *are* the kind of girl who likes to wear clothes large enough to accommodate at least three people at once."

She goes into my bathroom and comes out with some hair products. Before I can protest she's applied three different things and is styling my hair with her fingertips. It takes too much effort to argue, so I don't.

When she is done she stands back and smiles as she appraises her work. She reaches out without looking and grabs the dress off the bed behind her to thrust it into my hands.

"This won't fit," I grumble.

"It's too long on me," she replies in a saccharine tone, "so it'll fit you perfectly."

I work the material around in my hands, looking for another flaw. It is cotton, so I can't complain about comfort or the dress being too formal. But a halter neckline and the fact that it is backless make it feel too dressy.

"I won't be able to wear a bra." I raise my eyebrows at her.

"Please." She pulls lip gloss out of the pocket of her dress and dabs some on. "Women all over this country pay doctors good money to get boobs as perky as yours."

She hands me the gloss and turns to flounce out of the room as quickly as she came in.

"Mali, I don't want—"

"Good effing grief, Max," she says without turning around. "Just wear the effing dress!"

When I come downstairs fifteen minutes later, I am wearing the effing dress.

Thanks to Malin my hair is shaggy and mussed to perfection, and since mascara was the only makeup I'd had on, her lip gloss goes a long way towards helping me look less pale.

I hear conversation from the living room and start to head in that direction, but Landon finds me first, with a little shot clutched between two fingers. Miko is right behind her, holding one in each hand.

"Max, you look so pretty!" she coos at me.

The compliment makes me feel even more anxious. I shouldn't have worn the dress.

"Thanks," I answer quietly.

"Oh jeez." Miko pushes her way around Landon and thrusts a shot into my hand. "It's worse than we thought if you're being all demure and polite!"

They both look at me in confusion.

"What's going on, girl?" Landon asks gently.

I am not even sure where to begin. I shrug uncomfortably.

Landon's shoulders fall a little, as if she expected that response but hoped it would be something else. She holds up her little glass between the three of us.

"To Sandra?" she asks.

"To Sandra." Miko and I clink glasses with her without hesitation, and we all swallow the shot of Jack. It probably isn't the wisest course of action for me to have straight liquor, but it does take a little bit of the edge off the anxiety I can't seem to shake.

"You look just gorgeous!" my mother says, coming up behind us.

When I turn around she is beaming. She loves it when I wear a dress; it reminds her of someone else. I discard the memory with a quick shake of my head.

Over her shoulder I see Taylor walk out of the living room, laughing with my brothers. His face lights up when he sees me.

"Kenzie, why don't you ride with Daddy and me, and you can tell us how everything is at the bar," Mom says, pulling me towards the door. My palms get sweaty and my steps falter. She must have misunderstood the reason for my hesitation, because she calls back behind us. "Taylor, you come along with us too!"

"Yes ma'am," I hear him say.

All the stress I released with the alcohol comes back with a vengeance. My anxiety is getting worse.

———

At dinner I try to keep up with the conversation, but I am too wrapped up in my own head. I can't stop thinking about Taylor, my job, and all the lies I am keeping up with. I get more anxious with every passing minute. Everyone is telling stories, and I try to look attentive; I even laugh in the right spots, but I know Taylor isn't convinced. He keeps sneaking me questioning glances that I don't answer. I manage to eat most of my dinner, but only because I know my mother is paying attention.

When we get back home Malin demands a board-game tournament, and everyone heads to the game room to choose something. The room is big and filled with everything from pool to darts to pinball, which kept us occupied as kids. Now it also boasts a fantastic bar filled with top-shelf liquor to keep us occupied as adults.

It is probably stupid, but I think a drink might help me calm down or at least clear my head enough to understand why I feel so apprehensive. I kick off my sandals in the corner and head towards the alcohol. As usual, as soon as I get anywhere near one of them, my brothers call out drink orders. Everyone else follows suit.

Brody and Liam play darts, and the girls debate the merits of all the board games in an attempt to decide what we should play. My parents have parked themselves on the big sectional in the corner, and even though I don't look up, I can feel Taylor watching me. Making the cocktails is good, actually, because for about twenty minutes it gives me something to do with my shaky hands. Once everyone has a drink, I make my own and take a swallow that decreases the liquid in my glass by half.

"What about Scrabble?" Miko asks the room.

"No!" my brothers say in unison.

"Max will murder you at Scrabble," Malin tells her seriously. "You have no idea."

Taylor catches my eye and smiles. I look away and take another drink.

Landon and Miko are both sitting on the floor in the corner, and they go back to digging through the game shelves.

"What about Password?" Mom asks everybody.

"You cheat at Password!" Malin laughs back at her.

Mom's only response is a giggle and a raise of her eyebrows. My dad leans over and kisses her cheek as if even after all these years she is still the coolest person he knows.

Liam lets out a whoop when he strikes the bull's-eye, and I turn to watch him handing out high fives at the same moment Landon gasps. I don't turn immediately, because Landon is overly dramatic and could be reacting to anything. I start to take another sip of my drink when she squeals.

"Max, is this *you*?"

Everything in me stills completely.

I am walking across the room towards her before my eyes can even focus on what she is holding. I stop a foot away from where she and Miko sit in the corner. They are flipping through an old photo album, the kind that my mom used to have everywhere until I begged her to put them away. She put them here, along with all the other pictures of me from before, so I wouldn't see them and have to be reminded.

The blood starts pounding through my body, and my heart is beating so hard I can hear it in my ears. Nobody else seems to notice my distress. Landon and Miko are immersed in the pictures on each page.

Landon's voice is filled with laughter. "All this time you have given me grief!" she says without looking up. "How many blonde jokes have you told me? How many times have you teased me about the color pink? Max, you looked like a Barbie doll!" She laughs outright now.

Miko nods in agreement. "Seriously, dude, why did you chop your hair off? Even I want to make out with you in this photo!"

I rub my palms down the front of my dress, fighting the urge to be sick. Malin leans over the page to see the photo they are looking at. I don't need to get closer to see the images; I know what they show. A lifetime of shots of me with the same blonde hair as my mother and the same pampered outlook on life that Malin has now.

"Oh, she did that freshman year at Georgetown," she says flippantly.

"When were you at Georgetown?" Landon asks, turning the page.

"She went there for part of her undergrad." Malin reaches out and starts shuffling a deck of cards as she shares more facts. "Went away that year with this perfect, long blonde hair and a golden tan, then came back at summertime all angry goth. You'd actually probably die of disbelief if you knew what she was like then," Malin continues, blissfully unaware of her story's effect on me in the way only a sheltered twenty-two-year-old can be.

I start to have trouble breathing.

I feel Taylor come up behind me, but that only makes it worse.

"She was the sweetest girl you've ever met," Malin says with a smile. She searches her memory for more information for her rapt audience. "She was captain of varsity track from freshman year in high school on. Won every award there was. Straight As, most popular girl in school, never did anything wrong. The perfect goody two-shoes!"

Landon gasps again and Miko giggles.

I vaguely hear my mother call my name, but it is hard to focus on anything other than staying upright.

"I guess you decided to rebel, though, because you kind of . . ." She trails off when she looks up and sees whatever is on my face.

She jumps to her feet in panic.

"Max?" she asks urgently.

It is too much. Everything with Taylor and lying to my parents and trying to keep my job and now those pictures, and remembering that time before it all went so wrong, and . . . I feel light-headed.

My mom's face is in front of mine, and it takes me a minute to understand her words.

"You're OK, Mackenzie. Just take a deep breath," she says soothingly but authoritatively. "You're OK."

"I'm OK?" I choke out.

I take a step back from her and back right into Taylor. I jump away like I've been scalded. I look around the room wildly. Everyone is standing now, staring at me in concern. My mother starts to speak again, and I cut her off.

"I'm OK?" I ask again in wonder. "I'm OK!" This time it comes out like an accusation.

"I am *not* OK," I answer honestly. "I haven't been *OK*"—I spit out the word—"in a really long time!"

"Max," Malin says gently.

Anger comes then, swift and welcome. It is an emotion I can process better than the overwhelming urge to fall to pieces. It sweeps through every part of my being, becoming a rage I direct at Malin, at my mother, at anyone who's ever considered my coming home as a completely different person the result of a childish act of rebellion. I spear Malin with a look.

"You think this is what rebellion looks like?" I gesture to myself, this person I've become who is so unlike the shiny, perfect little girl I see in the photos before me. "You think I became this person because I was going through a phase? One I'd still hold on to six years later?" I swipe at my cheeks, surprised to find the tears there.

The group around me is utterly still; no one knows how to handle me.

I don't know how to handle me.

"Mali"—I choke on a sob—"you don't destroy yourself on purpose. Don't you get it? It's one stupid mistake, over in an instant, but then it's too late to take it back."

"Mackenzie"—my mother takes a step towards me—"sweetheart, let's get you upstairs and we can talk."

I take another step backwards and reach out to finger the bracelet on my wrist.

"Why upstairs?" I demand. "You've tried for years to get me to talk. Well, here we are." I throw my hands up in frustration.

"Honey, I don't think this is—"

"Why, Mom? Don't you want to hear about it?" I can't stop the words. I've held them in for so long, and I can't stop them now. "Don't you want to know about that first year of school? How excited I was to be on my own? How I thought it was finally my chance to have fun and go to parties like the other girls? And you told me. You told me so many times that I had to be careful with my diet, and that alcohol would affect me more because of my condition. And I knew better, but I so badly wanted to be like everyone else, and so I drank right along with them."

"Sweetheart, let's go upstairs," she tries again.

I ignore her.

"And the alcohol hit me hard, like you told me it would, but I was having fun, more fun than I'd ever had before." I shake my head at the memory, as if I could wish the rest away. "There was this guy there, and he seemed like fun too."

"Mackenzie?" My mother's voice is pleading.

"You can guess where this is going, right?" I ask her. "Because I couldn't. I *was* a goody two-shoes, just like Malin said, but I felt wild and so grown up. I didn't think about consequences, because I'd never done anything that had any real ones. You know, it was my first time, and I don't even know what his name was?"

I can never live up to their standards, and they may as well know all the ugly details.

"Sweetheart, please stop," my mother begs quietly.

Her eyes fill up and the tears run down her face, but I can't make myself stop talking.

"Don't you want to know the rest, Mom? How ashamed I was the day after, when I woke up in bed with a man I didn't know?" I feel Taylor flinch beside me. "How later," I say in a near whisper, "when I found out I was pregnant"—I hear sounds of shock from the people around me, but I can't be stopped—"all I could think about was how unfair it was? All I could think about was what this would mean for my GPA, or how"—my voice breaks on the words—"how disappointed Daddy would be with me?"

"Please, baby girl—" My father tries to reach me, but I cut him off.

"Don't you want to know how selfish I was then? How I wasn't even mature enough to make any decisions, because I didn't want them on my conscience? How I prayed every day that God would just make that baby go away?"

I lose the ability to speak, my throat closed off by words I've never told anyone.

A hand slips around mine.

I look down at Taylor's fingers holding on to my own. I can't look at my parents anymore. I can hear my mom crying, but the rest of the room is utterly silent. They know there is more; they are waiting for the bomb to drop. I feel Taylor's hand in mine like an anchor, weighing me to earth. I can't say the rest to them, but I can tell him; Taylor kept all my secrets. I look up into his eyes. They're shiny, but no tears fall from them. He'll be my confidant one more time.

"A month went by, and I tried to pretend it wasn't really happening," I tell Taylor. "But then another month meant it wasn't just an abstract thing anymore; it was a baby. And I started to wonder what he'd . . ." I swallow and try again. "What he'd be like. Or if his hair would be blond too . . . Or if he'd be a good runner."

I can hear both my parents crying now; maybe everyone in the room is. I have to say the rest. Taylor squeezes my fingers.

"I had an ultrasound, and I saw his heartbeat. It was so *fast*, Taylor. So strong. I understood something then that I hadn't before. I had made a mistake, but *he* wasn't a mistake. He was a baby. He was *my* baby. I didn't know how I was going to be a mom, but I knew I could figure it out for him." I take a breath, and when I speak again my voice sounds as hollow as I feel. "A week later I started bleeding. By the time I got to the hospital, they told me there was nothing they could do." I shrug, then say the words I've thought a million times and hate myself for the truth in them. "I guess God heard my prayers after all."

Everything starts to go dark.

Taylor catches me before I hit the ground.

Chapter Sixteen

When I open my eyes the next morning, the early sunlight of the summer day is streaming in through the drapes I forgot to close. I stretch out my arms and try to remember going to bed, because I am kind of obsessive about sleeping in a cave I so won't be woken by the sun. *I must have—*

My thoughts stall out as the memory of the night before comes back to me in a flood.

Oh no, what did I do?

I sit bolt upright in my bed and realize I am still wearing the wrinkled dress from the night before. They must have had to carry me up here after I . . . after I just spewed all of that out all over everyone. Six years of carrying around the secret, and it all came undone in one stupid crying jag in less than fifteen minutes! And everyone knows now. I cringe. My parents, my brothers, even Taylor and Landon and Miko. They all had front-row seats to my train wreck! And today they will want to . . . what? Hold hands and talk it through? Cry about it? Or worse, reprimand me? I can't handle that at all. I do a perfectly good job of beating myself up about everything that happened. If one of them starts in on me, it will break our relationship in an irreconcilable way. That is why I could never bring myself to tell them what happened. It is why I stayed away the rest of that year until I was sort of pulled together enough to come home. I hadn't come home as the same girl—not even close—but I did transfer to a local school so I wouldn't have to see reminders of the darkest period in my life. But I've done it now; I've spewed all of those secrets out into the world, and I can't take any of it back. After years of worrying about it, I am finally going to have to see my family's faces now that they know exactly what kind of person I am.

I reach out to pull my phone off the nightstand and see that it is only a little after six, which means that it is likely that only one other person is awake right now. Before I can think about it further, I jump out of bed. While I brush my teeth and wash my face, I convince myself that this is really the best option. I go back in the bedroom and throw on the first things I can find. I grab my backpack and my phone and hurry downstairs as quietly as possible. The house is utterly silent as I make my way through it, and the relief I feel at not running into anyone is profound. As I get closer to my destination, I hear noise, telling me my guess was right on.

When I walk into the gym, Liam's eyes fly to my reflection in the mirror in front of him. He hits a button that immediately stops the treadmill he's running on, and as soon as it slows down, he jumps off and turns towards me. He must not have been on it for long, because he hasn't even broken a sweat yet.

I look down at my feet, not sure what to say. I try to make a joke.

"So *that* happened," I say with as much sarcasm as I can muster.

"Yeah," he answers.

Apparently he is as much at a loss as I am. I feel sort of sick to my stomach and unsure. This is the kind of confrontation I've been trying to avoid for so many years. I look down at my feet again. If there is disappointment in his eyes, I can't stand to see it.

"Are you mad at me?" My voice comes out sounding like a child's, and I feel just as small.

I look up when Liam swears, but he is already in front of me, pulling me into his arms.

"Don't be an idiot! Why would I be mad at you?"

When I only shrug, he sighs.

"I'm sad for you, Mack. I am so fucking sad that you went through all of that. That you didn't feel comfortable enough to ask anyone for help." He holds me at arm's length and looks me over.

"I didn't want to disappoint anybody," I answer him honestly.

"So this was better, then? Letting it eat away at you for years? Letting what happened alienate you from your family? You haven't had a boyfriend. You haven't really had friends until recently. All that was better than being honest about what was going on? Why would you do that to yourself?" he demands hoarsely.

Tears burn in the back of my throat. I cannot believe there are any left in me.

"Please, Liam," I say almost desperately. "Please. I can't do this today. I need your help."

His eyes narrow, and he looks down at the backpack on the floor next to me.

"No way! You cannot run from this again!" he barks.

How can I explain this to him? I know my family and friends will want to talk about it in detail, but it isn't their burden to bear; it is mine. I deserve to handle it however I choose to, and if I piss everyone else off in the process, well, it won't be the first time.

"Liam, last night was"—I choke on the words—"last night was horrible for me. Don't you understand? It wasn't just the first time I told you guys; it was the first time I told anyone."

He swears again.

"I know I'll have to talk about it with Mom and Dad and every-one else, but please, just not today. I just need some time, OK?" I say, searching his face for some sign that he might be considering my plea.

He is looking away from me, staring at the wall, but really, who would want to have to look at such a screwup and know she is your sister? I fight the urge to cry again at the thought.

"My keys are by the front door," he says finally. "I'll face the wrath this morning for helping you."

"Thank you. I—"

He cuts me off with a look.

"But you'll talk to Mom, right? Take a few days to get your head on straight, but then you have to talk to her. Promise me."

"I promise," I say, grabbing my bag off the floor and turning to go. I've already spent so much time down here that I'll be lucky if I can still sneak out without anyone knowing about it.

"I'm serious, Mack," Liam calls after me.

"I know," I respond and hurry off to grab his keys.

I know he is serious, and I meant it when I said I would speak to my mom about everything. I just can't guarantee when that will be.

———

I wait all throughout my drive back to LA for calls and texts that don't come. I don't know what Liam had to say to everybody to keep them from sending out search parties, but I know I owe him a bigger debt than I can ever repay.

When I get back to my apartment after a few hours in some horrible holiday traffic, I drag myself upstairs. The whole way here I was thinking about how much I wanted to take a shower and put on pajamas and not have to talk to anyone for as long as possible. When I walk into the apartment, though, the emptiness seems absolute. The quiet is its own kind of noise; the hum of it makes me pause inside the entryway, not sure what to do now. Here I am again, alone. This was exactly how I wanted it, so why is it that I still feel anxious? How come I feel more like crying now than I did when I left this morning? I don't even just feel like it; I am pretty sure I am about to have another full-on, ugly cry.

The shower, I think. The shower is the absolute best place to cry. It covers the sound and the tears, even from the person making them.

I lurch down the hallway and into my room. Minutes later I am under the too-hot spray of the shower. When I finally shut the water off, it has run cold, and I have run out of the energy to sob anymore.

I towel myself off and put on the coziest pair of pajamas I own. I have to turn the air conditioner on full blast to accommodate the flannel, but it is well worth it for the comfort I feel when I snuggle up on the couch with a blanket and a bowl of soup. I can't find the motivation to turn the TV on. I just sip at the soup in the bowl and watch the shadows stretch across the patio through the sliding-glass window.

I'm not sure how much time has passed when I hear scratches at the front door, but I don't even have time to question what the sound is before the door flies open and Landon and Miko barrel down the hallway and into the living room.

"Thank God we got here just in time!" Miko says, dropping her duffle bag on the floor and walking towards the couch to give me a once-over. "She was about to drown herself in three inches of home-style chicken noodle."

Miko removes the soup bowl I am still clutching in confusion and then plops down beside me.

"Well," Landon says cheerfully, "at least it isn't clam chowder. We all know what cream-based soup does to the thighs."

I watch in disbelief as Landon drops two grocery bags on the coffee table in front of her and then starts to produce a cornucopia of junk food from their depths.

"Can you throw me the Red Vines?" Miko asks.

A package goes sailing over Landon's shoulder and ends up bouncing off the wall behind us and falling onto the unoccupied couch cushion.

"Close enough," Miko says to the licorice package.

She rips into it with her teeth and extracts a piece to masticate on. I finally find my voice.

"What are you guys doing here?" I ask them.

Landon pulls out a can of mixed nuts and puts it on the arm of the sofa next to me.

"We got you some stuff too," she says with a smile.

"What are you doing here?" I ask a little louder this time.

"It's a Sandra Bullock marathon!" Landon announces with the energy of a drum major. "Just like we always talked about doing!"

I shake my head, but neither of them pays attention to me.

"I think we should start with *Love Potion No. 9*," Landon says right before she opens a can of Pringles with her teeth.

"Classic Bullock," Miko agrees through a mouthful of Red Vines.

This isn't something that can be fixed by a slumber party or a girls' weekend. This can't be made better by a romantic comedy, and they can't just act cheery and pretend it never happened.

"I want to be alone," I tell them vehemently.

"Bullshit!" Landon yells, and all five feet three inches of her vibrate with anger.

In this moment, I actually believe that if she wanted to, she could kick my ass. Miko turns towards me with her eyes wide in shock. We rarely hear Landon curse, and we've certainly never heard her scream one.

"You do not want to be alone! You've been alone long enough." She glares at me. "I know you don't want us here, and you don't want to hear what I'm going to say, but that's too damn bad for you, because you're going to listen anyway."

I turn away from her and look out the window again, because I don't want to see her face when this conservative southern Republican tells me what she thinks of me now.

"Max, you, me, and Miko—we're best friends." Her voice softens. "I know you think I'm cheesy or immature when I say that, but it doesn't make it any less true."

She sits down on the coffee table facing me, but I still can't look at her.

"Do you imagine we'd think anything less of you because we understand now? I think you're one of the strongest people I know, and having the courage to admit what happened—that makes you stronger than ever."

Miko's hand finds mine, but I can't protest through the tears I am trying to swallow.

"Dude, we're here because we love you, and there is no possible scenario where we'd let you ditch us to spend Fourth of July alone in an apartment like an agoraphobic," Miko says.

She picks up a pack of turkey jerky with her free hand and throws it in my lap.

"Eat some protein; we've got about eight hours of quality programming coming your way," she tells me.

Landon walks over to our entertainment center and starts to dig through her DVD collection. I don't say anything in response to either of them. I've had enough emotion in the past twenty-four hours to last me a lifetime. I am pretty sure if I say anything, I actually might start blubbering like a toddler and tell them how much I love them and how thankful I am that they've come back for me.

"Now I want you to prepare yourself, Max," Landon says, putting a DVD into the machine. "At the beginning of this Sandra has really bad eyebrows and frizzy hair, but she'll get a makeover when the love potion kicks in, OK?"

I roll my eyes and pop some jerky into my mouth in response. The opening credits begin to roll, and they both settle in with various snack foods to watch. A few minutes after the movie starts, Miko interrupts.

"Max?" she says without taking her eyes off Tate Donovan.

"Yeah?" I ask, nervous we are going to have another heart-to-heart.

"I really liked that picture of you in those pink hot pants," she says sotto voce.

Landon guffaws while I roll my eyes and shake my head.

"Assholes," I grumble.

But even as I say it, I am smiling.

———

The next day I still feel kind of numb, but so much better than I did the day before. We stayed up late watching more Bullock movies than I'd even realized existed, and while I will never admit this to them, I actually loved *The Proposal*. Apparently, even I am not immune to Ryan Reynolds's abs.

I start to get ready for work, and I am eternally grateful that I am headed back to the normalcy of my job. It won't do me any good to sit around thinking about everything that happened. I don't want to face what my family thinks of me now. I don't want to see the look in Taylor's eyes now that he knows why I am such a wreck. I need to throw myself into my work and get past this as quickly as possible.

I pull on jeans and a thin cotton T-shirt, which is what I usually wear, but I take the extra time to do my hair and apply whatever makeup won't melt off around the ovens. I want to feel more pulled together on the outside than I am on the inside. A cheap ploy, perhaps, but I feel better just the same.

Back in my room I grab my bag and reach into my closet for my shoes. At the last second I grab for the orange pair of Natives, the ones I bought for my first day. I haven't worn them since then, and it is time to give them another try.

On the way out the door my phone rings for the first time in two days. I am not surprised to look down and see my mom's name on the screen. I debate for a moment whether or not to answer. I know I had promised Liam that I would talk to her, and I know eventually I am going to have to get it over with.

"Just not yet," I say to the empty hallway.

I flip the switch to silence my phone and drop it in my backpack.

———

I stand at a high table working out a large batch of the toffee pudding I served at the dinner party earlier in the week. Apparently it was such a hit that Avis wants it added to the menu. Making a large-batch recipe is surprisingly tricky. Sometimes all you need to do is increase the measurements exactly, but other times making something in large quantity subtly mutes the flavors that make it so special. A big part of my job so far has been to find the most efficient way to make a larger batch without diluting the quality of a given recipe.

I am busy grating nutmeg when Harris walks by on his way to the stove. He smiles when he sees me.

"Happy to see that one is making its way on the menu; it's excellent," he says over the din of the stand-up mixer my ingredients are spinning around in.

"I know," I say, lowering the speed so I can hear him better. "It's one of my favorites too."

"Joey is not going to believe how many new dishes you've added when she comes back in a couple of weeks. It's a whole new menu she'll have to learn to make."

I look up from the ingredients in my hand.

"What?" I ask him.

He clearly misunderstands the look of confusion on my face, because he tries to explain.

"I know it seems silly to refuse to tell her what's going on, but I don't want her obsessing over the kitchen. She already refused to take more than eight weeks of maternity leave. She'll be back soon enough to hear about all the things you did while you covered for her."

Wait . . . what?

"All right, my dear, that berry compote isn't going to make itself. I'll see you later." He waves at me with one of his meaty hands and heads off towards the back of the kitchen.

I blink stupidly after him.

What did he mean "when she comes back in a couple of weeks"? Since when is Joey coming back at all? I have to find Avis and ask her what is going on.

I find her braiding together pieces of dough to create individual challah rolls. She has both an unlit cigarette and a wrapped lollipop stuck in her bun, the way a librarian might stash a pencil. Her foot taps absently to the banda music that marches out of the speakers in the back of the room.

I walk up to her table but don't wait for her to acknowledge me before I ask the question eating a hole in my stomach.

"Joey is coming back?"

She doesn't look up from her dough.

"She has"—she stops working her fingers long enough to calculate—"a few more weeks off, I think."

She says it as if she's casually mentioning the weather or asking me to get her a drink. She says it as if it is the simplest of statements, as if it doesn't utterly rip apart everything I've been planning for myself since starting this new job.

"But . . . but," I stutter, "you never mentioned that this was temporary."

She looks up at me, her mouth pursed to one side.

"Did you cut your hair?" she asks unexpectedly.

"What?" I shake my head. "No. It's always been this short."

"Has it?" she asks absentmindedly, and then turns back to her dough. "A bit mannish if you ask me."

"Avis," I demand, "please focus! You never mentioned that this job was temporary. I was under the impression that—"

"I did so mention it. I called you Stork," she tells the roll in her hands.

"Because I'm tall," I try to argue with the delusional woman in front of me.

"No"—she shakes her head with a smile—"because storks help the moms get their babies."

I shake my head in a kind of mute disbelief and try to grasp for something, *anything* to say in response to possibly the most insane explanation I've heard from her yet. I start to protest, to argue, to scream, but really, what good will that do? Joey has been with her for years, and I've been here a couple of months. It isn't like she'd choose me instead, and I wouldn't ask her to. Also, because I work with payroll I know what the budget is for the kitchen staff, and they are already pushing it, salary-wise. My shoulders slump in defeat.

Crap. What am I going to do now?

Luckily Avis answers the question for me.

"Can you get me a Fresca? I'm really thirsty."

"Sure," I tell her before slowly walking away.

Too many things have happened in the last several days, and I don't know where I am going to go or what I am going to do now, but I do know one thing.

I am going to light these effing stupid, cursed orange shoes on fire.

———

As I walk to my car later that night, I finally allow myself to think about what I've learned today. Whether it is fair or not, in a couple of weeks I won't have this job anymore. I also haven't spent enough time here to warrant getting a job at this level anywhere else. I guess I could apply to be a stage in another restaurant, but that likely means going without any pay. It is one thing to juggle two jobs when I think I am killing myself to work alongside my idol, but working two jobs so I can start as a dishwasher in someone else's kitchen is utterly depressing.

And isn't this always the way? Don't I know better? Damn it, I *know* better! I wrote the freaking book on managing expectations, on not ever demanding too much out of life, because then you won't be disappointed when it turns out to suck all over again.

"Damn. I don't know what those shoes did to piss you off so much, but I'm glad I'm not them."

I look up at Taylor, who has parked himself on the hood of my car yet again. I didn't even realize I was glaring down at my feet until he mentioned it.

Ugh, please, could I just not have to deal with more emotional baggage for at least a day? Just one freaking day is all I ask!

I try my best to swallow my temper and everything else the last few days dredged up. Taylor has been incredible to me; he doesn't deserve my bad moods. In fact, he is way too good to have to deal with me at all.

"What are you doing here?"

He stretches his legs out and stands up, looking concerned by something he heard in my voice.

"I wanted to check on you, make sure you were OK after—"

"I'm fine." I cut him off.

"OK, of course." He holds both palms up in surrender. "Of course you are. I just missed you. I thought I'd see if you wanted to grab dinner or watch crappy TV or something."

Here he is once again, being this incredibly kind, wonderful man. Some twisted part of me wants to ignore everything else and let him be that for me. But how long will it be until my moodiness wears thin? How long until he grows tired of putting up with all of my crap? How long until I screw this up too?

I feel tired down to my very core.

"You shouldn't miss me, Bennett; it's a waste of energy." I walk around him to put my bag in the car.

He reaches out for my arm to stop me, and I pull it away like he might burn me. He looks at me in confusion.

"Since when did you start calling me Bennett again?" he asks.

"I don't think I can do this with you," I tell him quietly.

I reach up to fiddle with my bracelets, as if they can give me the energy to stay upright against the weight of his stare.

"What do you mean?" he asks just as quietly.

I take a deep breath.

"I can't do this!" I slam my car door and try to hurry around to the other side. I need to get out of here.

Taylor's voice is like a whipcrack; it echoes off the walls of the parking garage and bounces back at me in the empty space.

"What does the bracelet mean?"

I turn to glare at him. "Screw you, Bennett," I say vehemently.

"What does fifteen percent mean, Max? You wear it around like a talisman, only I don't think it's that. I think it's your own personal cross." He points at my wrist. "If whatever that stands for means that I don't get to see you anymore, then I at least deserve to know why!"

I don't remember moving forward, but suddenly I am in his face, spewing years' worth of anger and pain at the person who deserves it the least.

"You want to know what it means? Fine!" I scream. "Imagine being nineteen and scared out of your fucking mind. Imagine yourself as this naive little girl who, yeah, knew that bleeding probably wasn't a good sign, but still thought maybe, *maybe* her baby would be OK. And then this doctor comes in who's old enough to be your grandfather, and he can't hide the disgust in his face when he sees you there alone and without a ring on your finger to go along with the baby in your belly. And then he tells you that you're likely losing the baby." I'm shaking now, so furious at the memory. "*Losing* the baby, he said, as if I'd just misplaced him or something! Now imagine you're stupid enough to ask the question, because you're naive, remember? You ask, 'What are the chances that my baby will still be OK?' And he looks at you petulantly, like you're a child, and tells you, 'Maybe fifteen percent.'" Taylor takes a step back from the force of my anger, but I won't be stopped. I step towards him again. "I lay there for hours, and even while I bled and hurt and cried for my mother, I held onto that number, because fifteen percent was still something, *right*?"

He can't answer before I cut him off.

"Wrong. Fifteen percent is a lie! It's something you tell a patient to keep her calm, when all the while you know she won't still have a baby in her by morning." I hold my wrist up defiantly. "It's not my cross; it's my *reminder*. There's really only ever a fifteen percent chance of being happy, but I don't even deserve that much."

"Sweetheart," Taylor says, looking almost desperate now.

He steps closer, as if he might reach out or try to take my hand, but I can't stand any kind of affection right now. I'm not worth it. My thoughts stall and speed up, a flash flood of vitriol. Doesn't he understand yet that I am not sweet? I am hateful and mean, and the sooner he figures that out, the better off he'll be.

I could make him understand. I know exactly what I could say to push him away completely. I know how to be hurtful; I've had years of practice.

"You should go," I tell him. "It's inevitable anyway."

"What are you talking about?" he asks, but his tone is too sweet, too cajoling.

He is still trying to be kind.

"You're leaving. It's inevitable," I say, managing to fit hateful-ness into every syllable. "That's what the men in your family do, right? They run away?"

"What the fuck, Max?" he demands savagely.

I've pushed him too far now; he is the angriest I've ever seen him. One more line and it will be done.

"You gonna use those on me?" I look pointedly at his clenched fists. "I guess you're just like Daddy after all." I toss it out with feigned nonchalance.

Taylor takes a step back as if I've slapped him. When he looks at me again, his eyes are filled with shock, confusion, and deep hurt.

I've finally done it. I have destroyed this thing between us once and for all.

I get in my car and drive away, and I don't need to look back to know that he makes no move to come after me.

Chapter Seventeen

I don't remember that drive home.

I don't remember parking the car or making my way upstairs to the apartment. But suddenly I find myself standing in the kitchen watching Landon stare back at me, concern etched into her every feature.

I don't imagine there is any emotion on my face. I am utterly void of feelings. I have nothing left.

I am not aware I have the ability to make sound until the words fall from my mouth in a sob.

"I fuck up everything I touch," I tell her.

When I slide to the floor she is immediately beside me holding my hand.

"That's not true," she tells me earnestly.

It isn't worth debating it with her; I know I am right. My entire life and nearly all the relationships in it are evidence enough.

"God." I scrub at my cheeks. "I am so sick of crying."

"Max," she chides me softly.

Only Landon would scold you for using the Lord's name in vain even when your life is in a tailspin.

"Sorry," I respond.

"It's OK." She smiles at me. "And crying is OK too."

I start to roll my eyes, but she calls me out again.

"Come on, Max. The only way you are going to move past any of this is if you mature a little."

I am so affronted that my tears stop immediately. I look at her in shock.

"I'm older than you are," I throw at her.

She lets go of my hand and smooths a nonexistent wrinkle out of her pajama pants.

"I was talking about your maturity level, not your age," she says quietly.

I start to protest, ready to argue the point, thrilled to fall back into our familiar routine. But Landon looks at me, intent and serious, and suddenly I do feel younger and infinitely less knowledgeable.

"Max, you are gorgeous and funny and so smart. You're an amazing baker and sister, and even though you won't believe this, you're an amazing friend."

I open my mouth, but she quells me with a look.

"No," she says sternly, "it's time to listen now."

I snap my mouth closed.

"You are all those things, and I love you so much, OK?" she says.

When she waits for a response, I nod because that seems like what she wants me to do. I don't think it is wise to argue.

"But you're also emotionally immature in a lot of ways."

I fold my arms but continue to hold my tongue.

"You have to give yourself some understanding. When you lost the baby—"

I am so shocked she said it that it takes me a moment to try to scramble to my feet. I can't believe she has the gall to mention it to me so casually!

Landon pulls me back down. I cross my arms again and look at the ground.

"We have to talk about it, Max; *you* have to talk about it. It happened to you, and it was horrible, but keeping quiet is why you're so closed off now. Nineteen is still so young, and even though you're older, I wonder if some parts of you are still that nineteen-year-old." I look up at her in surprise.

"Running away, closing yourself off, alienating the people that love you, snapping at anyone who gets too close—those are coping mechanisms, and you're entitled to them, up to a point. You don't want to go through the rest of your life this way, do you?"

I should be offended, I guess, because she is essentially saying that who I am right now isn't someone I should want to be. I should feel angry or maybe even hurt, but there isn't a single ounce of malice in any part of Landon. I can feel her good intentions, how desperately she wants to get through to me, and with that realization comes another one. I *don't* want to be this way anymore, but I also don't know how to be anything else. I look away from her.

"I can't go back to the way things were; that's what everyone doesn't understand. My parents, my brothers . . . Even when they didn't know why I had changed, they still couldn't understand why I couldn't just flip a switch and turn back into the girl in those pictures."

"Of course you can't go back," Landon responds immediately. "You're not that girl anymore. But you can move forward."

This time I do roll my eyes at her.

"I did move forward. I just had to change a bit in order to pull it off," I tell her flippantly.

"You didn't," she says seriously. "You're still back there in that hospital room. You carry it with you every day. You beat yourself up."

I have nothing to say to that.

"I know you won't like me saying this, Max, but I have to tell you anyway." Landon reaches for my hand again, and I fight the urge to shake her off. "The other night you said that God answered your prayers."

My stomach turns at the memory. I hate hearing it on someone else's lips.

"It sounds like you're tearing yourself up because of an emotional reaction you had when you were a teenager. I'm sure a lot of women struggle with the news that they're unexpectedly pregnant. That's a natural response, and you were so young. It doesn't mean you would have been any less of a mom. You didn't lose the baby because God was punishing you. Losing a pregnancy just happens sometimes. It's not your fault."

I can't breathe for a moment, and then I take in too much air too fast. I look over at her in shock. How can someone with eyelash extensions who is unironically wearing poodle pajamas voice the exact fear that I've carried around like a yoke for years?

Even if some small, rational part of my brain knows I didn't wish the baby away, the guilt I've had about my initial reaction has overridden everything else. I realize with sudden clarity that she is right. I have let that belief—I have let that *guilt*—shape every other part of my life.

I take a deep breath and let it out again.

Landon is right, but what am I supposed to do with that information? It's not like I can just snap my fingers and stop being this way.

"So what exactly do you think I should do?"

My question comes out a little hostile, but she ignores the tone.

"I think," she says carefully, "that it would be really helpful for you to meet with a therapist."

I fight the urge to scream at the familiar request. That is what my mom has been asking me to do for years. I have no desire to sit with someone twice a week and rehash all of the things I fought so hard to forget. I do not want to yell at Landon, though. I know she is only trying to be helpful.

"Not going to happen," I say through clenched teeth.

Landon lets out a breath of her own. She looks up and around, searching the kitchen for inspiration. Her eyes alight on the fridge, and she jumps up to pull something out of it and rustle around in the cabinets. When she sits down next to me again, she is holding two shot glasses and a chilled bottle of tequila from our freezer.

"You want to get drunk?" I ask, confused.

"No," she says, pouring a shot for each of us. "I want us to drink this shot, and then I want you to tell me. One time, all the way through, from the beginning."

I look at her like she is insane.

"And then someone will know, and you had control over whether or not to tell them. Truly understanding that you're in control of the telling will really help you," she says simply.

"How would you know?" I snap.

"Because"—Landon looks right at me—"when you had your accident and I found you, I had nightmares for weeks. I couldn't close my eyes without seeing blood everywhere. Every time I put my key in the lock, I would start to panic because I thought I'd open the door and find you hurt or . . . or worse."

I have never, not once, asked her about that night. I imagined she must have been frightened, but I didn't want to hear the details. It had never even occurred to me that it might have been that diffi-cult for her to get through. I feel sick hearing about having put her through even more than I had imagined.

"Hey," she says gently, "I didn't say that to make you feel badly. That was another situation that you had no control over, right?"

I fight to deny it, but she is right. I'd gotten sick that night, but I would have never let it happen if I could have prevented it.

"Exactly," she agrees when I nod. "I told you because I wanted to explain why I went to a therapist afterwards. The therapist told

me to set an alarm on my phone and force myself to think about
that night in detail throughout the day for ten minutes at a time."

"What?" I demand, feeling defensive on her behalf.

"I know; it seemed crazy to me too. But the point was that I
needed to know I could control my thoughts. By scheduling time
to think about the worst of it, I kind of tricked my brain into not
thinking about it all the time. And then I didn't think about it at
all. So," she says, handing me a shot glass, "if you talk about it with
me, I think you'll feel a little more in control. And if you have a
bad day or you're feeling sad, you can tell me the story again. You
can tell me over and over until the memory loses some of its power
over you."

Landon looks me right in the eye then. "You can run or walk
or crawl past it if you have to, but you have to get to the other side
of this thing."

She smiles then, a little mischievously.

"Remember in *28 Days*, when she was really battling an addic-
tion to alcohol and—"

"Oh my gosh, fine!" I bark in annoyance.

She holds her shot between us.

"To Sandra?" she asks with a small smile.

"To Sandra." I clink my glass against her own.

We settle with our backs against the cabinets. I don't face her.
I look at the dishwasher, the rug from Ikea, even the baseboard
under the cabinet that hasn't been cleaned since the late eighties.

Finally, I open my mouth and tell her my story.

I talk about my biological father running out on us when I was
little. I talk about watching my mom work three jobs to try to take
care of Malin and me. I tell her about meeting the Ashtons for the
first time and how I thought it was a real-life fairy tale. I tell her
how perfect my childhood was after that and how hard I tried to
be perfect too, so I could fit in. I tell her about how I had my future
all planned out. How proud I was to get a track scholarship, even

though I didn't need one, how excited I was to go away to school by myself, how grown up I'd felt. I talk about the frat party freshman year of school. How I'd had just enough alcohol to make all the bad choices seem like good ones and how that made it worse, because in the end I'd known they were *my* choices. I talk about the pregnancy and everything that came afterwards. I talk and talk and talk, about getting the job and lying to everyone, how good it felt when I started to succeed there, and how upset I was to learn I won't be able to stay.

Through it all Landon remains silent. I can see her nodding along, and at some points she holds my hand to give me the courage to keep speaking, but she never once says anything. I tell her about Taylor and his stupid cat and how many desserts he has eaten on my behalf. I tell her about the kiss, and that I thought he might be one of my best friends. When I tell her about our conversation in the parking lot and how badly I've hurt him, I find out that as impossible as it seems, I still have tears in me after all.

"What am I supposed to do now?" I ask miserably.

She takes a big breath and looks right at me.

"First, you're going to get some sleep. Tomorrow we're going to make some coffee, eat that rabbit food you call cereal, and then we're going to get a manicure."

I wince in reaction to her ridiculous plan. I'm talking about the destruction of my personal and professional life, and she's talking about our nails. Landon is already standing up and pulling me along with her.

"Roll your eyes all you want to, but fresh nails make everything better." She has the audacity to wink at me. "You'll see."

———

A fresh manicure doesn't make everything better, but it helps.

Or really, I guess talking to Landon had helped. I can't fix everything overnight, but I can at least try to, well, try.

The first step towards anything is to figure out what I want to do now. I will be done working at Dolci in a couple of weeks, and I have to decide where I go from there. As pointless as it seems, since she is rarely lucid enough for intelligent conversation, I need to talk to Avis about it.

I find her in Dolci's small office, eating a Handi-Snack.

"I don't like the breadstick kind," she says as soon as I walk in. "Using the little red thing to dig out the cheese is half the fun."

She maneuvers the plastic stick in her hand to smear gelatinous orange "cheese" onto a cracker, which she then pops into her mouth. She raises her eyebrows at me expectantly.

That twitch of her brow makes her seem more perceptive right now than she's been in the entire time I've known her.

I take the chair opposite her.

"I thought I'd ask you for some advice," I tell her.

She lifts another cracker from her little box and starts to cover it with cheese like the last one.

If Gollum were a little old French woman with a snack pack . . .

"About what you should do next," she finally supplies.

I nearly fall out of my chair. Apparently she is cognizant enough to recognize the world outside of the one-foot radius surrounding her crackers.

"Yes," I answer, "about what I should do next. I was hoping you might offer some advice."

Or a letter of reference.

"Well, you could go anywhere," she says with a shrug. "Certainly any of the chefs from last week would be interested."

I sit a little straighter in my chair. I don't especially love the idea of being a stage, but the chefs from last week are preeminent. Any one of them would be incredible to learn from. I never considered trying to get a job with one of them, because I had spent so little time with Avis.

"You think they might need a stage?" I ask eagerly.

Avis's mouth twists as if she's bitten into something distasteful.

"What are you talking about?" she asks.

Oh damn, maybe I am losing her attention.

"About me being a stage for one of the chefs." I try to remind her of our conversation. "You said they might consider me."

"As a stage?" she asks slowly.

Maybe it is coming back to her.

"Yes, I didn't go to culinary school, remember?" I try to get the words out quickly, before I lose her attention again. "I've only been working with you for a little while, and I know that's not enough to list on a résumé, but I thought maybe if you put in a call—"

"Mary, mother of pearl," she says in wonder. "You really don't know, do you?"

I sigh. Now will come some crazy speech about storks or crackers, and then she'll ask me for a Slurpee. It isn't her fault she is a little off, though, and I had been hired to manage her.

"Don't know what?" I ask to placate her.

"You actually believe you're making *my* recipes," she says, peering closer at me.

Crap! Is this where she tells me her ideas come from lepre-chauns or the aliens she met at the eighth level of scientology?

"They're not my recipes, Stork." She points her little red stick at me.

I smile at her as kindly as I can; I have no idea where this is going.

"OK, so whose recipes are they, Avis?"

She reaches back and puts the little stick into her bun, along-side a mechanical pencil. She peers at me through her giant glasses.

"Oh, Stork," she says with a chuckle. "They're yours."

"What?" I ask stupidly.

It is almost as crazy a statement as the leprechauns would have been.

"What?" I say again.

Avis sits back, folds her bony arms across her chest, and smiles like the Cheshire cat.

"The first time, with the galette? I was messing with you."

"What?" seems to be the only thing I can get out.

"I was messing with you. I wrote a bunch of scribbles down. Thought you'd scramble around and try to figure them out. Thought it'd be fun to watch." She smiles. "But then you came back with a really damn good galette. I was intrigued. I wanted to see if you could do it again. And you did."

I am shaking my head in denial.

"No," I tell her. "I recognized ingredients. I could always see the start of a recipe."

Avis is shaking her own head before I finish speaking.

"I put down one thing, maybe two at the most—enough so that you'd think the rest of it must be real. There was no recipe there, Stork. Those came from your head."

"I'm not a pastry chef like you. I don't know how to create recipes at this level."

"Sorry," she says, not really sounding sorry at all, "those scraps gave you a safety net. I've never provided you with a single new recipe in the entire time that you've been here."

My mind whirls at the implications of what she is saying. *If I really have been creating the recipes the whole time, that meant that last week I served—*

"Marcus Balmain and his guests—"

"Ate a dessert sampler conceptualized, designed, plated, and presented entirely by you," she says, sounding utterly pleased with herself.

"What if I had failed?" I ask weakly.

"*C'est impossible,*" she says, dismissing the notion in French.

Words are utterly lost to me; I can't think of a single response.

"I have some advice, Stork," she says, folding her hands primly in front of her.

I nod, in a total daze.

"I wasn't exaggerating when I said those chefs would hire you. In fact, I'd be willing to wager Marcus would take you in a second himself if he wasn't locked into a contract with me for the next however many years. Whether you recognize it or not, you're in a rare position in your life."

Her words are so eerily similar to what Landon told me this morning that I lean in closer.

"Right now you get to decide what's next. Being the executive pastry chef in a five-star restaurant might be what you've always dreamed of; in fact it might be what's perfect for you. It's what I dreamed of and what I've enjoyed for the majority of my life. A dedicated team of artists, the space to be creative, the quiet to do it without having to deal with the public. The odd hours mean that you can interact with the rest of the world as much or as little as you'd like to." She sighs deeply and points to herself. "But that's what this looks like, OK? I'm sixty-two and I've never been married. I don't have children; I don't even have a cat. I don't regret my life or the choices I've made, because that's a waste of time. I just wish I'd gone in with my eyes open. You're in a rare position to decide what you want to do next." She picks up her remaining crackers and stands up to leave. "That's all I wanted to say."

———

Through the rest of the shift, my mind starts to pick up speed. I think back over every moment in the kitchen and all my interactions with Avis. When I realize the recipes she gave me are saved in the front of the binder with all the others, I go over each one in detail. Looking through them with new information, I am able to recognize the truth in what she said. They were all scribbles. Taylor had once called the writing gibberish, and he'd been absolutely right. It was like Dumbo and the magic feather.

I laugh at the absolute absurdity of it all.

I can't wait to tell him this news! I can't wait to—

But that isn't an option now, is it?

I think about it throughout the rest of the workday and as I walk to my car that night. Maybe Landon is right; maybe if I just try to . . . I don't know, but I have to do something! I don't know what to say or how to apologize, but I can't let another day, or even another hour, pass without telling him how sorry I am for what I said. I run the rest of the way to my car.

Taylor is sitting on the hood.

He stands up and walks over to me without a word.

I open my mouth, but he holds up a hand to silence me.

"I really thought about not ever speaking to you again." He looks down into my eyes. "Can you understand that?"

I nod. He shoves both his hands into his pockets.

"But last night I kept thinking about what I said. I told you I was your friend, and I told you I wasn't going anywhere."

He looks away, out at the other cars, and continues speaking.

"I'm so sorry that you were hurt. I'm sorry that you've *been* hurting, and that you haven't told anyone about it. I understand why you lashed out at me. There was a time I would have done the same thing." He looks back at me. "I don't want to lose you as a friend."

"I don't deserve your friendship," I tell him, because it is true. "Not after everything I said. But I'm so sorry, Taylor. You have to know how sorry I am for the things I said."

A friend shouldn't ever use your pain against you. Even when I was so vicious to him, Taylor never did that to me.

"Do you know much about grace?" he asks.

"Who's Grace?" I ask, totally confused now.

"Not who, *what*. My mama always said that grace was offering someone the opposite of what they deserve. Life's just full of opportunities for that."

"But—"

"You said you were sorry, Jennings," he tells me sincerely.

My shoulders slump as I sigh.

"It doesn't seem like enough," I tell him.

He looks away and then back at me with a slight grin on his face.

"What if you paid me for it?"

I smile back at him.

"Don't be stupid," I say, pushing at his shoulder playfully.

All of a sudden I am in his arms. I let my bag drop from my fingers and wrap my arms around his waist. I am so thankful to be there that I feel light-headed.

"I want you to pay me, like I said," he whispers into my hair.

"OK," I mumble to play along. "What do you want?"

"I want your bracelet."

I push back to look up into his face in confusion. His eyes are fierce, determined.

"I want the bracelet," he says again. "I want you to take it off and give it to me. I don't want you to wear it anymore."

I continue to stare at him, totally mute.

"Maybe it's wrong and maybe it's not my place, but I hate that you have it. You haven't forgiven yourself for a mistake you made *six years* ago. Whether you admit it or not, you wear it to hurt yourself. I can't be friends with you and watch you punish yourself anymore. I won't do it." He holds out his hand. "Please give it to me."

I look down at my wrist, utterly shocked to find my fingers already messing with the clasp. I drop it into his outstretched hand, and we both stare down at it without speaking. Without warning his fingers close around the chain, and he steps back from me and throws it, seemingly as hard as he can, into the darkness of the surrounding garage. I don't have time to think about its absence, because he is hugging me again.

I don't know how long we stand there, but it is long enough that I am aware of every single place where his body brushes against mine. I can't help but think about that night on his couch, and my lips tingle at the memory.

He pulls back to look at me, and I am surprised to see him looking playful and relaxed. Clearly he isn't concerned with thoughts of kissing or anything else like that.

"Jennings, I realized I probably pushed you too hard. But I understand now why you're not . . ." He rubs a hand along his jaw. "Why you're not ready to date."

I start to protest, but he holds up his hand.

"I don't want this to be weird, OK? I really care about you, and I don't want to lose you as a friend. We'll just be that, OK? You don't have to worry about any, uh . . . advances from me."

"I won't?" It comes out sort of strangled.

"No," he says, dropping his hands. "It'll be better this way."

He is right; of course he is right. I am a mess, and I've done nothing but emotionally vomit all over him since the moment we met.

He will be my friend, and I should be—*am*—so grateful for that.

I nod.

"It's better this way," I agree.

Chapter Eighteen

"And then you add nutmeg, right?" Joey asks as she stares down into the bowl beside me.

"Exactly," I answer. "But not until the very last step."

It feels a little weird at first to be teaching her the recipes we've added to the menu in the time she's been gone. But after a few days it is just par for the course. It is my last day at Dolci, and the entire team threw me a little party in the kitchen this morning to celebrate. Now I just have to finish out this recipe with Joey and update some paperwork, and my work in this kitchen will be done.

I am not any closer to knowing what my next step will be, but I have a little money saved up, at least enough to survive for a couple of months until I figure it out. I'll get to that whole "what the hell am I gonna do with my life" thing later. First I need to show Joey how to make this crème fraîche.

"Yo, Chef," Ram calls from across the room, "it's for you!"

There is an awkward moment when we both turn, and then I try to laugh it off nervously. Joey waves to him that she'll be right over and then turns to me with a smile.

"It's probably the nanny calling again. I'll just check to make sure everything is OK."

I nod and she hurries away.

She comes back a few minutes later with an odd smile on her face.

"It's actually for you," she tells me.

"The phone?" I ask, confused.

Nobody calls me here. In fact, very few people know I am here at all, and those who do would have just called my cell.

"No." She smiles again. "There's a customer who wants to give their regards to the chef. They loved the dessert sampler."

"But that's—" I try.

"That's all you, girl, and you know it. Now get up there. They're waiting at the front."

I run my hands down the front of my chef coat, feeling more awkward than I have in years. I watch my shoes as they eat up the distance between the back and the front of the house. Why does this make me so nervous? So some customer wants to tell me they liked my dish; it isn't a big deal. I will just smile and say thank you, and head back to where I came from.

I look up just as I come through the swinging door. I can see Haven, one of our servers, is at the bar talking to a customer. Since it is an odd time of day, the lobby is fairly empty, so I assume the person with Haven must be who I was meant to find. Just as I get close enough to ask, the server moves out of the way, and I look into my mother's face.

"Kenzie." She gives me a tight smile. "Perhaps we should talk."

When I nod in agreement she spins on her heel and walks away. She is all polish and shine in a typical weekday outfit of silk and cashmere and whatever other textiles DVF has put in her line this season.

I follow her back to a table in the corner, which has empty plates and the remainder of an espresso with my mother's lipstick stamped on the side. I sit down quickly, feeling very much like a five-year-old who is about to be scolded. I play with the untouched place setting in front of me, unsure what else to do with my hands.

"Liam told you," I manage to get out.

She raises her eyebrows nearly to her hairline.

"Liam," she says his name carefully, "said to tell you that you had a deal. Since I have called you exactly seventeen times over the last eleven days and you couldn't be troubled to answer the phone *even once*"—she glares at me—"you forfeit your right to secrecy."

I don't even know where to begin.

Apparently my mother does, because she keeps going.

"Am I so horrible? Am I really so meddling and terrible that you can't share such a big part of your life with me?"

She reaches into her purse for a tissue, which makes me feel like the very lowest kind of scum.

"Mom, that's not it at all—" I try to explain.

"You lied. *To my face.*"

For a moment I don't understand her meaning, which is to say, I don't know *which* lie she is talking about.

So actually I was wrong before; *now* I feel like the very lowest kind of scum.

"How many times have I asked you about the bar? How many stories have you made up to keep this from me?" She swings her hand around to encompass Dolci's empty seating area.

"I was still at the hotel," I say weakly. "I didn't lie about that."

"That's just semantics," she says fiercely.

My shoulders slump in defeat.

"You're right. I'm sorry."

She opens her mouth, I'm sure to yell some more, but she closes it again quickly and looks away from me. Twenty-five years of advice and lectures, and for maybe the first time ever, my mother doesn't know what to say to me. The thought makes me uncomfortable.

The urge to argue or to make an excuse, or even to leave, is strong. Then I think of Landon and how she told me I was immature. She is right; I need to try to stop acting like a child, and the first step, the *biggest* step, is to stop lying. I have to stop lying to my friends and my family, but most importantly, I have to stop lying to myself.

"I wanted to tell you," I say quietly.

She looks back my way.

"Did you?" she asks.

It isn't a question; it is an accusation.

I start to reach for the bracelet, an old bad habit, and then stop myself when I realize it isn't there anymore.

"Not all of it, no," I answer honestly. "Everything that happened . . . that happened in DC and afterwards . . . I didn't want to tell you about that."

She opens her mouth to argue, but I cut her off gently.

"I was ashamed and embarrassed," I explain.

"But you know how much we love you; you *know*," she says emphatically.

I nod.

"I do know. I also knew how much you expected of me, how high the standard was. That's why I was so afraid of letting you down."

Her lower lip starts to tremble, and when she does finally speak, the only thing that comes out is a broken, "Oh, Mackenzie."

I don't want to make any more of a scene. I try to steer us back to an easier topic.

"But about this." I point at the kitchen to our right. "This, I wanted to tell you about *so* much."

"So why didn't you?" she asks, her voice sounding stronger again.

"Because you were worried enough after everything that had happened in December, and I knew you'd freak out about my diet and the hours and—"

"I wouldn't—"

I raise my eyebrows.

"Oh fine," she says primly. "Yes, I probably would have. But we could have worked together; we could have found some way for you to—"

"Mom, I love you so much, and I am so thankful, and . . ." I search for a better word, and choose one of Landon's favorites. ". . . and blessed to be your daughter. But I am twenty-five years old. My life is not something that we work on together anymore. I know you care about me, and I know that you worry, but I'm not a little girl. I have to be able to make my own decisions and even my own mistakes. Fighting about them with me is only going to alienate me more."

She looks ready to argue the point. I reach out for her hand and tell her as gently as I can, "You can continue to be a big part of my life, but that means you have to accept me as I am. You have to stop trying to manage me."

"I'm your mother. Of course I'm going to offer you advice," she says, sounding a little exasperated.

I refuse to rise to her level, because that will only lead us into an argument we've had a hundred times already.

"Of course you're going to offer advice," I agree, "but there's a difference between offering advice on big things and judging everything from what I wear to what I eat."

She looks distraught. "Is that what it feels like to you?" she asks. "That I'm *judging* you?"

I hate how hurt she sounds, but I need to be honest.

"Sometimes, yeah."

"Oh, sweetheart, I never meant it that way. I thought I was being helpful or looking out for you. Sometimes you forget to eat right or you . . ." Understanding dawns on her face. "Oh good grief. I'm doing it again!"

Her eyes fill with tears, but her grin is self-deprecating.

"I think I've always been more protective of you," she says. "You were my first baby, my first real responsibility, and I wanted so badly to do a good job. When you were diagnosed I was devastated. I know it could have been so much worse than it is, but I hated that you had something wrong and I couldn't fix it. I think I thought if I could just keep a close enough eye on you, I could keep you from being hurt or getting sick."

"That's impossible," I tell her gently.

"I know that, Mackenzie. On a rational level I do know that, but I just get . . . carried away sometimes."

I snort in response to the understatement.

"I'm going to work on it. I'll get better, I swear," she promises sincerely.

"OK." I smile at her.

I know she won't be able to flip a switch and turn into a different person, but she will try.

"So if I'm allowed to advise you on the *big* things, then I have some thoughts," she says, sounding businesslike.

I can't help laughing. She has tried for exactly forty-seven seconds.

"Kenzie," she chides me, "you said I could give you advice on the big stuff."

"OK, you're right." I fight the urge to laugh again. "Go ahead."

"It's only two things," she says, sounding a little hurt.

I smile at her with genuine love.

"OK, Mom. Go ahead."

"It's OK to ask for help," she says succinctly.

"I know, Mom. I—"

"You don't know. I'm not sure why you don't understand that, but I'm positive that you don't. So I am going to say it to you over and over in a thousand different ways if I have to. It's OK to ask for help. We love you. Your friends love you. You are the most self-sufficient person I know, and I'm so proud of the independent woman you've become. But you can't be so independent that you run yourself ragged trying to prove you can do it on your own. No one will think less of you. Leaning on another person and allowing yourself to be vulnerable sometimes is its own kind of strength."

I think of her relationship with my dad, and I can remember so many examples of them leaning on each other over the years. Times when they were sick or overworked or stressed out, times when one of them shouldered more of the burden for a while. It never made them weaker; if anything, that kind of trust is what makes their relationship so strong.

"OK," I sigh. "I'll try to ask for help when I need it."

Her face splits with a grin, and I can feel her pride in me from across the table. She reaches into her purse for a second tissue— the first one has been mangled to death—and a mirror and starts dabbing at her eyes.

"What's the other thing?" I ask as she runs a finger under the line of her mascara.

"Hmm?"

"You said there were two pieces of advice. I'm wondering what the other one is."

"Oh." She puts both hands on the table. "It wasn't advice; it was just a comment. This," she says, tapping an empty plate that had once held the dessert sampler, "was incredible. I'm so happy to see you find your place. This is exactly where you should be."

I almost laugh at the irony.

I did promise I would be more honest . . .

"Well, Mom, about that . . ."

I explain everything about the job. From the very first interaction with Avis to creating the recipes with Taylor as a taste-tester and all the way up to today. When I am finished she blinks several times before finding her voice.

"Today is your last day?" she asks, aghast.

"Yep," I answer.

She asks me her favorite question: "What are you going to do now?"

In the past I would have evaded answering, but today I give it to her straight.

"Honestly? I have no idea."

To her credit, she doesn't freak out; she just looks at me as if I am a particularly interesting puzzle. Finally she asks, "If I asked you something, do you think you could be totally honest with me?"

Jeez, where is this going?

I nod.

"I know it's not in your nature to bare your soul, but just this once, don't second-guess it or overthink it. Just answer me honestly, OK?" she requests calmly.

"OK," I answer, more nervous by the second.

"What would you do if you knew you couldn't fail?"

My brows draw together in confusion. She slams her hand down on the table, startling me.

"Quick! Tell me the first thing that popped into your mind. Don't think about it!"

"I'd open the bakery," I blurt out.

She smiles and sits back in her chair.

I don't have to tell her *which* bakery, because this was a dream from before, something I'd talked about with her too many times to count. Apparently the dream is still alive, though I hadn't admitted it to myself, let alone to another person, in a really long time. When she doesn't say anything in response, just continues to look at me with that smile on her face, I make myself ask the question I really want to know.

"Do you think it's a bad idea?"

"I think," she says gently, "that this is one of those times you should ask for help."

———

I spend the next two weeks working on a business plan.

When I think about what I am doing, I start to freak out. More than once I almost talk myself out of it, because seriously, who do I think I am to start a business? But then there are Landon and Miko. They had the guts to do it, and while they aren't rolling in money, they are supporting themselves by running a business they love, and that business is growing and booking new clients all the time. If they can do it, then I can too, right?

I look up spreadsheets and figures, interest rates and rent per square foot. I learn the difference between storefronts and ware-houses, and which can best accommodate industrial kitchens. I want to throw up when I find out how hard it will be to deal with the health department, but I give myself a mental slap and keep on working.

For once, instead of being the last to know, my mother is the only one to know. She encourages me to tell my friends or even just my siblings, but I am not ready to do that yet. It feels like too much exposure. Since she has insider knowledge, I fully expect my mom to try to pop by with high-protein snacks or fight me to come to dinner as she used to during finals, but true to her word, she doesn't meddle even once. I get at least one text a day tell-ing me how proud she is and the occasional email with a motiva-tional graphic she found on Pinterest, but beyond that she is silent. Landon has been swamped working on some big event, so if she's noticed that I haven't left the apartment and have been constantly hunched over my laptop in yesterday's pajamas, at least she doesn't say anything.

After two weeks of work I have created—I think—a really intelligent-sounding plan. It is forty-two pages, single-spaced, outlining why my idea is a good investment. Sure, the economy isn't totally steady. Sure, three cupcake chains have just gone belly-up in the last six months. But I am not going to think about that. If I do, I will talk myself out of this whole idea. Instead, I print out my business plan and read over it for the seventeenth time. And then I am ready to throw it in the trash!

It is terrible. Nobody is going to want to read this. *I don't even want to read it!* It is dry and boring, and I am trying to open a bakery, not a mortuary.

I fall down onto the sofa with the stack of boring, stupid paperwork clutched in my hand. I am still fighting the urge to fling it across the room when Landon and Miko come in, sipping the giant glass bottles of juice that everyone is so obsessed with now. Landon sets one down on the coffee table in front of me.

"We got you one too." She taps the cap with her finger. "It's kale, lemon, ginger, and a bunch of other stuff. It's not as terrible as it sounds."

"Thanks," I mumble.

"What's that?" Miko says, landing beside me on the couch like an overeager puppy.

She is pointing at the paperwork I have in a death grip.

"It's . . ." I search for the words and can't come up with any. "It's this," I say, dropping it in Miko's lap.

She picks it up and starts to read it without comment. After a minute Landon leans over and starts to look too. I can feel their eyes look up at me occasionally, but I don't look back. I study the Royal Navy polish on my nails. Hey, bully for me! I've managed another new color in my repertoire. Maybe I could be a nail tech. I'm pretty sure the lady who does mine makes really good money in tips.

"You want to open a bakery?" Landon squeals.

They are both practically bouncing on the sofa cushions in excitement.

"Um, yeah, I guess."

"This is so rad," Miko says, jumping up to grab her bag. "You need our help, though."

My instinct is to make a snide comment and tell them how I don't need their help for anything. But that isn't true.

I can hear my mother's voice whispering in my head. She'd probably turn purple if she could see her sage wisdom playing out right now.

"How do you think you can help?" I ask.

"Well, for starters"—Miko pulls her laptop out of her bag—"that proposal is about as exciting as a pamphlet for psoriasis."

"Yeah, but at least with a medical packet there would be photos," Landon says with a wink.

"Look," I say, jumping up to reach for the paperwork, "I didn't ask—"

Landon grabs the papers first and promptly hands them off to Miko before I can steal them back.

"Calm down, killer." Miko starts to look through my work again. "I didn't say this wasn't well done—"

"Yeah, just boring and—" I say in exasperation.

"Max," Miko says sternly, "do you want to know what our business plan looks like?"

Landon starts laughing in reaction to the question. Whatever the joke is, I don't get it.

"We don't have one," Landon says in response to the scowl on my face. "We tried to write one out, but it was just so long and boring. And we couldn't really figure it out, so we just stopped."

I am too stunned to respond.

"This," Miko says, holding up my papers in her hand, "is impressive. It takes hours and hours of research and the brain capacity to lay it all out correctly. You did a market analysis of baked goods along the western seaboard, for freak's sake!"

I sniff primly. "I thought it would be important for potential investors to have that information."

"It is." Landon nods enthusiastically. "It totally is."

"But at the end of the day, you're not selling baked goods," Miko tells me seriously.

I open my mouth to argue.

"You're selling the *experience* of eating baked goods. Do you understand the distinction?"

I think of the hotel I have worked in for the last several years. From the lobby with its mismatched but congruous decor to the idea that you go to three different restaurants in order to have one complete meal. That is an experience. I think of Brody's club or my family's other restaurants and hotels, each one of them offering something far beyond the items on the menu. They evoke certain feelings in their guests, from playful and casual to luxurious and elegant. Miko is right; the experience is just as important as the food itself.

"I understand," I tell them.

"Then the first thing we need to do is polish this up," Miko says as she drops the bundle of paperwork back on the table. "Everything you present should look and feel the same as the experience you're trying to sell."

"I don't know how to do that." I look at them both desperately.

"Well, lucky for you, you're friends with a designer and someone who produces experiential events for a living," Landon says with a wink.

Together they start going through the report page by page, each making notations in the margins with Sharpies in different colors. I cringe when they rip out a section that took me two days of research to put together, but I keep my mouth shut. I do feel weird sitting there watching them work on my proposal without me.

"What should I do?" I finally ask.

"You"—Landon looks up at me for a second—"should figure out what you're serving to whoever you're pitching this to."

"I can't bring food into a formal business meeting. I'll seem like an amateur!" I bark at her.

Both of them raise their eyes to me, looking amused.

"Dude, you *are* an amateur," Miko says.

"And the best trick you have up your sleeve is the food you can create. Presenting one amazing dessert needs to be the opening volley," Landon adds.

"And then what?" I ask.

"Then"—Landon looks at Miko and back at me—"you present this killer presentation we're putting together for you, and they find you professional and trustworthy, and offer you buckets of money to build your dream."

Glinda the Good Witch couldn't have given that speech with any more optimism than Landon just did.

I snort in response.

"You think I can sell *professional*?" I point to my Betty White T-shirt, which has at least three stains of unknown origin gracing the front.

They look at each other and then back at me.

Landon says, "Maybe, uh, two or three desserts as your opening volley?"

Chapter Nineteen

A week later I am back in Taylor's kitchen working on a cookie recipe I've dreamed up. I have no excuse to be using his space, since Landon knows about my meeting and would be happy to taste-test for me. But I've told myself that it's good luck to create recipes here and that Taylor has already proven himself great at offering feedback. The truth is, though, that I miss him, and this is the best excuse I could think of to hang out with him again.

I am adding ingredients to the mixer when his hand snakes out and snatches some of the crumble topping I've already made and set to the side. I pull on my earbud, the sound of Paloma Faith falling out with it, and look over at him in question.

"It sort of reminds me of that toffee thing you made," he says, grabbing some more.

"It's the nutmeg and cinnamon—they were in that dish too," I tell him with a smile.

He pops another bite into his mouth and casually leans back against the counter. I wish I could feel so easy around him, but now I feel awkward. It is uncomfortable between us. Actually, Taylor doesn't seem to feel any differently than he ever did. He is affable and laid back, totally friendly. It is exactly what we agreed on, and I wish I could feel that way too. Unfortunately I keep remembering that kiss, which makes me think of everything that came after it.

It feels as if we've gone through too much to go back to being so casual now. But what is the alternative? Even if I could figure out how to have a normal relationship, he made it clear that he just wants to be friends. I am not about to press the point either; I don't want to think of a scenario where Taylor and I don't hang out anymore. I will just keep hanging out with him until I don't accidentally keep looking at his mouth. I'll see him often enough that I lose the desire to trace the words on his arm with my fingers.

"—tomorrow?" Taylor's question catches me off guard.

Crap, he's been saying something. I have no idea what it was.

"Sorry, what?" I shut off the mixer as if the sound is what was distracting me.

"Tomorrow. Are you nervous?"

I turn to look at him and lean one hip against the cabinets.

"Yes, but not for the reasons you think," I tell him.

He gives me a half smile. "Oh, I bet what I think is probably pretty close to your reasons."

I shrug. He is right; he probably knows exactly what is making me so nervous. There is no reason not to speak to him about it either; he's always been a good sounding board, and maybe if I talk through it, I can calm myself down a little.

"Well, I—"

At that moment his phone rings and cuts off my words mid-sentence. I realize, in that moment, that I have never heard his phone ring. Had he always kept it on silent before?

"Hey, sweetheart, is everything OK?" he says into the phone.

My heart lurches and my stomach rebels. It takes everything I have to keep the retching sound from leaving my throat.

Taylor holds up a finger to me and mouths that he'll be right back. I turn back to my recipe, my hands clutching the edge of the counter for support.

Of course he would date other people; we are just friends now, right? I have no claim on him anymore. In fact, I have never really had a claim on him. Something deep inside me starts to bubble and churn, and I want to scream. I want to rail at him and break his phone into pieces. I want to curl up in the corner and cry for days. But I force myself to take a breath, and then another.

If I can't deal with Taylor dating other women, I won't be able to stay friends with him. Some sick part of me would rather be hurt watching him move on than not be able to have him in my life at all. I've promised myself I am going to mature and stop acting like a child, and this is an excellent opportunity to learn to do that. So when he walks back into the kitchen ten minutes later, I force myself to smile and ask the kind of question one friend asks another.

"Did you finish that big conference table you were working on?"

He takes the lure as I knew he would. Taylor loves to talk about a piece of furniture; he can lose half an hour at a stretch just describing the finish he wants to use on a particular piece. I let the cadence of the words lilt through the air between us and melt some of the tension in my shoulders.

He is my friend, and I won't trade that away even if it takes me a little while to convince my heart that this is better for both of us. I don't even know if I am capable of a real relationship, and Taylor is one of the best people I know. He deserves someone who doesn't come with a cartload of emotional baggage. Why would anyone want someone this messed up when there are so many better options out there? When it comes to Taylor, I don't know many things for sure, but I know that whatever girl was on the other end of the phone can't be as messed up as I am. I can't blame him for his choice.

———

I hear the car doors closing out front, which means the people I most need to impress in the world have just arrived. Five different desserts sit on the island in front of me, along with beautifully bound copies of the gorgeous presentation Miko and Landon helped me with. Everything looks as good as I could possibly make it. There is nothing else I can do, except maybe throw up, which sounds like a great idea right about now! I look across the kitchen to my helper.

"I think I might be sick," I tell her nervously.

My mom grins back at me. "They're going to love it."

She walks over and gives me a hug just as my dad calls from somewhere in the house.

"Honey, where are you?"

"We're in the kitchen!" she calls back, a smile in her voice.

My eyes dart around the kitchen. There are still several excellent options for escape. The back door, for one, or I could slip out through the dining room.

"Too late now, Kenzie," my mom says just as my dad and my brothers come into the kitchen in search of food. We knew they would be hungry; they always come back from golf looking for snacks. We've planned it this way on purpose.

"What's all this?" my dad asks happily.

Liam walks towards the center island like a moth to a flame.

"Are those cheesecake brownies?" he asks.

I am struck mute by my nerves. My mom has to nudge me, twice.

Finally I find my voice.

"I—" I clear my throat. "Can I talk to you guys for a minute?"

All three of them look at me now, maybe alerted by something in my voice. Liam looks down at the desserts, then at the pile of paperwork, then back at me. He always sees more than anybody else.

I can see him fighting a smile, but it isn't teasing or patronizing; it is pride that turns his lips up at the corners. It makes me feel embarrassed, but it also gives me the courage I need.

"Why don't you boys sit at the table, and I'll get you some drinks?" My mother jumps in to play hostess, giving me the time I need to get my thoughts straight. "Kenzie made some really incredible treats for you."

The three of them agree and all ask for coffee. It is stupid, maybe, but I am inordinately happy they've picked something that will pair so well with dessert. I roll my eyes at my idiotic thoughts, as if the proper palate cleanser is all that stands between me and the crap-load of money necessary to pull this off.

Oh well, better get it over with.

Liam, Brody, and my dad all sit down at the table.

Actually, for today's purposes it might be better to think of them in their professional roles, the acting executive board members of Barker-Ash, one of the biggest players in the hospitality industry in the nation. The combined wealth of the three of them could easily fund this dream of mine. My fear isn't that they won't be willing; my fear is that they'll be willing out of obligation or love, and not because they think I have the talent necessary to pull it off.

I bring over the desserts one by one while they all look at me with bemused expressions. I grab the presentation packets off the counter, but when I walk back over to my family, I can't quite make myself put them down on the table. I am not even sure how to begin. What can I say without sounding even more ridiculous than I already do? I try to imagine either of my brothers in my place now, because I know they've pitched business ideas plenty of times as part of their job. But they are put together in a way I just don't know how to be.

Then I think of Landon and how she would handle the situation. Bright, cheerful, effervescent Landon. She would be honest and self-effacing, and people would find it endearing. Her personality is one of the reasons she's been able to snag clients so quickly. The three of them stare back at me expectantly, and Liam raises his eyebrows nearly to his hairline, prompting me into motion.

Well, here goes nothing . . .

"I don't know what to do now," I blurt out.

"Forks," Brody says, fighting a smile. "Forks would be a great place to start."

I almost slap my forehead at my own oversight, but my mom has already appeared with a handful of silverware. I hand a fork to each of them and begin my opening volley. Food is the one thing I can speak about intelligently in this moment. I point at the first plate.

"These are sour-cream coffee-cake cookies with a brown-sugar crumble and a drizzle of maple glaze. Next is a Milky Way cheese-cake brownie topped with sea salt," I tell them.

My brothers both reach for the brownies without waiting for me to finish. I smile and keep on going.

"This is a peach-cobbler cupcake with a bourbon cream-cheese icing. And an individual bananas foster pudding parfait with coconut whipped cream topped with a caramelized banana. And last is a spiced cake donut topped with maple icing and candied bacon."

Daddy has already started in on the cupcake and looks totally blissed out. When he finds his voice again, he asks, "You made all of this?"

"I did." I set a packet down in front of each of them.

Daddy is grabbing for a donut when he reads the cover and looks up at me with a smile.

"Of course, Max," he says. "You don't even have to ask. You know I'd love to help you. Just tell me how much you need."

My smile is a little strained, because it is exactly what I knew he would say. I sit down to face the three of them.

"Thank you so much for the offer, but I don't want you to give me money. I'm looking for a loan."

Brody and Liam have both begun looking through the proposal, and Liam glances up at me.

"With what collateral?" he asks, sounding, I think, exactly like he would in a boardroom.

"An equity stake in the company," I tell them.

"A silent partner?" Brody asks, because he more than anyone has constantly fought me on my need to do everything alone.

"No," I tell them. "I don't know how to start a company. I can run a kitchen, and I think my recipes are unique and, beyond that, delicious enough that I could sell them if I had the opportunity. But other than that, I'm running blind." I take a breath. "I need help, guidance far beyond the capital. I'm looking for partners, not a handout."

"Fifty-fifty?" Liam asks, raising an eyebrow.

"Thirty percent," I tell them deliberately, "and I'd like an option clause written in that I can buy you out if I can return your initial investment plus interest within five years."

Liam and Brody both laugh.

"Why ask all three of us when one would suffice?" Liam asks.

"I guess I thought it would be safer for you all if you were able to spread out the risk," I tell them honestly. "I'm terrified of failing and losing all your money."

"First of all," my father says, grabbing for a parfait, "this family doesn't fail at anything. Secondly"—he points his spoon at me meaningfully—"forty percent is the lowest I'll agree to. Even nepotism can't allow for a margin that skewed against us."

I straighten my spine. I need his help, but this man didn't raise a fool.

"Thirty-five," I say firmly.

A smile splits his face in half.

"Good girl," he says proudly. "We're in."

I look around at them in shock as they continue to plow their way through the desserts.

"But you didn't even get all the way through the proposal," I say nervously. "You didn't even discuss it with each other first. I—"

"Mack," Liam says gently, "you could pitch us the idea for a business trading old people cash for their gold fillings. We'd support you no matter what."

"But you need to be sure." I point at the report I worked so hard on. "Make sure it's a good idea before you decide. I don't want to mess up. I don't want to let you down," I say a little desperately.

My father reaches across the table for my hand and squeezes it so that I look into his eyes.

"You have *never* let us down," he says fiercely. "That's not possible, no matter what. OK?"

We aren't just talking about business anymore. I blink back stupid tears.

"OK," I whisper back.

"I like the name," Brody says, grabbing a cookie and swiftly changing the topic and the mood in the room. "I'm surprised you'd pick something so . . . cute. Where did you come up with it?"

My mother materializes again like a genie, though it is a miracle she's been able to hold herself back this long. She sits down in the chair next to my dad and starts to unfold an old piece of paper.

"She came up with that name when she was a little girl," she tells everyone, smoothing the paper out on the table for us to see. "It couldn't be called anything *but* this."

In the center of the page is a drawing my six-year-old self had painstakingly worked on so it looked *just right*. A yellow-haired crayon drawing of me is in the middle of the page holding a tray of cookies. Behind her is a cheerful-looking building with a big sign on the front that reads "The Flour Shop."

"Imagine that," Liam says with mock surprise. "She was face-tious even then."

"Or wise beyond her years," my mom says, playfully throwing a napkin at him.

"Or well versed in double entendre." I jump into the banter.

"Or lacking an ability to color well," Brody adds in.

"I was a little girl," I tell them with mock indignation.

"She's missing half her facial features!" he shoots back.

"Noses are really hard to draw!" I explain to him through my laughter.

"Clearly," Liam says, leaning over to inspect my drawing in closer detail.

I pick up another napkin and throw it somewhere in their vicinity.

"You guys are the worst," I tell them. The effect is lost, though, because I can't stop smiling.

———

"So they're going to help you?" Taylor says as we jog around the last bend at the end of our run.

"They are." I smile at him through my Wayfarers. "Did you think they might not?"

Taylor dodges a little boy who zips by us on a razor scooter, and his dad calls a hurried apology to us as he races after him.

"Not for a minute," he answers. "Your family is amazing. I knew they'd be happy to help."

"Do you think it's, I don't know, cheating? To use their resources, I mean?"

"I think"—he increases his speed a little as we get closer to our cars—"it would be idiotic not to. Jennings, people would kill for the kind of connections you have. It would be bad business *not* to look for every advantage you have when starting a new company. You are supremely talented at what you do, and knowing you, you'll probably work twice as hard to make sure their investment pays off. That's all any investor can hope for."

I nod along with his words. It isn't anything I don't know already; I just want, or maybe need, to hear it from him.

When we get back to our cars, we sit down in the shade of a nearby tree to stretch. Asphalt isn't the best surface to stretch out on, but after a six-mile run, I care more about not getting a cramp later than I do about whether the ground is clean or comfy. Taylor pushes up into a downward-facing dog and stretches out his calf muscles.

"So what happens now?" he asks me.

"Next week we start looking for a space. Liam and Brody have a friend in commercial real estate. We're supposed to see a bunch of stuff."

When I look over at him, I see that his shirt has slipped down, revealing his chest as he bends over. His abs are shiny after the long run.

"Where are you looking?"

My gaze slams into his.

"What?" I ask stupidly.

"Which area of town are you looking in?" he clarifies.

I bend over my legs in a butterfly stretch to hide the fact that I'm blushing as hard as Landon does. And that I'm a total creeper.

"All over, honestly," I tell him. "They have a list of require-ments, and so do I. Hopefully we'll find something that hits every-thing on the combined list before the next century."

———

"This has, um . . ." Landon kicks an empty beer can out of the way as she steps farther into the space. "This has real potential," she says judiciously.

I look around the cavernous space we are standing in. It is the fifteenth place we've seen in the last couple of days, and it's in the worst shape by far. It is covered in an inch of dirt and drywall dust that has settled in and has never been cleaned up. Apparently someone began a renovation to turn it into a restaurant the year before but ran out of money. They had only just started the process, and it sat untouched for eight months after that while they fought with banks and creditors. In the end, they weren't able to make any kind of a go at it, so it sat empty and beat up. Miko takes several more steps and inspects a broken piece of wall with rusted pipes shooting out of it in every direction. I vaguely wonder if she is up-to-date on her tetanus shot.

"It's a great area," Brody says as he comes to stand next to me. "This part of Ventura is really popular. You'd have a ton of foot traffic. Babe, please be careful. Those wires could be live!" he calls across the empty space to Landon.

She looks back at him with a sheepish smile and keeps slowly picking her way past debris to inspect the space. I can't remember a single time in all the years I've known him that I've ever heard my brother call anyone 'babe' or sound like a mother hen. I smirk in amusement but don't want to embarrass Landon by calling him out on it.

"I like the brick." I point to an area where the drywall has fallen away, exposing old brick underneath. "It would be cool to open up the whole back wall."

Liam makes a sound in the back of his throat but keeps his mouth shut. He has already preached on the value of finding a space that needs minimal improvement. He believes it is the best option, even with the added expense. He argued about it for so long and in so much detail on the drive here that we threatened to kick him out of the car if he didn't shut up. None of the other places were quite this raw, though, and I can tell it is killing him to keep his opinions to himself. While Brody likes the idea of renovation and working with the bones of a space, Liam prefers throwing money at a problem to ensure ease of use.

"There's tons of room, though," Brody says. "You could finish the kitchen and partition off areas for an office, and still have a small space where people can sit down to eat or grab a coffee or something."

Most of the spaces we have seen so far have been in high-traffic, high-rent areas, which means that the square footage is smaller. A smaller space means room for a kitchen in back, a bakery display and counter up front, and not much else. It isn't absolutely necessary, but I love the idea that people could sit down and enjoy their pastries if they wanted to.

"Does this door go somewhere—" Landon's call is cut off by a loud crash as she pushes her way through a door in the back.

"Babe," Brody calls as he hurries off after her.

He manages to fit exasperation, worry, and adoration into a single word.

I look over at Liam, who looks back at me.

"Babe," he says in a pretty good imitation of our brother.

"Babe," I answer, applying my own tone to it.

"Babe." He offers more nuance, and we both start laughing.

"You're both assholes," Brody calls from the far end of the room. "Come check this out."

We are still laughing when we step out onto a cement back patio. It is walled in on either side by the buildings next door, and the far side of it is closed off by a high fence covered with ivy. It is totally bare of anything else, save for some fast-food wrappers and a collection of pots that might have once held living flowers but have no evidence of them now.

"I guess you could use it for seating," Brody tells me. "I can't imagine you'd need it, though."

Miko turns around in slow circles, her eyes alight with possibilities. She looks at Landon.

"What does Diane charge for a room rental at Da Vinci's?" she asks her.

Landon is already nodding in agreement to something. "Fifteen hundred, plus a food and beverage minimum for weekends, and this is—"

"—twice the size," Miko finishes for her. "It wouldn't be hard to retrofit this for something rustic." She taps her foot on the cement.

"A plank would be nice. Maybe whitewashed? Like we did for the bar mitzvah last year?" Landon asks.

My siblings and I look at each other in confusion.

"Exactly." Miko continues to stare at a space only she can see. "Add some large-scale vegetation . . ."

"She means trees," Landon supplies. "With twinkly lights."

Miko snaps her fingers and points at Landon, letting her know she is right on, and I can feel Liam biting his tongue to keep from arguing the point with them.

"Twinkly lights are a must, or maybe some exposed Edison bulbs overhead." Miko looks up at the open area.

Apparently, Liam's ability to remain silent snaps.

"What are you guys going on about? We're looking for a bakery location, and you're talking about—"

"The potential to upsell," Miko says in challenge.

Liam looks at her as if she has sprouted a second head, then glances around the dirty patio for some kind of answer.

"What do you see that I don't?" he asks her in exasperation.

"In what capacity?" she asks him.

He gives her an impatient look, which only seems to make her happier.

"An event venue," she finally answers.

My brothers and I are all quiet as we examine the space with new eyes. I would have never considered it, and it is likely too small to gain notice from the two of them, whose venues host only large-scale events.

Landon reaches out for Brody's hand when she comes to stand beside him.

"Lots of popular restaurants have small rooms or patios for private events. They're great for showers or birthday parties. The room rate alone could probably cover your mortgage if you could book a few of them a month," she tells me.

I look around the space again, and I can almost see what they see. I have no idea how to produce a party or turn this into a venue, but I know they could do it. I kind of like the idea of getting to work with them on a part of the business. Apparently asking for help is going to my head.

"Mack," Liam says calmly, "this place is a dump. No one in their right mind would want something this messed up when there are so many better options."

His words hit me like a slap, because they are almost the same ones I'd thought about myself where Taylor was concerned. I feel, then, sort of desperately angry on behalf of this abandoned storefront. Sure, it has some issues, and it needs a little work done, but it isn't a lost cause. Just because something is messy and needs some help doesn't mean it isn't worth a second chance, right?

"This is the one," I tell my brothers.

Miko claps like a five-year-old while Liam glares at her.

"No way," Liam says at the same time Brody asks, "Are you sure?"

I ignore Liam. I know I am right. I have a feeling.

"This is it. I can feel it in my gut. If you think we can pull it off on budget, and it has the foot traffic and the neighborhood to help it succeed, I'd really like to use this space."

Liam's shoulders drop.

"You have no idea how much work this is going to take," he tells me. "This is impossible."

I smile back at him.

"The last time someone told me something was impossible, I talked my way into working for a lunatic, who also happens to be one of the world's greatest pastry chefs. Impossible is a self-taught baker creating six menu items that sell out daily at one of the nicest hotels on the planet. Impossible is creating and serving a dessert plate to a table full of the greatest chefs in the world. All of that without trying more than the tiniest bite in order to check the flavors. That," I tell him proudly, "is impossible. *This* is just a lot of work, and I'm not afraid of that. Are you?"

I can see Brody fighting a smile, but Liam's face is totally blank.

"Fine." He sighs. "But this has to stay on budget, and don't come crying to me when that means you end up having to paint this thing yourself or—"

I cut off his tirade with a bear hug, and even if he is annoyed, he hugs me back just as hard.

"Let's go check out the front again," Miko says when we break apart. "I had an idea for an art installation."

"You"—Liam points an accusatory finger at her—"are a bad influence."

"And you"—she points back a finger of her own, but the gesture ends up looking more like a fairy granting a wish than something aggressive—"need to chill out. I am an excellent influence. Ask anybody."

With that she grabs my elbow and pulls me away. If Liam has any kind of rebuttal, he isn't fast enough to get it out before we are out of earshot.

Chapter Twenty

Taylor pulls a drop cloth back with flair to reveal the smooth expanse of wood underneath.

"It's gorgeous, Taylor," I tell him as he folds the material back up.

"You've seen it at least a dozen times." He grins at me. "You're the one who helped me stain it."

Over the last few months I've spent almost every minute of my waking hours at the bakery trying to get everything ready. From the construction to the ordering to the minutiae of uniforms and learning a new POS system, it is unbelievable how much work it's taken to get to opening day. But whenever I've had a chance, I've sneaked away to Taylor's. Sometimes I test recipes, sometimes we go for a run, and lately, more often than not, I watch him work in his shop on new orders, including the one for this dining table, which matches the industrial, rustic vibe of the bakery's design. He finished several smaller tables weeks ago, but I was dead set on a long communal table in the center of the dining area, and he found a gorgeous piece of reclaimed hickory to build it for me.

"I know I've seen it"—I smile back at him—"but I haven't seen it here, in the space. It looks wonderful," I say wistfully.

And it does; the space has turned out so much better than I could have imagined. Everything is bright and airy with high, pristine-white walls, which despite Liam's grumbling, I didn't have to paint at all. The floor has a glossy finish over the existing cement. The clear varnish means that you can see every crack and discoloration, but it adds to the overall charm. The entire design has become a homage to celebrating and even highlighting the imperfections rather than covering them up. Taylor made all of the tables around us in the seating area from reclaimed wood. The countertop is a marriage of modern glass display case and French country kitchen. A large framed blackboard menu hangs on the exposed brick wall behind the register, announcing the day's specials, and below it is an espresso machine so spectacular we've dubbed it Magic Mike, because as far as Landon and I are concerned, access to Italian-grade caffeine at any time of day is right on par with Channing Tatum without his clothes on.

Coffee will be served in one of the mismatched vintage teacups my mom and I have collected over the last month or in a logo-emblazoned paper cup for customers on the fly. That logo is everywhere, from the napkins to the menu to the T-shirts and aprons the staff will wear. It is the prettiest thing I've ever seen Miko design, and her attention to detail and the seamless way she managed to weave it into the bakery makes me emotional every time I think about it.

"Are you going soft on me, Jennings?" Taylor asks, breaking my train of thought.

I straighten myself up quickly.

"No, never that," I tell him facetiously.

I grab a rag to wipe off the table simply to have somewhere else to look. I see him so rarely, and when we aren't together, I am so busy that I can convince myself I don't have time to think about him. But when we are together I have a hard time thinking about anything else. Like right now, for instance. I want to hug him so badly that I feel sick with it. But we don't hug anymore. We don't touch at all. We are *just friends*. I am fine with being friends, and I am fine hanging out with him without getting any weird ideas, as long as he doesn't smile or laugh or look at me for too long.

Ugh!

OK, so I am *mostly fine* hanging out with him without getting weird ideas.

"I heard we're hitting up bingo this week," Taylor says, putting away the drop cloth.

"Yes." I look back at him. "I've been told I work too much and that I need to lighten up." I smile at the memory of the mock intervention Landon and Miko staged last week. "Against my will, I have agreed to bingo, which should buy me a couple more months before they harass me again. So you're joining us?"

"I am," he says, but I can't read the expression on his face. "I have someone in town this week visiting. I thought I'd bring her along."

I look back down to rub at phantom dust with the rag in my hand.

"That sounds . . ." *I will not choke to death on this word. I will not.* "Fun," I say finally.

Taylor's response is enigmatic. "I thought so too."

He knocks once on the table. "I told Big Pretty I'd have his truck back by eight, so I better run. I'll see you Thursday, OK?"

It takes all six years of practice I had at schooling my emotions to look up at him with a smile.

"See you Thursday," I say as he walks out the door.

———

"What are you going to do?" Miko asks me.

Her eyes are as big as saucers and full of concern, but she still manages to reach over and add a stamp of color to I-19 on my forgotten bingo card.

"What can I do?" I nearly whimper.

My emotions are all over the place. I can't decide if I want to rage or cry or be sick or fight someone. I mean, really, the options are endless. Across the table Brody whispers something into Landon's ear and then kisses her neck when she giggles in response.

On second thought, maybe fighting someone is exactly what I should do.

"Don't take your ire out on them," Miko says, following my line of sight. "It's not their fault they're adorable together."

"I guess," I mumble into my drink.

"So he told you, point blank, he just wants to be friends?" Miko asks.

"Yes," I hiss.

"And you want to be . . ."—she purposely trails off, and when I don't pick up the sentence, she continues it for me—"more than friends?"

"What difference does it make now?" I say, folding my arms petulantly. It only serves to perk my chest up further in this ridiculous bra. I glare at Miko for assuring me that boobs would help this situation and insisting I wear this dress.

Nothing good ever came from wearing a dress when you were already feeling desperate!

"Have you told him how you feel?" Miko asks calmly before marking three of her four cards.

"No," I whisper-yell to her over the drag-queen bingo announcer calling out numbers. This time he's dressed as Kate Middleton, which is almost as upsetting as Miley had been. "He told me it was better this way. Then he found someone else."

"You don't know that," she says calmly.

"He called her sweetheart"—I count the points off on my fingers—"she's staying with him, and he's bringing her tonight to introduce her around to everyone."

The last one hurts the most. I know it isn't fair to wish he hadn't moved on, but I don't want to have to see her and pretend I am fine about it. But as far as he is concerned, we are just friends. And it has been months. I know it makes sense that he'd want his girlfriend to meet us, but that doesn't make it suck any less.

"Maybe"—I take another swig of my drink—"maybe she'll be hideous-looking."

"Dude," Miko says, looking over my shoulder, "no such luck."

I turn around because I don't want to have to face it when they are right in front of me. Better to see them from afar and prepare myself for it. At the entrance Taylor is following his date through the crowd. I might have wished for someone hideous, but I knew there wasn't a chance of Taylor dating anyone who isn't as gorgeous as he is. She is tall and thin with dark brown eyes and hair that falls in loose waves all the way down her back. She looks like a model, and that isn't just my self-loathing talking; she is stunning, and as she floats across the room nearly every man turns to watch her pass.

I wonder if this is what massive heart failure feels like, because I am sure I am dying.

They arrive at our table, and Taylor smiles and begins to make introductions. Before he can get two words out, I mumble something and head for the restroom as fast as my legs can carry me. I am not going to get sick in this godforsaken Hollywood bar, but I need a few minutes to get myself under control. I look in the dingy mirror and force myself to pull it together. I am going to handle this like a mature adult. I am going to smile and be civil and not do anything to hurt my friend or let him know how much his actions are hurting me. I square my shoulders and walk back down the hallway and over to the table.

As I come back up to the table, I notice that Taylor and the girl have left to go get drinks at the bar together. Miko spastically flags me down.

"Dude," she says.

"Hold on, Miko," I say.

I feel as if I am in a trance.

Across the bar Taylor points out something to the girl, and she laughs along with him at whatever the joke was. She looks so happy to be with him, so perfectly suited to go on dates and say sweet things and laugh at the jokes he makes for her. I am never going to be that girl.

Something in me breaks. Just splits apart into shards of glass and falls to the floor along with whatever pride I have left. It doesn't make me weak, though, doesn't make me want to cry or run away and hide. Screw that. He is mine, and she, with the perfect hair and the giraffe legs, can't have him!

I am in motion before I can talk myself out of it.

Behind me I hear Miko curse and call after me, but it is too late; I am at the bar next to him. I tap the giraffe on the shoulder.

"Excuse me," I say. She turns to me with a smile, and I barely succeed in not punching it off her face.

"What's your name?" I ask the girl, and she tells me the answer. I snort with response.

"OK." I spit out the word. "Is that Cassidy with an *i* or a *y*?"

"Two *e*'s, actually," she responds, beginning to look confused.

I snort again. "God, *of course* it's with two *e*'s!"

Taylor steps closer to me, concern all over his face.

"Hey, are you OK?" he asks me.

Miko and Landon run up behind me. Miko pulls on my arm.

"Dude, Max, can I steal you for one quick word?" she asks.

I know they are trying to save me from making a fool of myself, but it is too late. I have had a lifetime's worth of keeping everything inside me, and I can't do it now. I shake off Miko's hand and look back into Taylor's eyes.

"No, I'm not OK." I bite my tongue, some part of my body trying to stop my heart from ruining everything. "I'm not OK," I say, louder still.

People are starting to look at us.

Taylor reaches out a hand towards me. Maybe he's worried I'm ill. Miko tugs on my arm again. Landon grabs for my hand.

I don't know how the giraffe reacts. I'm not looking at her.

"I'm not OK," I say, each sentence louder than the last. "I'm not perfect or sweet. I'm not like her." I nod towards the giraffe at his side. "But I am in love with you."

Landon and Miko both gasp behind me. They stop trying to pull me away. Taylor goes totally still, and I swear no one in the bar makes a sound. Even the drag-queen bingo announcer has stopped turning the balls in the brass cage and is looking in our direction.

"I have . . . never said that to anyone before," I tell him earnestly, "and I don't know if you're even allowed to say that to someone you're not dating. I'm sorry. I'm so sorry I'm doing this all wrong, but I can't *not* tell you the truth."

Taylor opens his mouth, then closes it again.

"Look, I know I'm not perfect," I say desperately, "but I've got to be better than Casidee with two *e*'s."

Behind me I hear Landon call my name sternly. I know what she means with the rebuke. I look over at the giraffe, who seems surprisingly amused by all of this. Maybe she is a little slow on the uptake.

"I'm sorry," I tell her quickly. "I'm sure you're a lovely person and . . . and your hair is really shiny. But you can't have him."

"Oh no she didn't!" I hear from somewhere in the DJ's direction.

I know I'm making a fool of myself, but it is too late to stop. I look over at Taylor and fight back the tears in my eyes.

"I'm not perfect," I admit to him again. "I can actually be pretty rude sometimes, but there was a time . . . there was a time when you liked me back. And if there's even the smallest chance that you'd consider me again, then I had to try. If there isn't"—I shake my head—"that will suck. It'll crush me, actually, but it can't be worse than not trying at all."

No one moves or says anything, and Taylor just continues to look at me in shock. I guess when I imagined this all playing out in my head, I thought it would come to some huge crescendo, but the truth is that Taylor looks totally blindsided, as if he doesn't know what to do or say.

I blow out a breath.

"Hey"—I shrug my shoulders—"can't blame a girl for trying, right?" I say lamely.

I hurry away, grabbing my bag off the table as I walk by. More than one person calls after me, but God bless the gender-ambiguous DJ, who chooses that moment to turn the music back up, drowning them out.

I am halfway to my car before Taylor gets close enough that I can't ignore his voice anymore. The giraffe is with him.

"Great," I tell the empty street.

Because her witnessing my humiliation just makes this whole thing perfect.

Taylor has the gall to smile. I try to turn around again, but he catches my arm.

"Jennings, I didn't get to introduce you. I want you to meet Casidee Taylor," he says carefully. "My little sister."

Oh holy mother of pearl!

"I . . . I . . ." I don't have any words. "I'm so sorry."

She sticks out her hand with a grin that I now see is exactly like her brother's.

"It's nice to meet you. I've heard so much about you, Max."

I mumble something inarticulate, and she laughs and turns with a wink. "I'll see you back inside," she calls as she walks away.

I can't do anything but stare at the ground. I thought I was prepared to feel like an idiot for a chance at Taylor, but I didn't have any idea just how far I was going to push that. His fingers reach for my face, turning it up until I meet his eyes. I swallow.

"I'm sorry—" I start to tell him.

"Please, God, stop saying you're sorry. That was . . ." He searches for words.

"Embarrassing?" I supply.

"Oh, definitely embarrassing on some kind of epic level, Jennings!" he tells me happily.

I try to think of something to say in response to that.

"I know it was idiotic, but I guess I thought . . ." I trail off.

It is probably better to just leave it. I'll only make it worse, and his fingers on my face make me want to say something stupid again.

"You thought what?" Dark chocolate-brown eyes search mine. "That it's a special kind of torture to be in love with your best friend?"

I suck in a breath.

"That being around them but not being able to tell them how you feel actually makes you ache? That you had to say something or you thought the words might suffocate you?" He reaches down for my hand. "I know how that feels."

"Really?" I ask, not even fighting my tears anymore.

He chuckles a little and wipes my tears away with his thumb. "That was a crazy way to go about it, but also sweet and brave and . . ."

"Effective?" I whisper.

He smiles, and it is big and bright and just for me. Not for any one of a hundred other girls who might have deserved it more. This smile is for me, the girl who is still messy and broken. I have a long way to go before I know how to be in a healthy relationship. But I so badly want to try.

"Very effective," he says.

Between one breath and the next I am in Taylor's arms, kissing him with months' worth of emotion. The longing I've felt over the last several weeks comes crashing through the space between us. I feel that kiss all the way down my whole body—feel the absolute precious weight of hope for what this person means to me.

His arms wrap around me tightly, pulling me closer, and I feel safe for the first time since the night he took my bracelet. In that moment, I am positive that he is the only thing holding me in place so I don't float away with the breeze.

"I don't think I'll be very good at this," I tell him when the kiss breaks. "I don't know how to—"

"What if you don't think?" He asks me the familiar question.

"Really, Taylor, I'll probably screw this up," I say. "Even though I..."

I feel stupidly shy all of a sudden.

"Please say it again," he asks me earnestly.

"Even though . . . I love you," I whisper back.

He reaches up carefully to slide his fingers to the back of my neck.

"I love you. I am *in love* with you," he tells me, "and that's all that matters, OK? We'll figure the rest out."

He says it like a statement of fact. Like it is the most obvious thing in the world to admit that aloud. No one has ever said those words to me before. Maybe that's why it is so hard for me to believe them. It don't want to argue or ruin this moment, but that little voice in the back of my head, the one that had urged me to wear the bracelet forever, makes me worry.

"It can't be that simple," I say nervously.

Taylor throws back his head and laughs at whatever look is on my face. He kisses one of my hands and then the other. He kisses my fingers and my left shoulder and the corner of my mouth.

"Oh, Jennings," he says with a grin. "Wanna bet?"

Landon told me once recently that she finally felt grown up when she had the courage to try for the things she wanted. Over the last several months I know I have grown up in ways I didn't think were possible before, but I also understand that the willingness to chase after childhood dreams isn't going to be the turning point in my life. I know, with every single part of my being, that I will always trace everything in my life back to this moment. I will forever identify everything as either before or after it.

I will always remember this dirty street in Hollywood and the fact that he is wearing that faded blue T-shirt. I will remember this stupid purple dress Miko made me wear and the feel of his thumb tracing little circles on my hip. I will remember the sound of his laughter and the joy in his eyes. I will always remember this as the moment I felt truly grown up. The exact moment that I decided to let Taylor love me back.

Acknowledgments

First and foremost, a big gigantic thank you to Jodi Warshaw. Your interest in *Party Girl* was massively flattering, but it meant absolutely everything to me that you took a chance on Max's story after reading only twenty pages. Thank you for trusting me to finish it. Thanks too for the title; *Sweet Girl* is so good that I'm only disappointed I didn't come up with it myself!

Immense gratitude to Eryn Kalavsky, who I'm still convinced is a gift sent directly from God. Thank you for talking me through a thousand possible plot points and for reading all eighty-three drafts of this book. Thank you for Saturday morning runs and follow-up motivational text messages encouraging me to keep at it. I am truly grateful for your friendship.

Shout out to Susanna Kearsley for betting/daring me to finish this manuscript by Labor Day, mostly because you knew I needed a deadline. Thanks again. Your next vodka rocks sans garnish is on me.

Thank you to Lisa Olin and the amazing team at Cake Monkey (literally the greatest bakery in Los Angeles!) for letting me hang out in your kitchen, be inspired by your flavor combinations, and ask you weird questions about pastries. Massive appreciation to chef Elizabeth Belkind. I didn't even know Joey was a character until you walked in and inspired her! Any pastry/kitchen/chef/food mistakes are mine alone.

Thank you to Josh Jackson at Arbor Exchange for showing me your workshop and sharing your massive knowledge of furniture design. I'm sorry I didn't listen to you about the whole "it would be unsafe to build furniture while shirtless" thing. Taylor's abs didn't give me a choice.

Thank you to Cynthia Lavers, who once again answered all my medical questions with the patience of Job. Any mistakes are mine alone.

Last but never least, thank you to my Lamb, Dave Hollis, for your grace and understanding while I finished this book. Thank you for listening to me work out the story over many sushi dates and for allowing me to read you my favorite lines. You always laugh in the right places. This story is about two friends falling in love, and I'm writing from experience because I've fallen in love with my best friend again and again.

About the Author

Rachel Hollis founded the LA-based event planning firm Chic Events at only twenty-one. Six years later *Inc.* magazine named her one of the Top 30 Entrepreneurs under 30. She went on to turn Chic into the extremely popular lifestyle website TheChicSite.com, where readers log in daily for the tips and tricks she's acquired after years of planning fancy parties for celebrities. She has designed and produced fabulous events for many of Hollywood's elite, including Bradley Cooper, Al Gore, Jennifer Love Hewitt, Ivanka Trump, Rashida Jones, Jaime King, Sara Rue, and Cuba Gooding, Jr., just to name a few.

Rachel moved to Los Angeles to go to college and promptly met a boy named David, who was as handsome as he was funny. First she made that boy her best friend, and then she made him her husband. Eleven years later they have three equally handsome and hilarious little boys named Jackson, Sawyer, and Ford. They live in LA, where they spend their time doing super-cool and sexy things, such as going to soccer practice and hitting up any restaurant where kids eat free with the purchase of an adult entrée.

Take this friendship to the next level by hitting up Rachel on any of the websites below. She's so excited to be an author that she'd probably pee her pants if you actually brought it up on social media!

Twitter: @msrachelhollis
Facebook: /msrachelhollis
Instagram: @msrachelhollis
Pinterest: @msrachelhollis